I'M ALREADY GONE

Alexa Cleasby

KDP

For Ruby

CONTENTS

CHAPTER 1

When I was little my mum used to tell me a story about where people go when they die. But before you go thinking any nice tales about angels playing harps and golden gates welcoming us to a heaven in the clouds—stop. That's not the kind of mother I have.

This was the only story she ever told me. The rest of the time I felt more like an afterthought growing up. A mild irritation like noticing rain and then realising the washing was still out. A sometimes source of amusement like when, age four, I tried on her make-up while she was out and stomped to greet her at the front door, a tiny drunken clown. There was affection, but it was fleeting and only when it suited her mood. And those moods; they slipped across her face as easily as changing clothes.

But back to her favourite, *her only*, bedtime story. Where do people go when they die, Liv? All those negative feelings you've accumulated during your life, all those regrets, jealousies, hurts and anger, they weigh you down. They leach into your skin. Each fresh pain like another coat of paint. Too many of those negative feelings and you become like a pulsing dark beacon - a lure to *them*. You're an irresistible snack to the darkest of creatures that lurk on the edge of our world. Creatures that hide in the shadows, waiting to be seen. Waiting to be recognised —to feel *like* call to *like*. She called them Shades and told me the only way to avoid them when I died was to always be happy, always be kind, always think positive thoughts. So, where do people *go* when they die? If the Shades get you, they drag you back to their world to meet their masters. They watch as your soul is devoured and all that's left is a husk of the person you used to be. Just another bitter Shade, stuck in the periphery. Mostly forgotten, mostly invisible. Trapped. Watching and waiting to lure the next miserable victim.

If the Shades didn't get you, you'd be lucky enough to sleep the best sleep you ever had. The forever sleep.

It's a wonder I ever slept as a child.

I'd largely forgotten about this story. It became a tiny blip hidden in years of growing up. Buried under friends and memorising song lyrics and schoolwork and boys and exams. And most recently, memories of Tristan.

But when I started seeing strange creatures out of the corner of my eye and hearing voices whispering in the dark, the memory resurfaced. My counsellor tells me that I'm normal. She says everyone's brain can play tricks. The voices are not real, she's very firm about that. Just brain tricks. All my insecurities and doubts came slithering to the surface after The Break Up.

The Day that Tristan Left.

My life already feels divided into two halves. Before Tristan and After Tristan. And After Tristan, came the voices and that quiet sense of being watched.

As my final exam draws to an end, it dawns on me - life is meaningless. It is a long stretch of forgotten days and choices that never quite *click*. On that thought, the buzzer sounds and a mass of scraping chairs and clicking pens follows. We all spill out from the draughty sports hall into dim winter sunlight. I'm free, but instead I feel lost.

The best thing about my life has left me. Tristan is gone. And he's been gone for the last four weeks and three days. My finals exams briefly filled my time. They were an object, a worthy goal to blot out the empty days. It's all pretend though, as if these exams really mean anything worthwhile. As if I care about them anymore.

Poring over meticulous revision notes, colour coded, highlighted, and ordered. I wish for those monotonous revision days again, that beautiful looming end point in front of me. I wish for that goal before me, the idea that everything will be better once I've done this or that... Now, I'm here and nothing has changed. In the wake of my last exam is a hole. I feel it crack open, expanding as I walk.

I reach for my phone. He'd want to know how my last exam went. I remember that strict voice of his telling me these exams were important and the smile when he succeeded in dragging me from revision. I slip my phone back into my pocket. Tristan doesn't care anymore.

Students mill around me. Excitedly dispersing as they plan food and parties. No one looks at me. They all filter around me. I'm a stone amongst running water. I feel like I'm being dragged downstream, constantly pulled forward. I stop to sit against a wall and grab my water bottle out of my bag. Sipping cold water helps when I feel my temperature spike in panic. So does music. I fish through my bag for my earbuds.

Something dark snakes past my vision and I jump up. There is nothing there. This doesn't surprise me, just another brain trick. I often think I see things. Glimpses of dark creatures out of the corner of my eye. My counsellor, Miss 'call me Jo' Salter, has reassured me that everyone thinks they see things occasionally. But the memory of a bedtime story about creatures lured by sadness haunts me. 'You are the same as everyone else' Miss Salter likes to remind me. 'Everyone has fears. Everyone feels alone sometimes. It's normal. You're normal.'

I put in my earbuds and turn up my music. I keep my eyes down as I weave between other students. Contact avoided.

Where has Tristan gone? This is a question I often wonder. How did he turn the girl I remember into this mess? How did I not see it coming? A friend said to me once, 'you're too good for him, Liv.'
'Is that supposed to make me feel better?' I'd snapped at her. I haven't seen much of her recently. In fact, I haven't seen much of any of my friends since I'd met Tristan.

The Day That Tristan Left, he said, 'I can't do this anymore.' I could lose myself in those words. Stare into nothing and repeat them over and over until they don't even sound like words anymore and tears roll down my face. *Do* what? How could things have changed without me noticing?

I reach my dorm house and go straight up the stairs, bypassing the living room and kitchen. I hear a kettle boiling and the sounds of a TV game show. My housemates are used to my behaviour now. They no longer seek me out. In my attic room the music goes straight from earbuds to speakers. I can't stand a moment of silence.

I wonder where Tristan is right now. Who is he with? I force myself to stay away from my phone. Instead I sit by my dormer window and stare out onto the street below. I think for a moment that I see a pair of yellow eyes beneath my bed. But this is normal, this happens to everyone, right? They blink and regard me curiously from the darkness. I turn my head finally frustrated with their presence, but they are already gone.

Those words.

I Can't Do This Anymore.

How many ways can I analyse five little words?

I remembered when I first saw Tristan. It was back when I still worked behind the bar at Nectar Lounge. I'd just turned eighteen, but still ended up mostly on glass collect. Seeing all the people pressing into the bar, I was glad. Collecting glasses left my mind free to wander. I'd always loved to daydream and sometimes my mind felt like a creature entirely independent of me. I was the observer watching it dart from thought to thought. I built stories from chance encounters and vivid dreams stuck with me all day blurring reality and fantasy.

I was loading the glass washer in the kitchen when I looked through the plastic beads that separated the back from the bar. Rows of impatient people piled up against the bar and I created names and lives for them. My eyes skimmed over him at first. Yes, he was attractive, but so were others at the bar. And I remember absently thinking not my type. Sometimes it can make me smile recalling that. *Not my type.*

It was only when I looked back a little while later and noticed Tristan was still at the bar. No one paid him any attention. He didn't lean in or lift his hand for attention. His eyes wandered the faces of those around him. What surprised me more was how neither Kimi or Val had clocked him yet. They each served at separate ends of the bar, working their way along to the middle and then back to where they started. Tristan was technically on Val's side, but it was debatable and yet neither had served him. Stranger still, he showed no signs of impatience or irritation. Normally, both Kimi and Val were eager to serve and flirt with good-looking guys. Tristan was definitely the sort I'd seen Val go for. She liked dark eyes where the iris and pupil became one. I'd always preferred blue eyes. Until Tristan.

I turned away and grabbed my basket. If he wasn't complaining then let him wait. I couldn't dredge up much concern. Glass collecting cast a kind of apathetic spell over me that left me on autopilot. I was about to wander back out into the crowd, when a hand grabbed my arm. I glanced at it and saw the red nails. I looked up into Kimi's face.
'I'm desperate for a smoke,' she pleaded. 'Will you cover for me?'
'Sure.'
As I served the first girl I noticed Tristan again, patient as ever. I took pity on him and ignoring the glares of the girl who thought she was next I turned to him.
'Hey, what can I get you?'

And it was the strangest moment.

The people on either side of him both looked to see who I was addressing and seemed surprised to see Tristan being served. I even noticed Val glancing over and then giving me a look. I knew that look. It was a look that said she'd noticed the handsome guy, saw he was technically on her side, and that I'd crossed half the bar to serve him first.
'Pardon?' I forgot Val and looked back to him.
'What do you want to drink?' I spoke clearly in case English wasn't his first language. Our eyes met and he looked shocked.

Not long after we'd started going out, I'd questioned him about that. 'Why did you look so surprised to be asked what you wanted to drink in a bar by a bartender?'
'Did I?' He smiled.
'Yes!'

'I guess I was surprised you noticed me.'

'What do you want to drink?' I repeated, thinking perhaps I shouldn't have taken pity on him.

'Oh, I'll have … that.' He pointed to the pint of lager Val was currently pulling.

'A pint?'

'Yes,' he said after a moment of hesitation. He watched with fascination as I pulled the pint and placed it before him. There was an awkward pause where he forgot to pay and I had to remind him, while becoming very aware of the irritated patrons around him. He gave me a twenty and began to edge his way out of the crowd around the bar.

'Your change?' I called.

He looked confused. 'No, Tristan.' I frowned and again our eyes held. Our mutual confusion was interrupted by a pushy man at the bar claiming my attention. I dropped his change in the tip jar and forgot all about him.

Later, when I was collecting glasses, I glanced up and saw him standing at a tall table in a quiet corner drinking alone. After that I found it difficult to stop my eyes wandering over to him. Dreaming up a story for him … and then he caught me looking. I smiled politely and quickly looked away. After the third or fourth time being caught staring at him, I was glad for the dim lighting that hid my burning face. Did he notice the build up of glasses at the tables around him? I felt ridiculously nervous to get too close. He began to return my awkward smiles with a slow smile of his own.

For the rest of my shift I shouldn't shake my awareness of him. I felt him watching me. It was a feeling that lurched and tightened in the pit of my stomach. I felt tuned to his every movement. I didn't need to see him, just knowing he was watching consolidated my usually scattered thoughts onto that sole focus. I started making mistakes, dropping glasses, taking people's drinks before they'd finished and knocking others over.

One time, my eyes torturously jumped to his to see if he'd witnessed my latest clumsiness and I felt an odd mixture of disappointment and relief to see he'd gone.

Back in my room, I wipe the tears off my face before bracing myself to leave my room. I creep down to the kitchen, hoping to avoid all my housemates. In my cupboard I find a bottle of wine. As I pour a glass, a dark shape crosses silently from the door to the fridge. Just shadows and a brain playing tricks, I repeat in my head. I take the glass and the bottle as I head back to my room.

Tristan began to come to the bar a lot after that first time. I never figured out whether the other girls left him for me or whether he timed his bar placement, but I'd always be the one to serve him. His drink always changed, I noticed it became whatever he saw being served around him. 'I'll have that please.' He'd point after a scan of the bar. I'd watch him take his first sip and bite my lip in an attempt to maintain a neutral expression as some drinks caused his face to twist with distaste while others caused him to smile in delight. Sometimes when the bar was quiet, he'd see nothing to take inspiration from and then he'd turn to me and softly say, 'what would you recommend this evening?' I loved this peculiar behaviour and took it upon myself to never recommend the same drink twice. When Tristan walked in, I felt the excitement build in my chest like a drumbeat. I'd anticipate the question and burst into a ridiculous smile when he asked it.

What would you recommend this evening?

Even then I was hooked.

A few weeks later he beckoned me over on one of my glass

collecting forays.

'Would you like to have dinner with me, Liv?' His voice was so quiet, nervous even, that I wasn't sure I'd heard him right. His eyes met mine and I couldn't look away. I felt my throat dry up. All I could manage was a nod while my mind screamed YES! And I swear, the relieved smile he gave me was the most beautiful thing I've ever seen. I rested a hand on the corner of his table to steady myself.

'Perfect,' he whispered. I nodded again, feeling my face burn as I stood there like an idiot.

'Right,' I stammered eventually, once the silence was good and awkward. I nodded for probably the tenth time. I turned to go, stumbling over a chair as I went.

I finish the glass of wine and pour a second. I push aside the revision notes to make room for the bottle and my glass. I see the numbers and symbols briefly as the notes flutter to the floor and I wish I could be sitting at my desk working through problem after problem. The order and logic of science had always relaxed me in the past.

A shadow lunges in from my left and I step back, ducking, instinctively. Nothing there. More creatures lurk in the shadows, some are faceless shadowy forms and some blink slowly with yellow eyes like hulking wolves. Just a room full of brain tricks. Do not think about Shades. Banish all thoughts of Shades and shadow creatures, but the very command has my brain crawling all over the idea. It repeats in my mind, like the Candyman, daring me to say it out loud.

Shades.

Shades.

Shades.

I lie on my bed, eyes closed and turn my music up. Nothing can penetrate my world. I daydream about a time when Tristan is due to arrive soon. When he'd walk through my door and his eyes would light up to see me.

God, how I loved those eyes.

He'd lower himself slowly over me to kiss my lips. If my music was loud, sometimes, that kiss was the first I knew of his presence and my eyes would fly open. He would lie next to me and our hands would automatically reach for the other to touch and rest skin to skin.

A touch at my arm jolts me from my daydream. My eyes open expecting a housemate complaining about my music. Instead bright yellow eyes in a dark wolfy face regard me only inches away. Instead bright yellow eyes in a dark wolfy face regard me inches from my face. I flinch away, a scream choked up in my throat and the wolf darts away silently and is gone. The touch felt so real. I should tell Miss Salter that my brain tricks are now physically touching me, but I know I won't. It's only Tristan I want to confide in and he's the only one that I can't.

And Tristan has left completely. We have no friends in common. In fact, I never met any of his friends. There is no one to go to for news of him. He didn't do social media. He doesn't answer the phone or respond to texts (and I've already messaged a truly pathetic number of times). I don't even know where he lives or works. Still, he makes regular cameos in my dreams. Even the bad dreams are better than nothing and I scrabble to retain the details as they dissolve with the daylight.

I know I'm dreaming when I am by Tristan's side as he lies in a crisp white hospital bed. He's pale and shrunken, with a grey stony cast to this skin. Nothing like the boy I remember. 'I can't do this anymore. I'm ready now.' He whispers, turning away from me to look out the window towards an impossibly blue lake. I try to find the words, but all I can do is nod while the words clog in my throat. His eyes suddenly turn to lock with mine and they are full of hate. Those dark eyes had never looked at me that way before. I stumble back and feel myself falling. My body jerks and I'm awake. My heart still pounds from falling. The Shades around me evaporate as my mind clears from sleep. I glance over at the clock, three AM. An empty bottle of wine lies across the floor, whilst a second stands beside the alarm clock, the dregs remain. I take a gulp hoping to bring back sleep. I lie back and count sheep, but that never really works. I go through my exams and try to remember the questions and my answers, but that doesn't work either. I can't remember facts properly and instead my heart beats faster. I've failed all my exams. I know it. My face burns hot and then washes cold. The last two years of studying all for nothing. The money Mum has spent on this private sixth form college, my inheritance, wasted.

Liv, a voice whispers to me. *Stop worrying, come and play instead,* but I can't. I've failed my exams, what next? No university will accept me. I'm a failure that nobody wants-

I said stop!

I twist toward the voice and see a dark shape leaning over me. I blink expecting it to be gone when I open my eyes, but this time it isn't.

CHAPTER 2

The shadowy creature reaches toward me through the gloom. We can help you Liv. Come closer. Instead of shrinking back in fear, I lean closer. It is an invitation. I lift my own hand up to meet the wolf and meet nothing, but air. There is nothing there and I am alone curled up in sweat and bed sheets.

I am disoriented from lack of sleep as I trail down the stairs to the kitchen hours later. Normally, I'd try to be quiet and keep an ear out for any of my housemates, especially when I'm carrying two empty wine bottles that I clearly drank alone. I push the door to the kitchen open with my foot.
'Hey! How does it feel to be free?' The kitchen isn't empty. Nina is sitting at the table eating a bowl of cereal a newspaper spread before her. I see her eyes try to avoid the empty bottles. Immediately I think she means free from Tristan and angrily I drop the bottles with the rest of our ever accumulating recycling. Nina flounders before my hostility. 'You know, because you finished your exams?' she adds. I turn my back and busy myself getting a bowl and pouring some cereal.

I wish I was still in bed. I wish I could still be dreaming. Dreams and the first quiet seconds after a dream are my favourite place. That sinking sensation and tightening of my throat when I remember are the worst.

'Great,' I reply flatly, crossing to the fridge. I don't have any milk

I realise before I open the door and instead I lean back against it, facing Nina. We'd been close once, not really even that long ago. Not that long ago I would have asked to borrow milk and Nina would have said yes. Now I eat my cereal dry.

'I'm not finished 'til Monday.' She speaks with an exasperated smile as if she thinks I care. Why don't I care? I can't think of a single thing to say.

Why can't I talk to you anymore? Why has this become so awkward?

Nina is one of those girls everyone likes. It isn't hard to become close to her since she is so likeable. She has a long-term boyfriend, but she never lets that interfere with friendships. She never lets friendships fall by the wayside, except mine.

'Unlucky,' I finally mutter and push away from the fridge. In the past, bumping into a housemate in the kitchen could mean a leisurely chat over the TV; evening plans made and rushed teeth brushing before we dashed out the door for classes. I decide to eat the rest of my cereal in my room and turn to escape. Another housemate appears in the doorway. I've been so careful to avoid them, but here I am trapped between two of them.

It is Beth. She's never been my favourite. I doubt she's ever been anyone's favourite. I dart quickly past her with no acknowledgement and pull the kitchen door shut behind me. It never closes properly and before I retreat back up the stairs I hear their bright friendly chatter.

That used to be me. What have you done to me, Tristan?

I listen caught in faint nostalgia. Their talk quickly turns to a mutual friend. This friend of ours is happy. She has a new boyfriend and things are going well.

'She really deserves it though, doesn't she?'

'Yeah, she totally does.' How sincere they both sound.

She really deserves it.

What about the rest of us? It implies we don't deserve good things. She deserves to be treated like a princess, but we don't. She deserves to be happy and we don't. She deserves to be loved and we don't. Her life is so much harder than ours. Why not say we all deserve good things, but she's lucky? The word loses all meaning to me as I focus on my hatred of it.

Deserves. Deserves. Deserves. Deserves. Deserves. She *deserves* it.

Lack of food and drink means I have to leave the house for a food run. I wander the streets awhile with my rucksack, delaying my return home. The fresh air feels cold and calming. I follow the sound of music into a store, but when the first painfully familiar notes of a new song start I run right back out again. *Sweet Disposition,* it's Tristan's favourite song... or it was four weeks and four days ago.

Stay there, cos I'll be coming over.

Through Tristan, all of my music became new to me. I heard it all again hearing it through him. I was always looking for something new to impress him with. I was instantly happy when I saw from his face that I'd made a good choice.
'What's this?' Tristan would turn to me eagerly, tugging my hand. He loved the layers and the build up of separate instruments. He'd listen so intently forcing me to discover things about a song I'd never noticed before. Sometimes I'd *shh* him, indicating I was trying to listen and he'd do his best to irritate me until he had my full attention. I held out as long as I could, but when he lifted my hair to kiss the back of my neck I always lost. Music triggers so many memories of Tristan. The time we listened to *Night Drive* in the dark of my room, our hands roaming and our voices whispers. Or the time we went

hiking and listened to *Lark Ascending* at the summit, it was deserted and we stood sharing earbuds, feeling like the world stretched away from our feet. Even the first time I served him in the bar I remember *The Chain* playing in the background.

Liv, a voice calls to me. I turn my head and see a dark figure disappearing down an alley. I want to follow, but fear stalls me. The pavement is crowded and people push around me. As I stare, other creatures writhe in the corners of my vision. I close my eyes wishing them all away, but they are everywhere. Just brain tricks. Crawling, shaking up the sides and obscuring my view. Just brain tricks. This happens to everyone I tell myself and try to breath the way Miss Salter taught me. Am I dying already? Have the Shades come for me so soon? Someone knocks me without an apology and I stumble. For a moment I'm falling towards something beautiful, green and alive. I blink. I am back standing in the middle of the street still staring down that dark alley, remembering a bedtime story.

'Why don't we focus on another aspect of your life?' Miss Salter speaks to me in a voice I'd describe as patronising and a voice she'd describe as reassuring. Well, Miss 'Call me Jo' Salter, what other aspect do you suggest? Tristan has infiltrated every aspect. I'm actually sick of talking about myself. I wanted to talk about her. I wanted to ask her why she was such a cliché? Why did she wear her hair that way and why did she make those noises when she was biting her pen? 'I want to talk about your friendships,' she continues and all I can think is *you're not my friend.* I want to talk to a friend, not this impersonal pen sucker who thinks I'm overwhelmed. I could've told Tristan anything. I could have told him about Shades and Mum's story. I could have told Tristan about seeing things and hearing voices and he wouldn't have looked at me the way she does. He would have believed me.
'Are you seeing your friends?' Miss Salter asks. She says it in such

a way that I know she knows I haven't. 'Spending time with your friends, doing things you used to enjoy, will help you feel more of a connection with... the world, if you will.' I nod. 'You need to stop this self-imposed isolation.' I nod again, but I'm not listening. I'm thinking why ask questions you already know the answer to.

I remember Tristan and I once had a staring competition. There were no strict rules, we were allowed to smile, laugh, and blink but our eyes must not leave the other's face. It was one memory absent from music. I heard birds outside my window, someone somewhere was drilling, but mainly it was our laughter. Tristan was my best friend. I know it was wrong of me to allow him to become my only friend, but it was such an easy enticing slide.

'I'm giving you homework this week.' Miss Salter smirks over the word *homework* as if she's made a joke. I don't smile back. 'I want you to go out one evening this week with a friend.' I don't realise until her expression changes that I'm shaking my head. A friend? My mind is blank. Her eyes turn frosty and even *I* know I'm hard work. 'Meet me halfway here, Olivia. I'd like to see some effort from you, otherwise our meetings will amount to nothing.' I don't reply and she continues. 'We can agree that the amount of time you spend alone obsessing over Tristan isn't healthy.' I flinch to hear his name spoken with no warning. I clench my jaw to hold back the itching behind my eyes. 'Only you can change your life Olivia, no one else, just you.' You love the sound of your own voice don't you? I want to say that, but I don't.

In my room I lie on my bed and stare into space. *Silversun Pickups* are playing. I thought they'd be a safe choice since I'd never introduced them to Tristan. Today the lyrics seem to glare at me. They accuse and deride and I can't shake the feeling of a presence in my room. My thoughts drift in and out of focus. One of them is what friend could I do something with? Who still put up with me?

The evening after my first date with Tristan I walked with the biggest, goofiest smile on my face. I'd tried to stop, but it was irresistible. The second the door shut behind me, voices called from the living room.

'Liv! Get in here. Details please!' They were all there, excited and happy for me.

'Tell us everything!'

'Are you seeing him again?'

'How did you leave things? Did you kiss him?'

'Look at her face! She definitely kissed him.' And I sat between them and relived the entire evening again.

Another evening – only a few months after that first. The second the door shut behind me, voices called from the living room.

'Olivia, is that you?'

'We want to talk to you.' Nina appeared in the door, she was surprised to see me alone for once. 'He's not with her,' she confirmed to the others. And I sat between them silently.

'We never see you anymore.'

'We know what it's like when you're with someone new. And falling in love, but you guys are never apart. We haven't gone out with you in months.'

'He makes no effort with us.'

'We know nothing about him!'

'You never spend an evening alone.'

'We miss you, Liv.' They were sad, disapproving and annoyed.

Nina was the worst. She was quiet watching me with hurt eyes and I remembered our agreement. Back when we first became friends we'd agreed never to be *that* girl. The girl who disappeared when a guy appeared. The one who forgets her friends, cancels on them constantly and revolves her life around a boyfriend.

I'd become that girl… it had been easier than I'd imagined. Even now, single, I was still *that* girl.

They moved the final year students into real houses, just outside the sixth form collage grounds so they could keep an eye on us. Still, we relished the freedom as we lived like mini adults in our mismatched spindley terrace on a street full of other spindley houses and students. None of the furniture matched and we felt the winter air leach in under the front door, but up in my attic room the sun beat through the skylight and it always felt too hot. Tristan liked the warmth, he said it was one of the reasons we never stayed at his place. That and the lack of privacy. Privacy from who?

You think too much. Yellow eyes watch me from atop the hideous sixties wardrobe in my room. I don't bother to turn my head but I see them drift down onto my desk anyway. *That's right.* I hear satisfaction. *Dream, don't think.*

'Go away,' I mutter, closing my eyes.

Come with us.

'No.' I see red dancing circles inside my eyes. I open them a crack and see in the corner of my eye those yellow eyes. They wait at the foot of my bed. I shut my eyes. Not real, I tell myself. Stop talking to it then another thought says.

Then, the voice is a lot closer, next to my ear. *I can take you to him.* I flinch away, refusing to open my eyes.

The more I get to know someone the less I like them. This is something I had discovered about myself over the years. It is not a trait I am particularly proud of, but there it is. At first a person was mysterious and intriguing – they could be anything, they could be something special. They could think *I* was something special, mysterious and intriguing. I'd think about them and wonder. I'd look forward to seeing them, being with them, talking to them. At some point I can never quite identify, things would change. I'd see things I disliked, behaviours that irritated and habits I'd have to tolerate. They became predictable. They made mistakes. And disappointment set it.

This never happened with Tristan and I felt set free from a curse.

'Why do we never do anything with your friends?' I asked Tristan once. We were walking down a street in the city centre. It was warm and I enjoyed the sun while disliking the people it attracted to the streets.
'Why do we never do anything with your friends?' he countered.
I shrugged. 'Because I'm selfish with you?'
'You're selfish with me?' he smiled, pulling me to a halt. 'That is exactly it.' And somehow I was leaning against a building, Tristan sheltering me from the people passing us. 'I don't want to share you with my friends. I like it… just me and you.'
'Me too.' I whispered, unable to look away.
'I love how you see me, Liv,' he said before he kissed me.

It kills me to think the disappointment set in with Tristan. Somewhere along the line he started to dislike me. When did this happen? Show me the day, the time. Show me the first thing I did that set in motion the beginning of our end.

I'm a construct of other people, reflecting their expectations. I don't like who I am with some people, I am irritated with them for who they make me. Yet I can't stop it. Sometimes, I look at myself and wonder who I really am. I start to think maybe I've never known. I liked who I was before Tristan. I loved who I was with him and now I hate who I am without him.

The night is a sticky web of fever dreams. Endless repetitive cycles of broken dreams that plague me. I'm too hot and the sheets are steel around me, but I'm too cold when I fight them off. I pull the sheets back and they are blades cutting between my hands. Whenever I get a fever, the fever dreams follow, ever since I was little. I lie, twisting and turning, alone in the dark feeling like time has stopped and that I am completely alone.

When I finally deem it an acceptable time to get up and stop pretending I'm asleep, I rise and feel immediately awful. Physically awful. I ache all over, my skin burns and I am exhausted. While languishing in the shower, I remember the last time I'd felt this ill. Tristan had been there to look after me. I feel so heavy I have to sit down and rest my head on my knees. The hot water sprays on my back. The sky outside is still dark. For a while I watch it slowly lighten through the patterned glass of the bathroom window. When I was sick last time, Tristan wouldn't leave my side. I'd never known him to worry about anything, but he worried about me.

'I love the way you make my face hurt.' Tristan said to me once. I don't remember where we were or what we were doing. I know I was lying with my head on his lap.
'What?' I twisted to look up at him and I was already smiling. I was used to Tristan by now.
He indicated his face. 'This stupid expression you insist upon.'

I laughed and reached out to touch his face lightly. 'I like your face. I don't remember insisting it look this stupid though.' I paused thinking about his words. 'At least we look stupid together.'

'Nobody told me smiling could hurt.'

'Aren't you cute?' I wanted to sound sarcastic, but it was one of those moments where I could feel my heart beating.

I don't get out of bed all day. There is no part of me that doesn't ache, my stomach growls, but the thought of food makes me nauseous. I turn on the TV, but the colours are so bright they jump out and dance around my head. People talk on every channel and each word runs into the one before, until it is a car crash of words. I imagine the wounded bloody words piling up. I turn the TV off. I try to listen to music, but everything sounds out of place and rushed. I am the beat and it is with a constant effort that I keep each song going. I don't know what would happen if I stopped, but I don't want to find out. I drift in and out, but fight to stay awake and away from strange dreams. I try to read a book, but the words read like screams in my head. There is a horrible sense of urgency about every move I make, so I move slower to try and compensate for it. I put the book down gently. Confined to my room, I don't know what is real and what is in my head. I sometimes see yellow eyes and dark shapes moving about my room. Something small moves along my arm and my room fades and zooms back into focus.

Come and play, Liv. Only for a moment. My eyes are closed and I feel something lightly stroking my hair. Feather light, it trails from root to tip.

She's so open.

Perfect.

Especially now.

There are voices, huddled together in the darkest corner of

my room. I freeze thinking they won't notice me. There is a scurrying along the ceiling above me and a snap and rustle beneath the bed. I lie still. I feel exposed imagining any number of things rearing up to bite me, but I can't move. They'd know I'm awake if I move.

Let's take her.

And I feel the bed move.

CHAPTER 3

Bedtime when I was little often involved me believing my bed was flying. My eyes were closed somewhere between dreams and waking and I'd feel my bed rise and rush out the window. The soars and dips would flip through my stomach. I had to force myself to keep my eyes closed, otherwise I knew it would end. I wanted to see the night sky, to see us trail through the clouds above tiny sparks of light and people below, but that wasn't how it worked. Bedtime became an exciting time. It was a dream that came less and less often as I grew older. I missed that dream and the sensation of flying after it was gone.

So easy, now you can play, a voice trills.

I open my eyes. I'm not in my room anymore. I think maybe I can see it, strangely faint and out of focus, hiding behind soft shimmering grass. I'm not even in bed anymore, grass grows around me stretching up to my waist. I'm in a meadow dusted with white flowers rising up between the tall grass to meet a clear blue sky.

Such a beautiful imagination.

I feel weightless, what am I made of? What am I? I can't remember. I look down and see nothing. I lift my hands to my face, but I don't have hands. There is nothing. I feel the flowers brush against my non-existent legs and suddenly there they are - my legs, hazy and seemingly uncertain of a good reception. Yes I think, yes I want legs and they become solid. Solid and brimming with energy. I break into a run, the strength in my legs surges through me and I'm laughing. Ahead of me, I see a lake still like glass. Beyond the lake is a gloriously high green mountain. I want to run all the way to the top. I hear lots of voices coming from all around me. *Come and play.* I run and run until I reach the lake and the water laps my bare toes. I wade deeper until the cool water reaches my waist. Stretching my arms out wide I fall back, letting the water carry me. I sink and the feeling of tranquillity as I float down softly carried and submerged in water is indescribable. Nothing matters down here. I have so much time. I look up and see, shimmering through the water, that the sky has darkened to an angry grey. The rain begins, immediately hard and heavy. Raindrops, like bullets from a gun, hammer down above me. The sound is a quiet roar but nothing can reach me here. I sink down to rest on a flat shelf of rock. To my left I see the lake stretches further down into darkness. Bubbles rise from the depths dancing up to meet the rain. And to my right is a face, immobile and lifeless.

It takes a moment for me to realise it is carved from stone. A man's face captured in an expression of resigned acceptance. I reach out a hand to run my fingers over his forehead and down his nose. He's so lifelike. I wonder why and how long he's been here. A statue that toppled and fell down here to be forgotten. Or maybe the man was hated and his statue was pulled down and dumped here. An intrusive thought steals my peace. But where is *here?* The scenery skips a beat, blips like a TV screen. I see my room lurking. I feel like I've been holding my breath for too long. I rise up following the bubbles.

Don't go. Stay. There is so much more. Come with us. They chant swirling around me, yellow eyes watching from above the water. I break the surface of the lake and as I do I'm back in my bed. Sitting up through sweat-soaked sheets and faintly I still hear them.

Come back and play.

I need to get out. It's early, but I've done nothing except lie around feeling ill for days. The streets are quiet. I feel a little odd when I encounter another person. That slightly paranoid feeling when you haven't left the house in days. I avert my eyes and pretend they aren't there. It is mainly panda-eyed girls creeping home in the clothes they wore the night before. They are only too glad to ignore me right back. My flu is subsiding, but I'm groggy from lack of sleep. I keep thinking about the meadow, the lake, even the face behind the fallen statue. I keep reliving the uncomfortable clench in my stomach when I realise I'm no longer there. Why did being there feel so good?

As I walk random streets, my thoughts drift around in aimless circles. Shadows follow behind me. I catch squiggling glimpses of something out of the corner of my eye. A large shadowy hulk brushes by me. I realise I'm biting my nails when I taste the blood. I look down, angry with myself to see them all bitten to the quick. I turn into a park and find a bench to huddle on. I hide my bitten hands hidden in my pockets. It is cold and there is a fine mist across the grass. My eyes find a comfortable spot and I stare. I try to ignore the crawling on the edge of my senses. Sometimes I think I see a ripple, like a curtain blowing in the breeze. Hidden behind it is a green mountain and a glass lake.

Being with Tristan was not always easy. Sometimes he'd disappear and not answer his phone and I knew I'd just have to wait. The longest he'd ever made me wait was one week, right near the beginning. I'd been a mess, demanding of my housemates what was wrong with me? Should I call him again? Leave a message? Or a text? I hated game playing. I just wanted him to know I was his if he wanted me.

'No!' Nina warned. 'Do not text that.' This was back before my housemates had decided they didn't like Tristan. 'Don't text him. Stop calling him. Leave it alone.'

'But how will he know I want to see him again?' I cried.

'How hard is it to return a text?' She was indignant on my behalf, and perhaps this was the start of her campaign against Tristan. 'I've never seen you like this, Liv!' When he hadn't texted by the next day she took my phone off me. 'You'll thank me for this, I promise.' When I was alone I cursed myself for not memorising his number. I was in agony waiting until eventually she came to me two days later and placed my phone beside me.

'You can have it back now.'

'He texted?' I grabbed my phone. 'When?'

'Yesterday morning.'

'Yesterday! Why didn't you tell me sooner?' But I didn't look up to hear her answer and any irritation dissolved into a smile as I read his text and immediately began to formulate my response.

While the silences were never again as long as that once we were officially together, they continued. Few were preceded by any warning that he was going away and there was no pattern to them. Sometimes as far apart as two months and sometimes as close as two weeks. We'd started spending every night together. I began to assume if he went to his own place for the night that I wouldn't see him for at least a couple of days. He was so vague when I asked him where he'd been that I stopped asking and accepted it was just part of who he was. I told myself I wasn't clingy and that I didn't want to change him. But now I know I was afraid of making him angry. I was always afraid of the time he'd never come back.

It feels too quiet in the park. I don't want to give my thoughts a chance to begin their racing. I put in my headphones allowing my phone to randomly select the music. The song that comes on is called *Kolnidur*. I haven't heard it in a while, hadn't even noticed any special quality within it before. It is quiet at first, building, a soft foreign voice and piano. This time it captures me completely. The sound of strings slides across my skin like cold fingers. For the first time I listen completely, watching the mist rise. My eyes find that comfortable spot and I stare transfixed by this song; in that moment it is beautiful and sad. The park merges trapped between reality and mountain lakes.

One time when I woke up, Tristan was already awake and staring at me. I smiled initially, before self consciously hiding my face in the pillow.
'Liv, would you forgive me anything?' His tone was serious, his voice quiet and I felt my heart stop.
'What have you done?' I remember his sad eyes turned to the ceiling.
'If I'd lied to you. Could you ever trust me again?' I didn't say anything. I couldn't speak and he rushed on. 'You might say you could forgive me. But you'd never forget. *I* could never forget.'
Escape my mind told me. *Get out now.*
'No.' I finally whispered. 'I don't think I could forgive you.' Tristan nodded, but didn't say anything. We remained that way. I watched him, while he stared straight up. 'You can't say that and then just say nothing.' I eventually demanded beginning to feel angry. The only time I'd ever snapped at him. He didn't stay with me that night.

I leave the park and walk aimlessly. I can't go anywhere without a goal and each gap of time becomes a race. Can I make that lamppost before I see another person? Will I pass that bin before the jogger overtakes me? I am a coward, I set myself these insignificant challenges only after I am fairly certain I will win. I pretend someone is following me and I have a certain amount of time to reach a spot before I am safe. Their eyes will turn me to stone if they catch me, so I must keep moving. I play with my necklace absently. The pendant is smooth beneath my fingers and I rub it back and forth. Tristan didn't give it to me. Tristan didn't give me anything. I have nothing. Not even a photo. It's like he never even existed.

In dreams everything makes so much sense, until you're awake retelling it to yourself and realise it's all disjointed and strange. That was Tristan and I. We made sense, but now I look back and think why did I take no photos?

Why did I never meet his family or friends?

Why did I let him give me so little of himself?

'I want you to meet some friends of mine.' Tristan said to me, not that long before the end. I looked up from my book in surprise and his hand playing with my hair stilled.

'Really?'

'Yes.'

'Ok.' I was determined not to make a big thing of it. My friends hated him, we never spent time with them. His friends were always a complete mystery. His hand continued running through my hair. I tried to get back into my book, but I couldn't concentrate. 'Why now?' I asked innocently. My eyes didn't move from the words in front of me. I stared so hard they looked like lines, dots and random swimming patterns.

'It's time to share you.'

I pass the bar we met Tristan's friends in. I should say I pass the bar we were *supposed to* meet Tristan's friends in.

When we entered the noisy bar, Tristan held my hand. It was November, close enough to acceptably decorate for Christmas and the bar had gone all out. There was a massive tree by the small stage and yellow fairy lights framed the windows and laced the ceiling. Tristan rubbed the back of my hand with his thumb. He scanned the bar and I saw him grimace, but he was taller than me and I couldn't see.

'Come on Liv. Let's get this over with.' He led me to a large empty table, he turned to smile at me. His smile faded as I sat down.

'I thought they were already here.' I told him and watched, feeling confused, as his expression turned stony. He sat next to me, his hand releasing mine as he pulled a chair out. I watched the door, every person was my potential jury.

And the waiting started.

Once that night I went to the toilet and when I came back I thought I heard Tristan's voice, but when I reached the table there was no one else there. He sighed, he shifted, he ran his hand through his hair. I'd never seen him look so uncomfortable.

I ordered us some drinks and tried to talk about other things. I tried to pretend we weren't being stood up.

As the bar grew quieter, it became table service. A waitress wearing a Santa hat approached our table. And I've remembered this moment so many times, because even now I don't understand what happened. She came to our table smiling.

'Can I get you guys any more drinks?' Her eyes jumped between the two of us.

I picked up the cocktail menu and scanned it, fondly remembering another night when I'd first introduced Tristan to cocktails.

'You win.' It was Tristan's voice. Cold. I frowned and looked up, thinking maybe I'd imagined it. The waitress looked uneasy.

'Did you say something?' I asked. Without even looking at me, Tristan stood rudely pushing back his chair. It scraped horribly on the slate-tiled floor. He turned and walked out.

I stare into the bar for too long. I don't realise I've stopped dead in the street, remembering that evening. Remembering how Tristan left me there. My heart shrivels at the memory; it cringes and collapses in on me.

Suddenly reflected back at me is the field, dancing sparks of light race across the glass. Black shapes curl and ripple around the edges of my eyes.

They were there. That night. They were there.

I feel dizzy. I am falling. I am floating. I am fading. There is no reflection. Just shimmering glass and a place I suddenly long to be.

Yes.

No. A rational part of me asserts. What is happening? There is nothing I can hide behind, nothing I can blame for this. I am not asleep. I am not sick. I am not drunk… yet this is still happening. It all falters and recedes, the bar and its upturned chairs inching back in.

No. Don't think, Liv. The voice whispers. The black shapes won't let go. *Let us in.* I can see the mountains and darkness, like a hand trying to claw its way back in.

Let us in.

Those words shock me. They are so familiar. I feel rocketed back to a time near the beginning of Tristan.

'Let me in, Liv,' he whispered to me, his fingers gently running along the nape of my neck. 'Let me in.'

I stare into the darkened bar until all traces of the mountain are gone. I carry on walking, heading for home. I check my phone. One missed call. I savour looking at it, anyone could have called me. Tristan could have called me. I imagine if that were true and the scenario that would then take place. Still focusing on my phone, I step to the side to let someone pass me on the street. Looking back I realise I have dodged a phantom, nothing remains. Finally I press the button and see that the missed call is from the counselling office. I immediately miss having the potential of *one missed call*. I realise I've missed my appointment. A text bleeps, it says I have a voice message and I listen to a secretary explain that I need to call back and rearrange my appointment. She sounds impatient and is probably sick of flaky people avoiding appointments. I press redial and turn off the pavement into a small paved garden with flowers and benches. I perch on a bench, phone pressed between my ear and shoulder as I rub my cold hands together. When I get through to the counselling team, I'm glad it is an automated service. I listen to my options. I don't want to make a new appointment. I haven't done my *homework*.

I remember the feeling of deliciously sinking into that crystal lake, as satisfying as icy water on the hottest of days. I haven't felt that kind of peace in a long while.

Come back. I shiver hearing that whisper, but refuse to turn and look. *You don't have to see us to know we're here. Come back and find Tristan.*

Find Tristan? That catches my attention.
'Where is he?' I speak softly under my breath. The frost coating the earth holds everything rigid and still, no sound replies only the distant hum of traffic. The mist in the air is like a cushion between me and everything else. I think I can see mountains sliding through fog, out of reach and ethereal.

I want to go home. The thought appears in my head as if placed by a foreign hand. *Home* home. Back to the village I grew up in. I end the call and look up another number. One I haven't called for months. It rings for a long time, but I'd known it would. Eventually, 'hello?'

'Hello Mum. It's me, Olivia.'

CHAPTER 4

I never quite remember her voice right. Mum always sounds different and vaguely uncertain.

'Olivia?' There is a pause where I imagine her to be summoning up a smile and recalling details. 'How are you? It's been a while.'

'About four months.' I confirm.

'How's school?'

'It's over.'

'Oh, already? Well, I hope you celebrated.' There is an awkward pause, where we both search for what to say next. 'How's Tristan?' she asks. My heart starts hammering. I can't speak.

'Liv?' She sounds so far away.

` We broke up.' I hear the catch in my voice and hate how weak I sound. My eyes sting and I hope she doesn't ask me if I'm ok. I hate being asked if I'm ok when I'm not ok.

'Oh. I'm sorry.' I know she genuinely means it. She is probably the only person who genuinely means it. She'd liked Tristan. They'd met a few times and she'd been chattier than usual, which meant a lot coming from her. Tristan had been reluctant to meet her, only wanting to stay at her house when she was away for the weekend. He told me he liked her after they'd finally met. His exact words, *I like your mother's mind.*

'I'm thinking of coming home for a bit.'

'Really?' We are able to handle a few other exchanges before we say goodbye with relief and hang up. I imagine she'll forget I called by the end of the day.

Don't get me wrong, I love my mother and I know she loves me. I don't mistake her lack of attention for a lack of affection anymore. We are too similar in too many ways for that. She is often preoccupied and distant, but warm and kind when she does shine her light on me. She reminds me of a kite, drifting and likely to become lost if nothing holds her down. I don't hold too tightly to the string that binds us. We haven't lived together full time since I was sixteen when I moved to board at college. She's become more of a mystery to me these last couple of years.

It is dark again and I can't get to sleep. When I close my eyes I see Tristan's dark brown ones, so close to mine. It's like he's in the room. I open my eyes and it's dim, moonlight flowing faint through cracks in my curtains. No sound. I could be alone in the world for all I can hear. Time could stand still, this moment could last forever.

You are alone here.

I look without turning my head toward the cruel whisper. A creature is sitting on the easy chair in the corner of my room. It is hunched over uncomfortably, its head too big for its body. In the shadows it seems to have antlers, they sway as it shakes its head. I feel threatened by its hulking presence. Its eyes blink, yellow holes as its head bobs up and down.

Why do you stay?

It's a good question that rattles around my head long after I fall asleep. I dream about Tristan again, but it's a memory I dream about. A time when we were at Mum's house and we had it all to ourselves. The wind howled viciously outside and we cocooned up inside. The rain hammered the windows like it was desperate to get in and we lit a fire. The moment reminded me of a poem I read once so I dug it out of my mother's collection to read to Tristan. He watched me intently as I read, until I blushed self-consciously. In the dream though, I can't speak the words of the poem. My mouth is heavy and I can't get any words out. I try to stand up but my legs don't work. They are resistant and heavy. Tristan watches me grimly.

'Open your eyes, Liv,' he urges.

I wake twisted in sheets. My phone tells me it's after 11 AM already. I wish I was still asleep, even a nightmare feels better than here. There is a figure in my doorway, which I ignore. I have an appointment this afternoon with Miss Salter and then I have to catch my train home. The dark figure shifts, a hand outstretched. I turn to look just to make it disappear. The figure doesn't disappear – it's Nina.

'Liv?' Her voice is unsure.

'What do you want?' My voice is scratchy from sleep and lack of use. I sound harsher than I intend.

'I just wanted to check if you were alright. 'I've heard you coughing a lot.' Nina's room is below mine. 'None of us have seen you for days.' She looks concerned. It is then that I notice Beth has come up behind her.

'Oh, she's fine.' Beth's voice is flat, almost disappointed I imagine, as she calls this news down the stairs to the others.

'Everyone's finished their exams.' Nina says. 'We're going to celebrate tonight, do you want to come?' Behind her Beth sighs. She already knows my answer and she retreats heavily back downstairs.

'No, I can't,' I say quietly. Even though Beth is right that I won't come, I don't want her to hear me say it. 'I'm going to stay with my Mum.' Nina nods and smiles a little. She likes my Mum.

'What time's your train? Maybe you have time for dinner with us?'

'No, I have a … I'm busy before my train.' No one knows I see a counsellor.

'Lunch? You look like you haven't eaten properly in days.' I admire her persistence even though it makes me sad to refuse her.

'Thanks for asking, but I haven't really got any money and I need to pack.' My voice is awkward. Nina's shoulders slump forward and we both know once again her kindness has been defeated. Seeing her like this makes me feel like crying. I want to tell her to keep trying, to please not give up on me just yet. I don't speak and she backs up, closing the door behind her. My vision blurs as I watch her go. I feel tears slide down my face.

It's also after she has left that I think she'd given me the perfect homework to present to Miss Salter and I refused it. I consider lying. The thought is quickly dismissed. Those sharp eyes would find me out. They would pierce right through me. Besides, I have no energy to lie. I feel like I have no energy for anything, except when I think of that other place. Running through that meadow, beating against the wind and slicing through the tall grass.

'You have some kind of power over me. I want to do one thing, but I end up doing the other.' Tristan almost sounded angry. 'It wasn't supposed to be this way.'

'How was it supposed to be?'

'I don't know,' his voice quietened and I took his words more seriously than I did the moment before. 'I've never felt this way before. I can't stand the thought of anything hurting you.'

'Nothing's going to happen to me.' I took his hand and interlaced our fingers.

'I won't let it,' he promised. 'You're mine. I am yours.' His eyes were a little resigned when he told me. 'I love you, Liv.'

I watch the rain hit the window. It strikes the glass and races jerkily away from me, dodging and merging with other raindrops. It is all darkness outside though and I imagine the train isn't really moving at all. There is always rain when I come home. I shift uncomfortably. The train is busy. I hate busy trains.

I hate the forced enclosure. Feet fighting to avoid feet under the table, small apologies, painful angles, strangers' bodies brushing yours as they pass and tired glares from those trapped standing. It always starts on the platform, people edging forward, elbows poised as the train approaches, guessing where the doors will stop. At least today I got a seat. A positive thought, I think Miss Salter would be proud. She forgave me today.

'We'll count going home as your homework.' She'd leant forward with a conspiratorial smile, as if she was doing me a favour and it was our little secret. 'Spending time with your family, with the people who love you, will be so good for you.'

I almost didn't have the heart to disappoint her, but I also liked to trip her up. 'I'm an only child and my father is dead.' I pointed out, maybe more deadpan than was necessary. My mum is my only family. She was an only child too. I come from a long line of 'only child' children. Miss Salter had shifted awkwardly at my delivery of the dead dad news. I think she realised we'd spent so much time covering Tristan and my exams that she knew nothing else about me.

'Well,' she amended. 'A mother's comfort is sometimes the best cure for young love and a broken heart.'

How can she use these stupid words to describe what is going on inside of me? She gives things nice little names like 'young love' as if that changes the mess left behind. She has more words too, 'worry time' and 'change cues'. It makes me angry and I don't even really know why. Maybe because it belittles me and everything I feel to have her sum me up so shortly. How I feel is the most real thing I have. What am I without it? Behind the loneliness and anxiety I'm afraid there is nobody here anymore. I'm afraid there's nothing left of the person I used to be.

I have no memory of my father. He died before I was born. When I tell people he's dead, I always get the same expression and the

same words. The pity and the *Oh, I'm so sorry.*
And I think, sorry for what? I don't miss him. I don't even miss the idea of him. There is no daddy-shaped hole inside of me, no sense of incompleteness. Why should a man I've never met have any say over who I am? I don't know how he died, but Mum once let slip that he'd been in and out of hospital with problems to do with his mental health. I've only ever seen a handful of pictures of him, all with my mum. I remember it was always her face I fixated on, never his. She looked the happiest I'd ever seen her in those few photos. I'd given up a long time ago trying to recreate that expression on her face. You needed a soulmate to look that happy I'd surmised as a little girl. It was then that I'd also decided that I didn't look like either of my parents. I wasn't *like* either of them. I didn't want to be bits and pieces of someone else. I didn't want their flaws and vices. I was brand new.

The train grows quiet as each stop takes passengers with it. When I have the table to myself I take out the questionnaire from my bag and stare at it. I've seen a similar questionnaire once before, years ago a friend showed me. Not long after, my friend was diagnosed with depression. Depression is too big. Too consuming. Once diagnosed, it will persist on and off for the rest of my life and that thought alone drains me completely. I don't want a life that hard, I don't have the strength for it. I don't want medication just to feel normal. I don't want the Shades to be waiting for me when I die.
The black dog that barks in the night. I don't remember where I heard the phrase, but it has always haunted me. A lurking companion that never quite leaves. Now, it makes me think of the yellow eyes.
I am to return with the completed questionnaire in two weeks, although Miss Salter tells me in a serious and concerned voice that I am to go immediately to my doctor if I score highly.

Do I have little interest in things I used to enjoy? My options; Never, Sometimes, Often, Always... I can't remember the last time I did anything I enjoyed.

Do I feel down and hopeless? Always. Is this how my father felt? I stuff the questionnaire back in my bag. I'm not ready to face this. I stare out the window. Reflected animal eyes meet mine.

I don't know who looks more surprised. Me to see my mother waiting on the poorly lit platform or her to see her daughter step from the train.

'You remembered,' I say as we step close for a moment in something resembling a hug. She touches my hair and smiles. I follow her from the station pulling my suitcase behind me. My mum never changes and knowing that makes me feel a small measure of comfort. Mum wears the same faded charity shop clothes and handmade creations that she wore when I was a child. This evening it is her cardigan I recognise as one of her own, it hangs uneven and bulky around her shoulders. The arms are slightly too long and rolled back, the colour I can guess was aimed at purple but somewhere in the dying process it has turned a murky brown. We pass the car park, which she never uses, and find her old green car on double yellow lines on the main road. I know she won't have bothered to lock it so I go straight to the boot to dump my case. I hear her jewellery jingling behind me as she roots through her bag to find the car keys. The car journey feels longer than it probably is. We don't talk, but I keep waiting for questions. I watch her hands on the steering wheel, six out of ten fingers bear rings. The most familiar to me is a thumb ring with two silver rams' heads staring each other down. When I was little I would sneak into her room just to find that ring and add it to all my games. She'd tear through the house looking for it if she ever noticed it missing, but she never thought to check if I had it. I always sneaked it back before she found out it was me, afraid of what she might do.

Throughout school, my friends would disappear to 'phone home' or jump up mid conversation...*hang on my mum's calling*. What are you calling home for? I'd ask and receive a shrug or a confused look... *just to talk*. I'd never called my mum just to talk. It was with a curious mix of indulgence, smugness, and mild jealousy that I viewed these constant interruptions to their lives. What do you talk about, I asked Nina. *Everything*, she replied. And I wondered why I didn't want to share my life. Why didn't I want this woman to hold my secrets and listen to my problems?

I've made a mistake coming home. I don't know why I thought nothing could follow me here. My room looks like the room of the little girl I used to be. I doubt Mum comes in here much. She's found a home for an old loom of hers on my desk, but even that looks dusty with lack of use. Nothing else has changed or even been moved. Stuffed animals clutter shelves, dog-eared teen novels I used to love are still strewn about. The walls still hold my blu-tacked posters of places I wanted to travel. Notebooks with things I'd written that no longer make sense to me are hidden in all the drawers. I read through some wondering at the mind inside that girl. I find detailed maps of made-up lands, cities and villages, woodlands and mountain ranges. It catches me off guard, but I think Tristan would have loved to see these. He loved fantasy and all things imaginary. When we stayed here we stayed in the spare room because it had a double bed. I'd only let him glance in this room, embarrassed by how little I'd allowed it to grow up. Now I think he'd have loved me more if he'd seen it. I hide the notebooks back in their drawers.

I don't even consider staying in the spare room I'd last shared with Tristan. I don't go near it. In my room I can lie still and almost pretend I've imagined the last five years of my life. There's an old bright yellow stereo, but I can't plug my phone into it so instead I listen to CDs I find scattered around the house. Mum tends to disappear, often for hours at a time, and when she comes back she is usually found sitting by the fire with her spinning wheel, methodically feeding in wool and moving her foot up and down on the treadle.

The rain stops on my second day back home and I take the chance to escape outside. Mum's house is at the bottom of a hill by a river on the edge of the village. Surrounded by hills and trees, it doesn't have any views and is often dark inside. It's the kind of house I would always pace restlessly wanting to leave, but once outside the house would glow invitingly. If I walk long enough away from the village, through fields and small woodlands, I feel entirely isolated. It was a feeling I loved. I could pretend I was in a different land, an explorer, a survivor trekking through deserted foreign lands.

But now I feel watched.

I see shadows moving behind trees and swaying figures sitting in branches. I cross a small wooden bridge into a sloped woodland, there is a narrow path between the wild garlic and bluebells. The garlic smell always knocks me back to childhood. Further up the path I cut to the left through thick plants and thorns. I feel the smooth give as my boots sink into mud with each step. Near the riverbank there is a tree with thick branches that grows out over the river. Its great exposed roots make it an easy climb. I hoist myself up like I have done hundreds of times before and walk carefully out over the river. The branch is slippery with moss, but it's a balance I know well. I used to love sitting out here, hidden from view from the path, but able to see somebody coming from all directions.

'Thank you for bringing me here, Liv.' Tristan smiled and laced his fingers through mine.

'I knew you'd like it,'

'It reminds me of home.' Tristan's voice was uncertain, enough to make me turn from studying the river. Tristan never spoke about a place called home.

'Where's home?'

'Far away from here. Remote, but beautiful like this place. You would like it. I do wish I could take you there.'

His wording implied he wouldn't ever actually take me there, but I didn't ask.

'I knew you were a country bumpkin too!' I squeezed his hand. I wanted to know where, when and all the little bits in-between. Why didn't I ask? Because I was always afraid of the answer.

Tristan pulled out his phone to Google the phrase (he did that a lot during our conversations). A moment later, 'hey!' He replied indignantly, knocking my shoulder gently with his. Our eyes caught and held fighting smiles. 'Actually,' he confessed with a mock sigh, 'that does just about sum us up.'

Us? I already knew better than to ask Tristan for more, but my mind wrapped around that word and played with it. We sat in silence for a while, listening to the river and the birds. 'You come here a lot?' Tristan spoke eventually.

'Yeah, since I was about eight or nine.'

'I like the thought of you patrolling this land as a child. Guarding your village.'

'Hardly,' I laughed. 'I just always felt safe here.'

'Safe? On your own?' Tristan pulled me to my feet and, arms outstretched, we balanced our way back to the trunk. 'I always thought people felt safer in numbers.'

I shook my head. 'Nah, I've always felt safer by myself.'

Tristan smiled as he helped me down from the tree, but it didn't quite reach his eyes.

Yes, there was a lot about Tristan I didn't know. An embarrassing mountain of basic facts. But I always thought that I knew the things that mattered.

I knew his kindness and his generosity. I knew his playfulness and his attention to detail. I knew the little things like how he took his coffee (Tristan hated tea) and how on cold mornings he liked to use my hairdryer to warm his clothes before putting them on. I knew that he ate fried eggs with a teaspoon. I knew that he loved Dr Suess and TV shows about home renovations. He hated anything scary or sad (why would you make yourself feel that way on purpose, Liv?!) He didn't have a side of the bed and slept wherever, but always curled around me. He knew I liked the cold side of the pillow and turned my pillow for me if I got up in the night. He loved the stars and learning all the constellations. He loved to take long walks, either aimlessly around the city or mountain hikes. He liked to feed the squirrels in the park and he'd always capture a spider and release it outside rather than killing it. He was gentle and thoughtful. He noticed me and did things for me before I even asked. He made me feel special. He made me feel loved.

'Tristan…is that you?' My mobile crackled against my ear.
'Hi Baby.' I tried to keep the smile off my lips when I heard his soft voice and words. Tristan knew I hated the endearment. A character in a film we'd watched once said it a lot and Tristan, like a sponge, started using it on me. More so when he realised it made me cringe.
'Where are you? Is your signal bad? This line is terrible.' I took my phone from my ear to turn the volume up and missed his next words. 'What did you say?'
'I said I miss you.'
'Then why aren't you here?' The line crackled more, his words skipped and jumped. 'Where are you?' More words were lost between us as the connection played with our conversation. Tristan wasn't one for phone conversations. I realised we'd never spoken on the phone for longer than a few minutes before. I walked around my room hoping to improve the connection and

switching between hellos and 'can you hear me?'. I ended up standing on my bed with my head sticking out of the skylight. It was cold and the sky was as clear as I'd ever seen it. The stars looked amazing. Tristan sounded far away, but it was comforting to think he had the same clear starry sky above him. 'Is there a reason you called?' I asked when the line sounded better.

'No, I just wanted to hear your voice.' He sounded sad.

'Are you alright?'

'Yeah. I feel better for hearing you. I just....' Something that wasn't the line stopped him talking and I heard other voices, but I couldn't hear what they were saying. He came back with a sigh. 'I have to go.'

'Look at the sky.' I told him suddenly, thinking a night as clear as this he'd love. A night as clear and calm as this can put things in perspective.

The line picked up its crackling again and he sounded distracted and sad. 'Yeah, it's a beautiful sunset.' I looked up again at the stars.

'When will I see you next?' I asked instead of what I wanted to ask.

'Tomorrow I hope you'll see me.' The line went dead. I closed my skylight, but left the blind open so as I lay on my bed I could see the stars. Tristan sounded far away because he *was* far away. A different time zone far away. I put on some music, but I barely heard it over the roaring question in my head.

Where are you, Tristan?

I turn my music up to drown out stray thoughts of Tristan before I lower myself to sit on the branch. *Biffy Clyro* blasts out. Go away, Tristan. I close my eyes on a deep breath.

That's right, the voice says.

I open my eyes slowly, but I don't look around. The river ripples below me, a silvery grey shadow. Through the running water I see inviting glimpses of the green mountain. I shake my head to clear it away, but it remains a field of green hidden under the water. I lean forward, my hands digging into the moss and bark of my ledge.

Yes. Come with us.

I remember what it felt like running through that field, the calmness of the lake. The gentle tracing of my fingers over that face of stone. The feeling of isolation was a beautiful retreat. It was a retreat from exams, college, friends, my mind and even Tristan. I want that.

Come closer.

My vision shifts and shakes, little black creatures crawl all around me. I barely notice them on the periphery. The river, the woods, it all falls away like thousands of little blocks. Behind them is my meadow, this time it is in bloom with more flowers, waving yellow and white. I feel the sun and I lean into it. There is a faint feeling of disorientation and falling and then I am there, lying spread like a star in the grass.

Come to the lake.

Don't be afraid.

Come closer.

The voices are louder in the meadow, more real. They can't be ignored here. I sit up and see the mountain directly in front of me. Before I realise what I'm doing I'm up and running toward it. My legs stretch and I feel my muscles burn with the rush. There is no sound other than what I make, my feet hitting the ground, my breath and the rustle as I slip through the grass.

The lake seems alive; it moves gently, lapping at the dark sand in slow measured breaths. In places the grass grows right out into the water. A turquoise dragonfly hovers up soundlessly, dancing between flowers.

You could stay here.

The voice is close. At first I don't see it, but then I see the eyes. Still yellow eyes hidden in the grass watch me.

'What are you?'

That doesn't matter. There are other voices and I see more eyes dancing between the grass.

What matters is you can stay with us.

For as long as you want.

Come with us.

Come closer.

'Where to?'

Come with us to the other side of the mountain.

To Tristan.

There's his name again. They all clamour to be heard, patient persuasive voices, but all overlapping with each other.

He wants to see you.

Give us a chance.

Come with us.

Come closer.

The idea that Tristan wants to see me are words I've longed to hear. Maybe he's trapped here, maybe he needs my help.

'Is Tristan alright?'

Come with us to the other side of the mountain.

To their village.

He's waiting for you.

I look up at the mountain. Its peak soars proudly into the cloudless blue sky. The lake is a long sprawling thing, stretching far off in either direction.

Swim.

Come with us.

Come closer.

'Does Tristan need my help?' I press, but it's hard to dredge up much concern. Something about this place is too relaxing for worry. The creatures suddenly break through the grass and I see them clearly for the first time. They are strange beasts, their movement and size remind me of giant wolves, but their shapes are indistinct, the edges blurred.

Come and help Tristan.

This is his home.

Come closer.

They pass me to enter the lake, breaking the water silently. Their heads dip low and they swim just below the surface, dark shapes drawing on the mountain. I knew the answer even before they said it. It slots into place and makes so much sense. Of course, this is Tristan's world, his home. I always knew he had secrets. I knew he was sometimes far away. He didn't fit in with my friends, the city or anywhere. He didn't fit with anyone except me. He didn't fit in my world.

My world. When I'm here I easily feel like I don't belong there either.

The warm water laps around me and I walk until my feet can't sink into the sand. I duck my head under the water and start to swim. From somewhere I hear a noise, in this quiet place it doesn't sound right. Ahead of me the wolves stop and lift their heads out of the water to look back at me.

Keep swimming.

Stay with us.

The noise continues, it jars with the beauty around me. I try to think what it could be. It sounds like a bellowing animal. The mountain blips and blurs, everything around me shudders. I tread water, looking all around me.

Come closer, stay close.

They all speak the same words to me and all I can think is I *want* to, I want to stay. The noise gets louder and is joined by a higher pitch howl, suddenly I feel a great pressure on my lungs. I try to breathe, but there's no air and I'm sinking. The entire scene around me is shaking so violently it begins to crumble and behind it I see grey darkness. I am cold and the noise is a roaring in my ears. The wolves sound faint, already like something from a dream and I feel real solid hands grab me. The mountain crumbles away and I'm gone, plunged into icy cold darkness.

CHAPTER 5

Hands drag me up and my chest hurts as I struggle to breathe. The roaring stops abruptly, sounds change with a pop and I'm breathing again. I take great coughing gulps of air. I hear a dog yapping nearby and a man's voice.

'Can you hear me?' I am dragged out of the river and feel hard pebbles, sticks and roots as I stumble and drop to the bank. The yapping is louder and all around me. 'Hello? Can you hear me? Get away, you!' The yaps' intensity recedes briefly, only to return seconds later. I open my eyes and the white sky through the trees hurts my eyes. 'Thank god you're alright!' A stranger's face obscures my view. I turn my head, still coughing and am confronted with two white furry faces. The man pushes them away from me as I sit up. My chest aches and my throat feels raw. I put my hand up and feel stickiness in my hair. Blood coats my fingers. 'Just a scratch I think,' I hear the man say. 'It looks worse than it is.'

'What happened?' I whisper.

'I was just walking the dogs. We heard a splash and they took off barking towards the river and then we found you.' The man shivers. 'Floating face down in the river. I've never been so scared in my life!' He puts his hand to his brow and I know it's an image he'll never forget. He's probably in his fifties, a navy fleece covered in dog hair and muddy wellies, he's soaking wet. I notice then how cold it is, it's just started raining and the wind is chilly on my wet clothes. 'Come on. Can you get up? We should get you warm and dry. Do you live nearby?'

'Yes.' I stand shakily, accepting his help. The dogs are quiet now. My soaking earbuds trail from my pocket to the ground. I wonder if my phone survived. 'I can get home by myself.'

'No, I couldn't leave you. Let me help you home. You might need a doctor.'

'No. I'm fine. I must have slipped. Stupid really.' I cough to strengthen my voice. 'I'm fine honestly. Thanks for your help.' I back away from him. 'Thank you.' I mumble again and stumble away. I hear him speaking, calling me back, but he doesn't follow. I turn and run, pushing through leaves and branches.

I could've died. I didn't feel myself fall from the branch, even hitting the water and banging my head didn't wake me from wherever I was, whatever trance I was in. If that man hadn't been walking his dogs, if he hadn't heard me fall, then I would be dead. Against my will I think of the Shades again. Mum said they waited for death to stake their claim, but could they lure you to it?

If I hadn't woken up, I'd still be swimming in the lake towards Tristan. Really? I'm sceptical. None of this can be real. Shades and talking wolves aren't real. I must've fallen, banged my head and imagined the whole thing. Or maybe I'm losing my mind. Maybe I'm crazy just like my father. I feel like I've been slipping since Tristan left me and struggling to keep hold of anything. Is this what a nervous breakdown feels like? More likely than the world disintegrating around me.

Sometimes when I'm stressed by exams and work, or just dwelling mildly in a depressed hangover, thinking about this garlicky woodland makes me happy again. The river, the birds and my branch make my insides ease. There is an eternal and unhurried pace to it all. The same as witnessing a magnificent star-laden sky, thinking of this sanctuary where nothing really matters is like taking a deep breath.

It's like everything unwinds and takes a step back.

It's like a pair of glasses coming off and a sighed 'my god, but you're beautiful'.

Nothing seems so important that it's worthy of anxiety. Everything is simple. No matter what happens, this woodland full of wild garlic, flowers and birdsong will always be here, a sky filled with stars will always be above me.

After today, I wonder if it'll still feel like my safe place.

Mum's car isn't in the drive when I get home. I'm glad I don't have to avoid her. I leave a puddle behind me as I prepare and drop my wet phone into a tub of rice in the kitchen and then go to the mirror in the hallway. Rivulets of diluted blood run down a pale face. The cut is only an inch long, almost lost in my hairline. I touch it softly, hissing as I feel the bump. I press it again, just wanting to feel the pain. It is a reminder of where I am now. A reminder of what is real. My eyes leave the bruising cut on my forehead and trail to explore the rest of my face. I step back to see my whole body and I think *who* is this person? The more I look the more I see a stranger. I stare so hard I am freakish and inhuman. I am just a collection of shapes and colour. What *mak*es this any more real than the lake I just swam in? Than the meadow and the wolves? I touch the bruise again. It feels real. I hear a car on the drive and look out the window. I watch my mum drift out of her car and towards the house as if it isn't even raining. I run upstairs before she reaches the door and head straight for the shower. I make sure the water is hot before I step under it. It hurts in a good way. I wash the blood from my hair and as I watch it wash down the plughole I know I have to go back to the meadow. My knees shake and I feel tremors spasm through me. I drop to a crouch, resting my palms against the tiles. Even if I don't find Tristan I have to go back. Even if it's part of my imagination. I want to try.

Downstairs, I can hear that Mum is back at her spinning wheel. I hear her humming beneath her breath.

'Is that you, Liv?' she calls as the stairs creak. I bypass the living room and don't reply, who else would it be? In the kitchen I put the kettle on. As it boils I notice how still everything seems outside. It is dark, but the rain has stopped and not even a breeze disturbs the trees or grass. The clouds in the sky hang low and ominous. It's like looking at a painting. A muted and dull painting compared with the vibrant greens of the mountain and the life in the waving flowered grass. I check on my phone, the screen flickers unhappily. I drop it back in the rice. Does rice even work with drowned phones?

I open the back door and am struck by the instant cold that greets me. Without thinking, I scan for yellow eyes and figures in the trees. Nothing is out there. Maybe, they are gone for good. Maybe, they've given up trying now.

A gentle tug on my wet hair makes me jump. Mum wanders past me to the kettle.

'Shut the door, would you? It's supposed to be below freezing tonight.'

'Sorry.' I murmur, closing the door. She gets another mug from the cupboard and sets about making the tea. I sit at the kitchen table, watching her and wondering if she'll mention the large yellow bruise that's developing on my forehead. I wonder if she's even noticed. Is the old bedtime story she told me years ago actually true? I dare myself to ask her if Shades are real and whether she's ever seen one. But still I sit there mutely watching her. Do Shades drag humans back to a meadow to meet their master? Never being in that meadow again makes my breath hurt. It makes my heart feel like it's sitting in my throat trying to escape. The meadow didn't feel like the end, it felt like a beginning. Without it the pointlessness of everything is suddenly overwhelming. Where do I go from here? A mug of tea is placed in front of me.

'Give it time,' I hear Mum say softly. I nod, not trusting my voice and unable to look at her. I feel her gentle tug on my hair again. She leaves the kitchen.

'Oh, Liv,' she says from the doorway. 'Be careful, won't you?' I turn around confused, but she's already disappeared through the door.

It's the first night in a long time that I sleep soundly. No weird dreams, voices or flying beds. It's the first time I wake up and feel clear headed in weeks. The light from my window is strangely bright. Drawing the curtains, I find the world blanketed in thick clean snow.

I hate when it snows in the city. I hate how quickly it becomes trampled, dirty and old. I hate how it lingers, unwanted, for days until left behind is just lethal patches of ice. But in the countryside, I love snow. I love being the first to break fresh snow. I love how I can find pristine untouched fields. I love the feeling of leaving the cold and warming up by an open fire.

Mum's boots are missing and I see prints wandering off up the drive. I don't bother with breakfast and wrap up in my coat and a brown knitted hat, one of Mum's creations with flaps and tassels that cover the ears. I pull on my boots and head off in the opposite direction of her footprints into the fields. The wintry sun provides little warmth, but turns the fresh snow into a dazzling crystalline crust across the fields. Snowdrifts rear up along the hedgerows. I kick my way through, my destructive side relishing the demolition. I reach my woodland and stomp through the snow, listening to it crunch and creak beneath me. I head towards the path towards my tree over the river and hear the gentle gurgle of water. The ice stretches out from both sides, but doesn't quite meet in the middle allowing a thin stream of water to meander through. For a moment, I imagine my body suspended in the river surrounded by ice.

The base of my tree is deep in snow so I allow myself to fall back into it. Through my thick coat, jeans and gloves I don't feel the cold, just softness. I close my eyes and refuse to let my thoughts intrude. I try to chase away exams, graduation and having to move out of our student house. It's the end of a chapter and I have no idea what's coming next. University feels scarily big and final. I try to chase away the image of myself face down in the river. My phone is still convalescing in rice, but I found an old iPod in a drawer in my room. I have no idea what's on it, but it's all I've got. Soon I'm lying in my snowy bed just listening to music. Music the me of a decade earlier had deemed worthy.

That's right, a voice whispers. *That's nice.*

Once you don't try so hard it comes so easily.

I open my eyes and see something hanging in the trees. For a moment it is a dead body, hung and swaying in the breeze and then I see the yellow eyes smiling. I smile back and the meadow is shimmering.

My transition to the meadow is the smoothest it's ever been. I lie cocooned in the grass for a moment, just happy to be back. My legs are bare and stretched, soaking in the sunlight. I'm wearing a pair of frayed denim shorts I haven't worn in years. The edges had curled up and inwards until they were borderline indecent, but unwilling to throw them away I'd hidden them in the back of my wardrobe.

The wolves are waiting for me at the lake.

Come closer.

Don't think.

Come and see Tristan.

I enter the crisp water. For a moment, I'm tempted to sink down and rest, to lie with my statue friend for a while.

Come and see Tristan, they urge.

I turn onto my back and watch the brilliant blue sky as I swim backstroke towards the mountain. I am safe. I am warm. I am real. I feel content. A feeling so foreign to me I revel in the glorious simplicity of it.

Stepping out of the lake on the other side, the sun dries me like I was never even wet. The wolves swarm around me, indistinct they blur into each other. I look up craning my neck to see the very top of the mountain, but it's out of view behind the trees. Still my heart beats faster. Tristan is up there.

The mountain seems alive as I draw closer. The air smells like the sky before rain and soon I catch the scent of sweet flowers. I feel warm humid air radiating from the mountain. It is dense and lush with trees. Not the polite woodland I'd expected from the other side of the lake. There is a low hum that at first seems like a warning growl, but then I realise it is the hum of insects. Underneath the green canopy, everything is vibrant and teeming with life. I see busy insects zig-zagging and I watch a large iridescent pinky-purple dragonfly hovering between the flowers. There is the regular chirp of crickets and bird song warbles down from the higher branches.

Come with us.

Come closer.

Come to the other side of the mountain.

The wolves bounce and blur at my feet. They are excited they've got me this far. It's infectious and each step of my bare feet in the warm sand feels like a step towards something I crave.

'Is Tristan up there?' My voice against the jungle chorus seems strange. The mountain takes my words and swallows them up like they never existed and I get no reply. I follow the wolves into the trees. The sand turns to baked mud, and we start the climb.

'Why can't I see you clearly? Are you…Shades?' I ask the wolves this as we walk up the mountain. We've been walking steeply uphill for a while now, but I don't even feel out of breath. I am made of power. My legs are all energy and burn.

You don't understand what we are.

You have imagined our appearance just as you have created your own.

I look down at myself and see a hazy shadow at first and a moment later my legs become clearer, bare and clad in denim shorts. Just like the first time I came here. I am nothing, until I think it. From somewhere in my mind a memory surfaces softly. Mum taking me to see a play when I was little, it was Hansel and Gretel. All I remember of it is the yellow glowing eyes of wolves dancing in the woods, behind a thin curtain. At the time it terrified me and now I think my mind must have created these creatures based on bedtime stories and half memories.

Your mind tries to make you fear what it can't explain.

It doesn't know any better.

Come closer.

Don't fear us.

And I don't. They are nothing like the Shades from Mum's story. There is a rough trodden path we follow and I wonder who uses it. Does Tristan walk here? Does his family? I remember the 'us' he mentioned once. The track is winding and steep in parts, sometimes I have to use my hands to clamber over rocks and logs. Like the meadow this jungle carries its own sense of peace. It says to me work and you will be rewarded. It is simple. Climb. One foot in front of the other. I can do this.

I feel sweat trickle down my back and wisps of hair stick to my face and neck, stray branches scratch me as I pass. I barely give my appearance and small scratches a second thought. It isn't important here. I feel like I belong and that's all that matters. It feels like home.

I know I am smiling as I power on up, my fingers trace the outline of my lips. I've missed you.

The wolves run ahead, darting in and out of the trees. They nip and chase each other, startling birds, and always running back to check I'm following. We are a team. We are excited. I imagine I am one of them and we all merge and blur hazily together like some beautiful dream.

You never have to be afraid again.

Come closer.

'Why are you staring at me like that?' I put my book down, frustrated and unable to read with him watching me.

'I want to make sure I remember you exactly as you are.'

'Are you planning on going somewhere?' My book slipped out of my fingers, falling closed and losing my place.

'I just don't know why you put up with me.' Tristan pushed my hair back from my face and leaned over me. We were so close our chests crushed together and our breath mingled.

'You are hard work,' I said slowly, my eyes wide like I was talking to a child. I saw the amusement light on his face. 'But I put up with you because I love you.' I thought he was going to kiss me, but instead he pressed his forehead to mine and whispered 'Please keep putting up with me.' He picked up my book from where it had fallen to the floor. He leant back and after flicking through the book briefly passed it back to me open. It was on the right page. 'How did you–'

'Details are important, Liv,' he interrupted. 'I like to see all the details.'

There is one wolf that travels alone, yet lingers the closest to me. This one doesn't play excitedly like the others. Sometimes padding softly directly into my footprints and sometimes hidden, just a pair of eyes behind me. Smaller than most of the others and delicate. I doubt these creatures have gender, but I decide she's female. The more I notice her, the more recognisable she becomes and the more I see details. She is paler than the others, a pearly grey. She senses my attention and fixes intelligent yellow eyes upon me. They are assessing and cold. Her blurry face blooms into definition as we slow our pace, regarding each other. The hair is darker grey around her small eyes with spears of longer white hair above them. Her eyes appear delicately outlined with black eyeliner. Towards her nose she turns white with black whiskers and black canine lips with hints of brown. I see white teeth, her long tongue hanging out in the heat. Her ears are mismatched in colour, white and grey, but they are both in tatters. The white ear especially is bad, cut jaggedly down the centre from tip to skull. It leaves the smaller half to droop forlornly. The larger half flaps as she trots, revealing scarred and shiny pink flesh. Have *I* imagined these details? Or did she already look like this? Her eyes evaluate me and I'm certain she can't be purely my creation. She is real. I name her Rip after her ears and vow not to forget her details. We break eye contact at the same time as she drops back. The other wolves move fast, snapping and moving as one, they drive Rip away from me. I am unable to focus on any of them long enough to distinguish any from the pack.

Despite being chased away a couple of times, Rip always eventually returns to my side.

'Is Tristan your master?' My words are quiet. Rip is the only creature to hear.

No. I hear bitter amusement at my question. I hear a low rumble. She is growling, I realise, deep in her throat.

A blur of wolves rush out of the jungle again, snapping and baring teeth at Rip. She senses them and runs before they reach her. I hear them all thrashing about in the dense growth with growls and pained yelps. I try to fight my way through plants and vines towards the noise, but some others appear behind me.

Not that way.

Come with us.

Tristan is this way.

Hearing his name is like being pulled back by a lead. I follow them back to the path. The wolves keep closer to me now. I glance back and see Rip trailing behind us. She skulks at the rear, head hung low and dancing submissively back when one of the others gives a warning snarl.

I don't quite pinpoint the change, but gradually I notice it's not so warm anymore. The thick blanket of humidity has receded. A breeze whispers across my neck. The jungle has morphed around me. The trees are less dense and now impossibly tall and covered in a soft, almost luminescent, green moss. I wonder how long I've been walking. It could have been five minutes, it could have been five hours.

Sometimes a confused thought niggles at the edge of mind. A thought I can't quite structure. Something about me or this place? I don't know. When I chase the thought, the wolves' ears prick up and they renew their pleas.

Come with us.

Come closer.

Not much further.

The trees give way abruptly to a rocky summit.

See how far you've come.

I follow them to where the largest rocks jut out boldly. I climb up for a better view, the wind is stronger here and whips my hair back. I stand at the top feeling elated from the climb. I can see over the forest and jungle canopy. Far below I see the shining edge of the lake, like a shard from a broken mirror. The meadow beyond is an intricate pattern of swirling flowers.

I pause for a long moment to take in the beauty. When I finally turn back I realise I'm alone. No wolves and all is quiet, even the forest sounds of the birds have stopped. I climb down, feeling close to uncovering something big.

'Well, aren't you a clever thing?'

I miss the last foothold and land jerkily, spinning around. A man is standing a few feet from me. His hand shields his eyes from the sun and his stance is relaxed, yet I suddenly feel wary. Others are waiting behind him. They all watch me with smiles hovering on their faces. No Tristan though. The disappointment is sharp across my chest and I release the breath I've been holding.

'How did you get here, little lamb?' The man takes a casual step towards me. He looks nothing like Tristan, but something about him reminds me of Tristan. Something in his smile draws me. Despite this, the wariness niggles in the back of my mind.

'Who are you?' I attempt to sound brave, but my voice comes out small. I look around hoping to see the wolves for some back up. Am I finally face to face with a Shade? Mum's stories never made them sound so human.

'Perhaps she followed someone, Cillian?' a voice brimming with laughter calls. It is from the only woman in the group. Her pale red curls tumble and dance in the breeze. She pushes the strands away with one hand while the other covers her mouth as she tries not to laugh. 'A young shepherd, maybe?' Her features are striking and although not conventionally attractive, when she speaks it renders her beautiful. The man, Cillian, turns toward her as she approaches to get a better look at me. She rests her chin on his shoulder, her arm loosely around his neck. She smiles at me and I notice how green her eyes are.

'Is that it?' Cillian asks, his dark eyes moving back to me. 'Does Orla have it? Did a careless shepherd lose his lamb?' I hear laughter behind him. I take a step back and am pinned against the rock.

'Wandering so far from home,' they murmur. 'Who is she looking for?' One calls lightly, so airily, like he doesn't really care. Mum's soft warning voice plays through my mind, *you'll be an irresistible snack to the darkest of creatures if you don't behave. Don't tell them anything they can use against you.*

Tristan. I almost form the word in my mouth, before I decide not to tell them. They look friendly, but they don't feel friendly. They could take me to Tristan, he could be one of them. Or they could take me to their master to devour my soul. Everything feels oddly like a dream.

'Yes.' Cillian agrees. 'Who are you looking for? Maybe, we can help.' He reaches out a hand and gently runs it up my arm. Orla steps back from him and turns away, but I can hear her laughing. Her laughter distracts me for a moment. I find myself thinking, I could listen to her all day. 'What is your name, lamb?'

'Olivia' I whisper, the word feels extracted from my lips as I listen to Orla.

'Come with us to the village, Olivia. You can rest in the sun and tell us how you found your way here.' Cillian's voice is gentle. 'I know Tobias would love to meet you.' I stare at his hand resting lightly on my arm. I think how tanned and warm it looks, and that thought revolves around my head even as I nod dimly at his suggestion.

Rest in the sun. Rest in the sun.

The niggle rears its head. This isn't right.

Where am I?

How did I get here?

I climbed the mountain – no, before that.

I swam the lake – before that.

I lay in the meadow, resting in the sun. Resting in the sun?

The sky isn't blue.

There was a white sky.

White sky.

I try to follow that thought, but it's too confusing. I look up and see the blue sky. *Don't worry, I am blue,* the sky seems to say to me. *I am blue and you are resting warm beneath me.* Big blue arms cradle me.

I walk with Cillian and the others back into the giant pine trees. They send broken splinters of sunlight spilling across the forest floor. I think I catch glimpses of gleeful yellow eyes hidden in the shadows, but too soon they are always gone. Gradually, I hear the faint strains of music. It comes from all around, whispering through the trees and down from out of the sky, but the others don't seem to notice.

I'll place the sky within your eyes.

The words are sung around me and then I see falling snowflakes. They scatter lightly in all directions as if gravity is nothing to them. The sky burns blue above us all.

'Do you see that?' I whisper to anyone who can hear me. They are talking back and forth over my head and I don't think they hear. I feel tiny surrounded by them.

There's such a fooled heart beating so fast.

Where do I know this song? It bothers me that I can't remember and the trees shudder. Sunlight catches the snowflakes and they glisten as they float around me. I reach out and catch one on my finger. It doesn't melt. I shiver just looking at it resting so benignly on my fingertip.

In search of new dreams, a love that will last.

'You look cold, Olivia.' Cillian says with concern.
And that is all it takes to shatter the world around me.
Cold.
Cold.
Cold.
You look *cold,* Olivia.
The trees, the moss, the lying blue sky it all splinters and falls away. Behind it, I see a cold white sky.
Olivia? Come back, little lamb. Already Cillian's voice sounds distant. I see them all as they disintegrate. None of them are laughing now.
I watch the snow making its unhurried gentle float down to coat the ground. It has all the time in the world and I envy its lazy approach. The song through my earbuds is louder now, but soon quietens as it fades to an end.
It's funny, I think, that people say snow is cold. It really isn't. But it isn't warm either. It just *is.* I am numb. I let my eyes drift closed. They feel better that way. My limbs are heavy, and moving is too much effort. Why move when I'm so comfortable right here in a soft white nest?
Someone disagrees with me and I'm faintly aware of hands gripping me beneath my arms. I am heaved to my feet. A coat is draped around my shoulders and for a moment arms hug me tightly from behind. I know that smell. I *love* that smell.
'Baby, you're like ice.'

CHAPTER 6

I fall back into the scent and it feels like falling back in time. My mind is numb from the cold and all I can say stupidly is, 'Is it really you?'

I try to twist around to see him, but the arms at my side and the chest against my back hold me still. We walk slowly through the snow. I can't open my eyes. The more I try to fight my body and stay awake the heavier and sleepier I become. My feet don't work properly and I stumble.

'I'm so tired, Tris.' The arms tighten and then I'm lifted off my feet, cradled against that Tristan smell I love. I close my eyes and each time I open them I have the feeling more time has passed than I realise.

'Don't leave,' I beg. 'Just let me close my eyes a minute.'

Everything after is distorted images and sensations that jumble together. The heavy white sky that hangs around us. Mum's house. A woollen blanket rasping against my arm. The soft lick of a fire. Kitchen sounds. The smell of lemon and honey tea. Birds hopping madly on the feeder outside. Snow falling across the window.

I shiver. All over my body, uncontrollable shivers and nothing makes me feel warm. I want to go sit in the fire and let it burn my insides. I try to shake free of the blankets, but my fingers just fumble and a hand stops me.

'That's a bad idea.' Those hands wrap around mine and slowly I feel a prickling itchy feeling of warmth returning. It hurts, but I don't care when I have those hands holding mine.

And then all my cloudy images are of Tristan. Tristan helping me drink warm tea. Tristan tending the fire. Tristan watching me as I wake between bouts of confused sleep. He hasn't changed at all, except now his dark eyes look unhappily at me. Why don't you look at me how you used to?

I say nothing, my teeth chatter and no words come out. He talks though. Words I don't want to hear.

'Please stop, Liv,' he says, looking away from me uncomfortably. I close my eyes so I can pretend he isn't talking to me. 'Don't do this to yourself. You're better than this.' My head shakes slightly in decline and a tear rolls down my check. I used to think I was better than this too, but I'm really not. I daren't look at him. I feel something hot and sickening burning in my stomach. 'I'm so sorry, Liv.'

You've ruined me, I want to scream at him.

'Let me go,' he whispers and it's too close to words from our past. *Let me in, Liv. His lips soft against my ear, his fingers sending tingles down my spine.* I take a slightly ragged breath and curl back up to lie on the sofa. I curl up tight and it helps.

The next time I open my eyes I immediately look to the chair Tristan was sitting in by the fire, but it's empty. It takes me a moment to realise hours have passed not minutes. It's dark outside, the fire glows with dying embers and I hear the whirr and creak of Mum's spinning wheel. My body protests as I drag myself to a sitting position, but at least I don't feel numb or cold anymore. I imagine how much worse it could have been if Tristan hadn't found me when he did. Would I still be lying in the snow? Would I still be with Cillian and Orla on the mountain? Would I be dead?

I know he's gone, but I ask anyway. 'Is he still here?' Maybe I'm wrong. Maybe he's in the kitchen. Maybe he's resting upstairs.

'Liv! You're awake.' Mum smiles, noticing that I'm awake. She's been watching the TV on mute, whilst spinning her wool.

'Is he here?' I repeat.

Her foot stops its gentle push on the treadle and the wheel slows and stops. 'I made some dinner. I left you a plate in the oven.' She stands wiping her hands on her dye-stained apron. 'I'll get it for you.'

She comes back with a plate of one of her food inventions, a homemade bean burger, roast potatoes with a purple and yellow salad. My stomach remembers it hasn't eaten all day and rumbles loudly. I'm about to ask again about Tristan, but she cuts me off.

'You've brought back a city cold.' I take the plate and watch her settle back at her spinning wheel and take the TV off mute. 'You've been asleep all afternoon.' She adds, eyes on her wool. 'You looked skin and bone at the station. No wonder you're catching colds.' I'm surprised she noticed enough to think that. I wolf the food down and realise it's the closest thing I've had to a proper meal in weeks. All I can remember of my diet the last few weeks' is breakfast cereal and toast.

'Did you see him?'

She pauses a moment before looking at me with her standard vacant frown. 'Who?'

'Tristan,' I whisper. 'He was here.'

There's another pause. 'Really? I must have missed him.'

'You just came home and found me asleep?' I ask, angry at Tristan for leaving. This is exactly him, flitting in and out leaving no trace.

'That's right.' She doesn't look at me, preferring her wool, preferring the documentary on TV. 'You had a good talk with him though?'

I feel like she's lying to me. She hates lying so I can't see why she'd lie about this. Maybe he did leave before she got home, maybe as soon as I slept he crept out, desperate to escape.

Suddenly, I can't be in the same room as her. I feel sick thinking of Tristan. 'Thanks for dinner. I'm going to bed.' I drop the itchy blanket on the sofa behind me.

'Night, Liv.' I hear her call as I climb the stairs.

At the top of the stairs I pause, my hand reaching toward the spare room I shared with him, but at the last moment I withdraw and go back to my old room.

Next to the spare room is a tiny box room. Inside this room is Mum's ancient laptop. Despite the fact that laptops are designed to be portable, this one has never left the box room since my mum bought it second hand and plugged it in five years ago. I'm amazed it still works and can only tally it up to her barely using it. She only got WiFi when I complained I needed it for school work one summer.

After failing to sleep for a few hours, I go to the box room. My phone is still having issues since its dunk in the river. I turn on the laptop and wait impatiently for it to turn on. It may still work, but it is irritatingly slow. I look out the window, but it is pitch black and I just see my face reflected back under the glare of the computer screen. I don't see someone I immediately recognise as myself. I look away with a shiver. While trying to sleep I was willing myself back to the meadow, but it didn't work. Once you don't try so hard it comes so easily. That is what the wolves whispered, but that's easier said than done. Just thinking of the meadow makes getting there harder and when I try to sleep it's all I can think about. How can I get back there? How can I feel that strong again? How can I be that thing made only of power and peace?

Tristan said to let him go. Did he mean to leave the meadow, mountain, Cillian and Orla alone as well? Did he know I'd been there? The wolves say he wants to see me, he says please stop. I know what I want to believe, but I'm afraid of the truth.

I move the mouse back and forth with my hand, waiting for the cursor on the screen to respond. Eventually it does, but then loading the internet browser is equally slow and irritating. I remember impatient times when I bashed my hands on the keyboard in anger waiting for signs of life from this laptop. I think of Mum sleeping across the hallway and restrain myself. I wish I'd not left my own laptop behind at uni. When the browser opens, my fingers type in my email out of habit.

There amongst the junk and graduation service emails is one from an old pre-boarding school friend. She'd largely been unaffected by the whole Tristan thing. They'd never met, I hadn't seen her myself in over a year and our monthly email was one friendship I'd managed to maintain throughout Tristan. In fact, she may have been the only friend who liked him. My emails had been brimming with stories of him. I actually hadn't emailed her since before Tristan left, so I'm surprised to see her email when it's still my turn. It is full of concern and support. She tells me she's called, but my phone is always dead. I wonder briefly how she found out before realising it must have been Nina. Nina was full of good deeds. At the end of the email she wrote, *'Remember how you felt about Dean? And think about how you feel about him now. This will get easier, I promise.'*

There was only one proper boyfriend before Tristan. Dean. We were happy. My first love. At one point if someone had asked me what we'd break up over, I'd have struggled to answer. Nothing could break us. I trusted him completely; he'd never cheat or lie. We laughed at the same things. We barely argued. We lost our virginities together at sixteen and fumbled our way through, learning what the other liked. He even had honest blue eyes; he was my type in every way.

Later on, if someone had asked me what we'd break up over I'd have struggled to narrow the list down to just one thing. I don't know when it happened, but gradually reasons appeared. They started to pile up back to back on a mental list I carried. He was rude to his parents. He was a know it all. He played video games for hours on end, swearing constantly at the screen. He couldn't cope without WiFi. He started drinking beer all the time. It wasn't long before I was scrabbling for reasons we should stay together.

Still getting over Dean felt hard. My friends surrounded me and I carried on. Now, when I think of him, I feel nothing. Not even a twinge of sadness or a glimmer of what might have been. Just nothing.

The thought of feeling that way about Tristan makes me so sad. I don't want Tristan to become nothing. I'd rather love and hate him than feel an apathetic void. He was important to me and why should that ever diminish?

Many rants with friends followed the Dean break up. Did we break up for any specific reason on my list? Or did we break up because I'd made the list? Since then I'd always believed I had the power to destroy anything just by overthinking it. My head was stronger than my heart.

There is only one band that Tristan ever introduced me to. The band is called *Delays*. I haven't listened to any of their songs for weeks. I'd rashly deleted them (and many other Tristan related songs) from my playlists. The cull had cost me a lot of my favourite music.

It sometimes felt like Tristan didn't exist when he wasn't with me. We didn't really talk about his life before me. It had frustrated me at first that he remained such a mystery, but my happiness soon overwhelmed any doubts. When he turned up with an actual CD and made me listen to *Delays*, I found it in equal parts unnerving, quaint and flattering.

One, I hadn't listened to a CD in years.

Two, the reminder that he *really* did live a life somewhere outside of his time with me was a shock. I was jealous for the time I was missing, jealous of the other people he surrounded himself with.

Without thinking I'm typing in Delays and the name of the song Tristan said should have been written about us. The search engine ponders this and then there it is, I click it even though part of me shies away. I lean over to firmly close the door to the tiny room and I turn the sound down low on the ancient speakers. The song is exactly how I remember as it starts to play. A happy song, a song I'm embarrassed to admit I thought of as *our* song. Now it's just a song about an old boyfriend. I bring my knees up close to my chest and wrap my arms around them.

> *Without a second thought you put your hand on my shoulder, without a second look you took me miles away. What happened after that, I couldn't see and I lost you. And I stumbled around until you found me again.*

Those words, *until you found me,* stick in my mind.
I love how you see me Liv, Tristan said once. I think about that night we were supposed to meet his friends and the whisper of wolves...*they were there.* I think of when I first saw Tristan, waiting for a drink in a bar, and how no one noticed him until I did. When will I see you again? I'd ask every time we parted. Soon, I hope. You'll see me soon, he'd reply.
The chorus of the song starts.

> *You are my only hideaway. You make the world seem bigger.*

More words from Mum's story creep back to me. Of Shades waiting to be recognised, waiting to be seen. Was Tristan the Shade rather than the master? I don't understand the train of my own thoughts. Am I seriously considering that Tristan is a creature from a bedtime story? All the answers are in the meadow, up the mountain and in that village.

> *I know that you're waiting and your patience is failing*

We listened to this song so many times together and they were such good happy times. Tears drip down my face. They are warm, but leave a cold tingle in their wake. I feel them gather about my chin and, heavily, one drips to my chest. I close the browser to stop the song. Nothing happens immediately, angrily I hold down the on/off button and obediently the laptop shuts down with a quiet whine. My finger remains on the button and I think how bony it looks, like an old woman's. I creep back to bed and fumble around the sheets for my earbuds and the iPod so I don't have to face the silence.

The next morning I wake early, the calm fog of dreaming drifts away until I'm left with the usual tension. Outside, the snow lingers. Just looking at it causes a shiver to run down my spine. I imagine people finding my body in that snow. If I hadn't woken up back in Mum's house I could have believed I'd imagined Tristan completely.

I don't bother showering or dressing, the house is cold and my pyjamas are warm. I pull a pair of joggers over my pyjama bottoms and wander downstairs. Mum is nowhere to be found, the thought of breakfast makes me feel a little sick so I make a cup of tea, light the fire and sit in front of it. I sit where Tristan sat and stare at the sofa where I'd curled up in pain less than twenty-four hours earlier.

I don't know what to do with myself. Normally, I'd go out for a long walk, but I'm afraid to leave the house after what happened yesterday. I turn on the TV and find a mindless reality show. My arm and leg nearest the fire grow uncomfortably warm, but I don't move. Burning is better than freezing and better than feeling numb.

As I watch TV, I see movement on the sofa. I don't turn to give it my full attention, but watch from the corner of my eye as the yellow eyes in a great dark body clumsily turn in circles on the sofa trying to get comfortable.

When are you coming back, Liv? The creature settles awkwardly on the small sofa, tail over nose, but its eyes are on me.

'Now?' I whisper, turning to look, but as if I've broken the spell the wolf is gone. I stare back at the TV with an internal sigh. I see a meadow. I see a mountain. I see tall trees, they are fragile and delicate and I freeze so I don't scare them away. I drink the details and my heart hammers against my chest – that's where I want to be.

Come closer.

Come with me. Yellow eyes slink out from behind the spinning wheel.

Yes. I am nodding and staring at the mountain. I close my eyes and take a deep clearing breath. When I open them, I'm there.

Orla is sitting in the lotus position beneath a pine tree.

The sky is fierce with colour as the sun sets. The rocks and the trees are coloured warmly with orange. Orla's skin glows and her pale hair is cast pink. Her eyes are closed, her hands resting delicately on her knees. I take a step toward her. I don't make a sound and yet she opens her eyes and fixes them steadily on me. 'Livvy,' she purrs, with a slow smile. She unwinds herself and rises in one smooth motion, stretching her arms above her. 'I'm so glad you came back.' Her voice catches me like it did before and I am smiling back at her, feeling like I've come home.

'So am I.'

Orla steps towards me, and she moves so gracefully that I simply stare. She reaches out her hands towards me. 'Come to the village with me?'

It isn't really a question. She takes my hand and bends my arm to tuck her hand through like I'm the one in charge of where we go. Her hand is steel and there is no question who is directing who.

'Why are you here, Liv?' Her words are quiet and her fingers tighten about my arm. Tristan's name is on the tip of my tongue, her voice makes me feel so safe I want to tell her everything.

Don't tell her.

The voice catches me off guard, it's Rip. I twist around searching for wolves. Looking for Rip. I think I see eyes watching me in the dark of the forest, but they fade away. Orla shows no sign of hearing anything. She is looking at me waiting for my answer. We hear yelps and rustling not too far from us. Rip.

'Did you hear that?' I twist towards the sound, taking a few steps toward it. Orla's hand falls from my arm as I move away. The sounds of fighting die down and a pale hand grips my shoulder.

'Take no notice of them. I don't anymore.' Orla smiles with exasperation and pulls me back to the path.

'You heard them fighting?'

'Everyone sees and hears them differently. That doesn't change what they really are.' Orla starts walking again and I'm forced to walk alongside her or fall. The fighting continues intermittently behind us as we move away from it. 'I see them ... like rats.' Orla's lip curls in disgust, her voice even when hard is still beautiful. 'Filthy, scavenging vermin. Ignore them. Don't listen if they try to talk to you.'

'What are they?'

'They're really not worth your attention. Not even worthy of a name. They're not like you and I, they're ugly reminders of old mistakes. Look,' with her free hand Orla points before us down the mountain. At first I'm not sure what she's pointing at. On the other side of the mountain is a wide green valley that stretches lazily and runs directly away from us for miles before it curves to the left. I faintly hear running water, but can't see any for all the pine trees that hug the mountainsides and valley bed. The bright colours of the sunset have faded and leave the bottom of the valley in shadow. Then I catch the metallic flash of the last of the sunlight against a tall building. I shield my eyes trying to see the building properly, a glass tower. Something so modern doesn't fit with the world I've been imagining. I have no idea what I'm about to walk into and the thought is unnerving.

'Your village has skyscrapers?' Just looking at it makes my stomach clutch with an excitement bordering on anxiety. Is Tristan down there? Should I be walking in the opposite direction?

'Oh, we have everything, Livvy dear.' Orla wraps warm fingers around mine. 'Come on before it gets dark.' Orla's stride is fast and confident, whereas I would be happy to slow our pace. I need more time. I'm not ready to face Tristan. His last words still ring in my mind. *Please let me go.*

Yet, here I was intruding in his idyllic world.

How idyllic is this place really though? It feels idyllic, it feels like a place I never want to leave. But underneath something is very strange. It is only when I allow that thought in that I feel things flickering around me.

I feel at home in a world where I know none of the rules. I don't understand the animosity between Orla and the wolves, or even their attacks on Rip. I'm in jungle heat humidity one moment and cool wind and pine the next. Things shift and change subtly like quiet thoughts. Despite all the confusion, I know one thing for certain. I am happy here. I've felt more peace here in a few short moments than I have known in the last month back there. Thinking of where I've come from causes my skin to grow hot and itchy, everything around me wavers uncertainly. Orla hums a tune I don't recognise beside me. When I focus on her everything feels more stable around me.

'I see them as wolves.' My confession causes Orla to laugh and I am drawn to the sound. Everything is so amusing to her and already I want to make her laugh again. Her beautiful laughter snares me firmly in the dark woods beside her. 'Wolves are cool, Liv. Trust me they are nothing of the sort.' I want to press her for a proper answer, what are they ugly reminders of? Orla changes the subject though. 'You said last time that you weren't looking for someone, right?' Her voice now has an edge. I feel like the answer to her question could change a lot.

'No one.' I say as calmly as possible, taking Rip's warning seriously. 'I just kind of stumbled here by accident. The wolves helped me.' I don't realise we've stopped walking until a breeze through the trees causes me to shiver and blows the curls across Orla's face. She releases my hand to pull her hair back and ends up playing with a lock. Curling it tight around her finger and then letting it go. She's thinking, she's deciding what to share and what to withhold from me. I stare her down, silently defying her to call me a liar.

'And you haven't met anyone new recently?' Her eyes search mine and I feel like they can see into my soul. Her voice is soft, like a lullaby. 'No one just a little bit different?' Her voice curls around me. 'No one mysterious?' She works some kind of magic and I feel myself relax. I feel myself wanting to open up. Tristan, I think. I'm looking for my mysterious best friend, Tristan. I open my mouth and I can feel the words rising and gathering behind my tongue, almost against my will.

Suddenly, I see yellow eyes behind her. They move forward with a limp. I see a pearly blood-smeared face lit weakly by the moon through the trees. I make out the savaged ugly ear. I focus back on Orla, the words drying up in my mouth. I shake my head. Orla smiles and I feel the tension dissolve. She glances behind her and sees Rip still standing not far off in the shadows. I see revulsion cross her face.

'Memories. That's all they are, Livvy. Just old memories that have taken a tangible form. Don't attribute more to them.' Orla drags me away, her voice has lost some of its melodic charm. Rip doesn't move, but watches us leave. 'They don't concern themselves with anything but their own misery.' I look back at Rip one last time. Orla is wrong, I'm sure of it.

'What are they memories of?'

'Mainly the memory of how they died I think.' She shrugs, like she hasn't given it much thought. 'They're all that remains of what they were before.' Orla's hand tightens. 'But I shouldn't say anymore. Not until you're confirmed.'

Confirmed. Tristan obviously didn't think I was good enough to come here. If I am confirmed, maybe he will love me again.

'You're so beautiful, Baby.' I opened my eyes and smiled. The best part of my day was the time Tristan came over. I was lying on my bed, pretending to study while speakers played my latest playlist.

'You ain't so bad either, Baby.' I drew out the *Baby* in a terrible southern American drawl and pulled a face at him. Tristan laughed gently, taking off his coat.

'I love the look on your face when you're listening to music. Lost in your own world.' Tristan pushed my papers aside and came to lie beside me. His fingertips ran lightly over my face. I shifted to accommodate him, feeling my heart jump about my chest.

'Care to join me in my weird little world?' I felt my face burn as he nodded slowly, his eyes, playful, stared into mine.

'I'd like that,' he whispered before he kissed me. My textbooks fell to the floor as I arched up to meet him. The feel of his lips against mine, his hands skimming over my body, in that moment it was all I knew. Everything about Tristan drew me in. It was as exciting as it was scary. I squirmed beneath him and pushed him back. I moved so I was on top of him straddling his hips and began to undo the buttons of his shirt. 'I like you up there.' I gave him an amused look from beneath my eyelashes, but continued unbuttoning his shirt. Once I'd finished, Tristan reached forward to lift my top up and over my head. I laughed as he got my top caught on my head and once freed, I leaned down to kiss him, resting my chest against his warm skin, so close I could feel his heartbeat. His hands moved to my sides, running up and down. His light touch caused me to laugh against his lips and I felt his mouth curve in response. 'That tickles.' He tickled me properly then, until I fell off him on the bed laughing and begging him to stop. I heard *Hey Girl* by Delays playing in the background. 'I never want to leave your weird little world, Liv.' His beautiful face obscured my view of everything else.

CHAPTER 7

Village is a very loose definition of the place Orla leads me into. It's too dark to see properly with only the moon and dim street lamps, but I make out scattered buildings, none of which match. Not just small variations, but completely different styles, periods of architecture, materials, and size. There is only the merest indication of a rough stone street running through them. Orla picks her way between them, glancing back at me occasionally. The streets turn cobbled as we pass a cosy thatched cottage, with flower boxes and shutters about the windows and then a spindly red brick terrace house standing alone like the sole survivor of an earthquake. I spy the bright white of a caravan down one grass-eaten street. Another side street looks like a pristine and wide leafy American suburb. I see what looks like a shipping container as I pass from cobbles to concrete. I wonder if we pass Tristan's home. The air smells green, like pine, fresh water and moss. I can smell burning wood, but there are no signs of life. No scents of cooking, no lights in the houses, no one else walks the crooked streets.

'Where is everyone?'

Orla glances around as if only just noticing how deserted the place is. 'They're probably all at the Night Cafe or out. We don't spend too much time at home.'

'The Night Cafe?' In a brief flash I remember Tristan sampling neat whiskey. He gulped down the large measure and choked as it burned down his throat. *Give me that again,* he'd asked moments later.

'Oh, not a cafe as *you* would know it, Livvy. We are sentimental creatures, I think most of us have fond memories of being in pubs, bars, and cafes in the Otherside.' She smiles dreamily. Her voice is almost a whisper when she mentions the Otherside.

The Otherside.

She means where I come from, but I force myself not to dwell on that as the buildings shiver and shake when I do.

Orla turns me down a new street. This street is old and cracked tarmac with faded double yellow lines. It is such a familiar sight in the strangest of places that I feel a jolt of discomfort. It looks like any old road in an English town, and yet I feel like it's my road. The street changes to fresh black unlined tarmac as we walk. I glance back but can't quite make out how or where the two sections meet.

We pass the first building that is actually lit up and it's the glass tower I saw earlier. It probably doesn't merit skyscraper status, but it is the only thing taller than the pines. It has a cream canvas marquee held up by two golden poles over the entrance, *1049* in a swirly font adorns the canvas. Inside the foyer is empty.

'The Night Cafe is the only communal place in the village. We have it for our get togethers.' Orla motions me to follow here down a narrow path between two dark buildings. 'It's kind of neutral territory since it belongs to no one. Everyone here is very particular about their homes.'

'I want a stable door.'

'Like for a horse?' Tristan frowned while he played with my fingers.

'Yeah kind of, the ones that split in the middle so the horse can stick its head out.

He nodded. 'What else?'

'I want it to look ramshackled and old on the outside, but be modern, clean and cosy inside.' I loved dreaming up the future with Tristan. It made me feel excited and yet so safe. '... and beams,' I added belatedly. 'What about you? I suppose you have to want to live in it too.'

'I'd like to be near a lake, surrounded by lots of trees.' He sighed contentedly and lay back in the grass. The botanical gardens were busy on such a sunny day, but we'd found a semi-secluded spot to sprawl out with food and a blanket.

'Ok, I'm getting 'no one will hear you scream murder' vibes, but I can work with that.'

Tristan pretended to ignore me. 'You can fill the place with as many beams and doors as you like as long as I get my lake.'

'Why do you want a lake so bad?'

'They remind me of my own mortality.'

'And you just cemented the murder vibe. I fail to see the connection between lakes and mortality.' I frowned. Tristan shrugged and I knew he wouldn't explain himself. I'd learnt to move on swiftly in conversations when this happens. 'Ok, so lakes remind you of death and that's a good thing and not at all creepy.'

'More or less.'

'Fine, you weirdo. I want a veranda then, so I can sit outside when it's raining and watch the water-'

'-and a pier going out into the lake for diving.' Tristan finished my thoughts. 'I like the sound of this house. When do we move in?'

Orla stops before a rustic log cabin. Her eyes shine as she stares at it. It is set back from the main streets down a narrow muddy track.

'Is this the Night Cafe?' I look around us confused.

'No, don't be silly!' Orla smiles indulgently, but doesn't look away from the cabin. 'Does it look like a cafe? No, this is my home.'

'Oh.'

'The Night Cafe will be better tomorrow, a lot of people are away tonight. It's a Saturday on the Otherside. Tomorrow will be busier, we'll go tomorrow.'

I don't know what I expected from Orla's cabin, but I definitely didn't expect it to be so normal and down to earth. I'd have dreamed up elegance and expensive pale colours for Orla, but inside the cabin is small and cosy, filled with worn patterned furniture and dark wood. Orla busies herself with lighting the fire, and for a moment I watch transfixed that she even knows how to build a fire. Across the room there is a massive TV mounted to the wall and a games console below it. I definitely can not imagine Orla as a secret gamer or even watching TV. At the other end of the room is a small and basic kitchen. I take a seat in one of the surprisingly comfortable old armchairs and continue my perusal. Two doors lead off to the rest of the cabin, but there is nothing in this room that tells me Orla lives here. In fact, the whole place is completely masculine. Everything is functional, dark and, aside from the tech, slightly shabby. Orla drifts around the rooms in her white floaty dress with perfectly imperfect hair cascading down her back. She gets fire lighters from the kitchen and moves back to her fire humming softly. She's so graceful she looks like she's dancing. Finally, I notice the first evidence that she might actually belong in this little log cabin. Above her head, on the mantelpiece is a wooden picture frame. Inside the frame I see a laughing Orla frozen in time and staring delightedly up at the man next to her. His mouth isn't smiling but his eyes are warm and crinkle at the sides as he stares at the camera, one arm is around Orla's shoulders and the other wraps around her front. She looks tiny and so feminine within his arms. Mostly, she looks happy. When I hear the first snicks of baby flames, Orla straightens with a satisfied sigh. She follows my gaze to the photo and looks startled, like she forgot it was there.

'Is that your boyfriend?' I ask.

Orla laughs abruptly, but it sounds strained, bordering on a shriek. 'Oh no! That's my...that's John.' She picks up the picture frame and it is the first time I've seen her flustered and unsure.

She glances around her before crossing to the kitchen and putting the picture facedown in a drawer.

'I'm sorry.' I don't really know why I'm saying sorry, it just seems like the only words. I'm sorry my question reduced Orla to anything less than perfect.

'No. Don't be silly.' She waves a hand dismissively. Her green eyes look glassy. 'Everyone says your first is the hardest.' This time her laugh has an edge of determination. 'We're such a maudlin bunch, really.' Orla sits down in the armchair nearest me; her long fingers reach out and take my hand. 'You'll understand when it's your turn, Livvy.'

I have the best sleep I've had in months. It's the kind of sleep I have no memory of. I shut my eyes and when they open time has passed. A sleep that I feel throughout my body, just blissful, warm, cushy, soft peacefulness. I lie still staring up at the unfamiliar wooden ceiling. I wonder where I am, but can't dredge up much concern that I don't know. I wait for the dread to settle, for anxiety to wrap its arms around my chest – but nothing happens. I can't remember feeling so comfortable for a long time, perhaps, ever. I could doze here happily forever. For a moment, I wonder if I'm dead and this is heaven.

'Livvy.' Orla's voice sing-songs from the doorway. Her face appears like an angel before me. I could be dead. She could be my guardian angel. 'It's time.' She purrs and pulls me up.

'How long have I been asleep?' I look around, I'm in a large bed with dark grey sheets. The wooden walls tell me I'm still in her cabin, but I don't remember coming to bed ir even falling asleep. Sunlight battles in through the tired curtains.

'Not too long. I'm so glad you're still here, Livvy. I never have guests. I thought you might slip away in the night.' Her hair is down and she is wearing silky pyjama bottoms and a vest top. They make her look so normal and human, but then that thought surprises me – when did I decide that she wasn't human? She draws open the curtains and moves around the room, rearranging and touching things lightly, her smile serene. She is elegance and control again, although with her hair down and in pyjamas she looks young and vulnerable. 'I'm making breakfast. Come with me.'

I hear her moving about in the other room and the sound of an old kettle hissing. The bedroom is small and just as masculine as the living room. There is one picture on the wall, a dramatic green landscape with rugged mountains. I don't know whether it's a real place or not. The thought catches me off guard and things start to shake around me.

What makes a place real? Is the picture of a place here or a place *there*?

No, I do not want to leave yet. I try to focus on Orla and her cabin, but it doesn't seem to work. My body burns down my left side and I hear faraway voices, a buzzer and clapping.

Then I hear Orla singing softly and something about it stills the commotion around me.

Her voice is beautifully sad and is almost a whisper at times as she moves around in the kitchen. I don't know the song, but I think I've heard it before. I want to sing with her and I find myself trailing though to the living room to hear better. When Orla sees me standing in the doorway she smiles, but doesn't break her song. The kettle whistles and still she sings as she makes the tea. She is now wearing a silky green dress and almost like a dream the mechanics of when she changed seem insignificant.

Near the kitchen is a small table, only big enough to seat two. I cross the room and take a seat on the hard wooden chairs. There is a violin case in the corner that I didn't notice last night and I wonder if Orla can play as well as she sings. She reaches the chorus of her song and it is in another language. I wish I knew what it meant.

Hovan, Hovan Gorry og O, Gorry og O, Hovan, Hovan,
Gorry og O, I've lost my darling baby, O

She passes me a mug of tea and I'm content just to sit and listen
as she sings. I can smell bacon and toast, but even these normal
smells don't shake my surroundings. I feel like the more time I
spend with Orla, the more control I have over whether I stay or
not.

I notice with surprise that the picture of Orla and John is back
on the mantelpiece. I get up with my tea in hand to take a closer
look at it. I assume if Orla put it back out she doesn't mind my
curiosity.

John is a handsome guy, in a burly outdoorsy kind of way.
Watching Orla float about in her beautiful dresses, I'd find it
hard to believe they were a couple if I didn't have the proof before
my eyes.

'Livvy, table.' Orla's voice pulls me away from the photograph.
She moves so silently that I am surprised to find her standing
right next to me, a scowl marring her face. 'John.' His name is
a brittle sigh mixed with anger. She takes the photo and storms
back to the kitchen, this time she drops it in the bin.

'Why did you put it back out?'

'Sit down.' She sounds impatient, but she keeps her back to me
for a moment before joining me at the table. I sit and take in
the food she's prepared. I don't feel hungry in the slightest, but
I don't want to appear rude so I pick up the knife and fork
that she's placed out. Orla takes the seat across from me, but
doesn't touch her food either. For a while we each sit in silence
contemplating breakfast.

'John used to love when I made him food.' Her words break
the silence and once broken more words pour out of her like
water. 'Forget you saw that picture, it shouldn't still be here.' She
delicately places her hand over her forehead and looks slightly
embarrassed. 'Don't tell anyone we spoke of him. I'm trying
to forget him, but...you humans.' I see her jaw clenching. 'You

make it difficult.'

You humans, she'd said.

'I'm sorry.' I know it's a pointless word, but it slips out again. Orla finally looks at me and gives a tiny short laugh.

'You're sorry?' It is then that I see the tears in her eyes and they make me feel uncomfortable, like when I'd interrupted my mum crying once. I'd rather walk in on her on the toilet than interrupt her crying. Crying felt too private a thing and was inexplicably sad. A child should never see their mother cry. 'John said sorry a lot. Another human thing.'

'Where is he?' I can feel my heart flip beneath my ribs, it climbs up my throat and drops pathetically down to my stomach. Over and over. Orla glances out the window. I follow her gaze and see nothing but the rigid pine trees.

'He's gone.'

I want to ask if she means dead. Or like me is 'gone' her way of slowly realising he's left her and is never coming back. My eyes feel itchy and my nose tingles. The symptoms caused by my own internal battle, my own refusal to cry. Orla stands abruptly, picking up both our plates and marching to the kitchen. She drops them both, plates and all into the bin. 'Only John would eat this much food,' she murmurs angrily.

I stay still, feeling vaguely stunned and embarrassed for her. 'Livvy,' and I can hear the control and forced cheeriness in her voice. 'I won't be a moment. Just wait right here.' She manages a wobbly smile before disappearing into the bedroom and closing the door behind her.

There are no clocks.

There is no time.

I could have sat obediently waiting for her for minutes or hours. Hours and minutes where I feel an internal struggle. What am I doing here? If she calls John human, what does that make her? What does that make Tristan? The master or the Shade, or something else.

At times some dulled and gagged panic tries to claw its way to the surface and the room vibrates around me. Parts drip and drain away. Behind it, a darkened room lit by firelight waits and the glow from a muted TV.

I half expect Orla's house to disappear completely, but some violent angry part of me shoves that panic down. I want to know the truth and if I could belong here. I want to know what Tristan is. I want to know the boy I'm still in love with. The cabin surges back and solidifies.

I knock gently on her door. 'Orla?' I open the door to the bedroom and feel more irritation than surprise to find the room empty. Closing the door behind me, I drop down on the bed. My sense of urgency dwindles without confrontation to keep it alive. I glance around the room looking for a clue of where Orla has gone. Nothing about this room is anything less than ordinary.

Still, I can't imagine Orla living here. I can't imagine her settling down to watch TV or doing the laundry. I glance down at myself and there is nothing for the briefest of moments and then I see the familiar faded denim shorts and legs. I think I'm getting good at this and also...I guess no one does laundry here. I open the wardrobe wondering if it's just for show, but it is full of clothes. Men's clothes. Flannel shirts, plaid jumpers, fleeces and a single black suit. Everything is dark shades of blue, green and grey and this makes the shoes stand out; a pristine pair of white satin heels, with circular diamante crusts on the front. They are nestled between walking boots and trainers. I close the wardrobe quickly like I've discovered a secret I shouldn't have. I cross to a chest of drawers and inspect each drawer. Again it's all men's clothes. John's clothes? Then I feel smooth paper beneath socks and boxers. A photograph. I take it out, once again feeling like I'm prying into secrets I shouldn't be but unable to stop. The photograph shows a laughing couple on their wedding day. John is wearing a kilt and sporran, a champagne flute in hand raised to the photographer and his other hand gripping tightly the hand of his bride. She is leaning across him, caught in the middle of trying to lift his kilt. The bride is not Orla. I've never seen this woman before. I drop down to the edge of the bed and notice writing on the back of the photo.

Presenting Mr and Mrs John McAulay! All the best to you and Amy, love Claire and Aiden x

Something scratches at the door, I jump to my feet guiltily, dropping the photo. The door clicks gently open and a grey nose pushes its way in.

'Rip!' I am relieved it isn't Orla.

What?

'Oh, I made up your name.'

I already have a name. A real one, not a dog's name. Her black lips curl as she snarls at me. The anger dies quickly though and her next words are an uncertain after thought...*I don't remember it though.*

The photo lies on the floor between us. I scoop it up and push it back into the depths of the bottom drawer and close it. The photo feels too real, the names and the people are all too real. Part of me doesn't want to accept this place as anything greater than my own fantasy. 'Are you allowed in here? I don't think Orla would want you in her home.'

I don't do what they tell me. I'm not theirs to control anymore.

'They controlled you?'

What do you think happened once she was done with him? I feel sick realising she means John.

This is not real.

Where do you think John is now?

This cannot be real.

He didn't survive, just as none of us survive their kind.

My face burns. This is not a place I want to be. The thought is so violent and powerful that this time there is no gentle sliding away, everything shatters in an instant.

CHAPTER 8

My body jumps with a start and I am back, sitting by the fire. The fire has long since died to embers and it is dark outside now. My body burns itchy down my left side where I've spent hours in front of the flames. 'You're back.' I turn to my mother's voice, she sits across from me on the sofa behind her spinning wheel. Only candles and TV glare light the room so I can't see her eyes, just two dark pockets in her face. I rub my hot cheek, unsure if she means back from sleep or back. I see the flash of the whites of her eyes as she turns them back to the TV.

'He was here the other day, you know.' She speaks mildly like she's talking about the weather.

'Uh?' I truly have no idea what she's talking about, my mind is still caught up with thoughts of John McAulay.

'Tristan.'

That catches my attention. 'You said you didn't see him. You lied!' I sound like a child.

'He was here,' she continues calmly, like she didn't lie less than twenty-four hours before.'and I asked him to leave.'My heart hammers hard against my ribcage. Her wheel continues spinning even as I surge to my feet. The homemade blanket she'd placed over me falls forlornly to the floor.

'Why? Why would you do that?' Shaking, I bring my hands to my face, my throat, my heart and then clench them to my sides. 'You don't understand. I need... I need to see him.'

'You don't need him.' She cuts me off and I've never heard her voice sound so sharp. Beyond her I see my angry reflection in the glass of the French doors. Like a loyal hound I see the faint yellow eyes at my side.

I look back to my mother. 'You know nothing about what I need. You know nothing about what I've been through. You know nothing about me!' My voice gets louder with every word. I haven't raised my voice to my mother in years.

Half the battle is already lost when you have to raise your voice, Mum used to say when I was younger. It was one phrase that never sounded at home on her tongue – like it was borrowed, like she was repeating something she'd been told.

'Tristan told me how he found you.' I hate how calm she sounds, as if her daughter is not standing furiously before her. 'You're being careless, Liv. You don't know what you're playing with.'

'And you do?' I snarl. I don't want her to know what I'm playing with. I don't want her to make it anymore real than it already feels. I don't want her to be a part of it.

I am brand new.

The yellow eyes glow in the glass. They aren't real. Yellow-eyed creatures are something born out of my imagination. Shades aren't real. John McAulay isn't real. Rip and Orla aren't real. My mother's crappy bedtime story is just a story to shut me up when I cried or wouldn't sleep.

'When you were little you used to ask about your dad.'

'Don't change the subject.'

'You're more like him than you know.' More pairs of eyes join the first in the glass. They press forward like they want to break it.

Where do you go when you die? What is left behind?

'I don't want to talk about him. Just tell me about Tristan, what happened?'

Finally the spinning wheel stops. 'He said he doesn't want to speak to you. He said he doesn't love you anymore.'

I was afraid to let Dean in. I was more afraid to let Tristan in, but Tristan left me no choice. Tristan was everything. He was a gentle and relentless force. He captured me completely.

I wish I knew what had changed with Dean. I wish I knew *when*. All I know is that it was me who slowly, haltingly, reached the conclusion. It was me who looked at Dean and thought I can't do this anymore. I thought if my feelings had withered away, surely so must his. I dreaded telling him, yet part of me hoped that when I did he'd breathe a sigh of relief. *Thank god,* he'd say, *I've been thinking the same thing.* But that didn't happen.

I thought he must have felt how strained we'd been. This could not be a surprise for him. Yet it was. He cried, he fought, he told me he'd change…*anything.* His begging only cemented for me that it was over. His vows of love didn't feel beautiful or flattering…instead they were an uncomfortable cloying burden. Something I wanted to crush out of him. I don't love you anymore.

And that's what really scared me.

It was not a fear of losing someone else's love. I was afraid of losing my own. Dean was perfect. And I still created reasons to end it. I still fell out of love with him.

I thought about all my past encounters. It was always me. I always left. I always got bored first. I never texted back. I barely visited or called Mum. I never asked about my father. What was wrong with me? Was I incapable of loving someone? I never let anybody in. Until Tristan and god knows what he was.

When I was little I asked questions about my father. Back then I wanted to know him, where he was, who he was, what was his favourite colour. And back then my mother didn't want to talk about him. Back then she left the room, turned the volume up or suggested a game. I stopped asking. I'd filled and papered over that crack a long time ago.

Her words stick in my mind. *You're more like him than you know.*

No. I'm not. No, I'm brand new. I will not become like you. I will not become like him. I'm brand new. I will not make either of your mistakes.

So, you want to talk about my father now? I couldn't bring myself to call him Dad. It felt too cosy. I wasn't a girl who had a dad. I felt uncomfortable, my skin felt tight. It was like fingernails scratching and inching their way in. Finding purchase and pulling, uncovering what I'd worked so hard to hide. It's too late. I cared back then and now I don't. Now I don't want to know. Knowledge, family, love—it was all an anchor pulling me down. Maybe I *was* incapable of love.

The laptop beeps unhappily at me as I turn it on. My stomach rumbles, but I can't think of anything I want to eat. My hunger feels like a strength, like a hard ball of power inside of me. It's something I can control. I'd waited for quiet before I left my room. I listened, back resting against the door of my room so I could hear her go to bed, so I could avoid her.

I type John McAulay slowly into the browser with one finger, my other arm wraps around my empty stomach. When the results pop up, they show a multitude of John McAulays on LinkedIn, Facebook and Twitter. There are addresses and phone numbers for masses of John McAulays, even a Wikipedia page for a John McAulay in the Scots Guard decades ago. I click images and scroll down through pages and pages of faces.

I'm determined I won't see him. Just like Orla, he doesn't exist. John McAulay is a figment of my imagination. Tristan is not some creature from another world, he's just a boy who stopped loving me.

But I finally do see John's face amongst the pictures.

A sickening clench descends on my body and I think I might vomit. It is a wedding photo, this one more reserved than the one I'd found. Family and friends line up beside the bride and groom in a pristine garden. A grand house with stone pillars, surrounded by fir trees and pink flowers stands behind them. I click the link and it leads to the website of a wedding photographer, their names and the date are above the photograph. It was taken eight years ago. John and Amy. I'm not sure how long I stare at the photo, willing it to change, willing some other couple's faces to appear. Everything that's been happening to me is real. How else could I have dreamt up John and Amy?

I click back to images and continue scrolling through them. I don't know what I'm looking for now… proof that John is still alive? I feel increasingly anxious as I search for clues to this stranger's life. Please let him be alive.

I've almost given up. I'm skimming each picture wearily now, when suddenly I notice a violin in one of the pictures I've already passed. It makes me think of the one I saw in Orla's cabin. A man in a wide-brimmed hat is leaning into the instrument as he plays it. From the angle it's taken, the violin and hat obscure most of his face, but I see the line of his lips and a straight nose. I click the link curiously and end up on the website for a pub in Edinburgh. It's a proper Scottish pub advertising live folk music, Gaelic fayre and ceilidhs. I click onto the events section and see a list of past performances. Down near the bottom I first see his name, *John McAulay* and I stare at it until it blurs. I click his name. A new picture loads with a short biography alongside it. He picked up his first guitar at four, his father taught him to play the fiddle. He comes from a village in Fife called Crail. He moved to Edinburgh for university where he met his wife, Amy. The picture is dark and grainy, but the laughing man I see on the stage is Orla's John. I scan around the page almost desperately for a date. Tell me this was taken yesterday, I beg the computer. My heart stalls when I see a small note underneath the photograph.

Please join us for a remembrance tribute to Amy and Holly McAulay, two beautiful souls, a wife and daughter that brought so much happiness to John. Our thoughts and prayers go out to John at this most difficult time.

It's dated four years ago and there are no further updates on John. Frustrated, I notice the email address for the pub in the page footer. I quickly write an email pretending to be an old uni friend and asking if they have any recent contact details for him. I feel vaguely productive. Once I find him, we can talk and figure out what's happening to both of us.

How awful to lose a wife and a daughter.

I know my break up with Tristan is absolutely trivial in comparison, but it doesn't stop the awful anxiety inside me. It doesn't make my feelings realise they are inappropriate in the face of true grief. They don't bow out gracefully, conceding to a bigger victim. They remain pulsing below the surface. I almost go back to Google and type in the names of John's wife and daughter, but at the last moment I don't want to know how they died. I close the laptop without turning it off properly and it flashes angrily as it dies.

I wake up cold after a night of broken sleep dreaming about all the ways John's family could have died. Mum has never believed in turning the heating on if there are more layers you can pile on so, shivering, I make my way to the bathroom. I stare at my reflection in the mirrored cabinet. I am unkempt and hollow cheeked with the bruise on my forehead now a faint yellow-green. Fed up with the sight, I open the cabinet just so I can hide from the mirror. Inside are only a few sparse toiletries, likely gifts Mum has received rather than active vanity. I can't see her browsing products, choosing wrinkle creams or caring about foundation or mascara. Everything I know about wearing makeup I learnt from YouTube and friends from school. It feels like a different life.

The clock in the hallway reveals that it's nearly midday and even though I'm cold I want to know if my email from last night has a reply. I even consider emailing some of my old pre-boarding school friends, thinking how proud Miss Salter would be.

I rescue my phone from the rice. If it's ever going to work again, the rice has done all it can. Reluctantly, it turns on with only two percent battery. There is no reply to my email about John. Instead of messaging any of my friends I scour their lives through Facebook, feeling forgotten and lonely, until the phone dies. I go for a shower and turn the water hot until it burns my skin.

Mum is waiting for me at the kitchen table when I return. I'd left my hair wet and I feel the damp patch spread across the back of my jumper. I see her and pause between running away or ignoring her.

'Liv, please listen to me.' Not one for confrontation, I'd expected her to drop the topics of either Tristan or my father. I sit down across from her as she runs a finger around the rim of her mug of tea. I can smell the chamomile and it reminds me of early mornings before school. Her hands are covered in rings as usual and they clink mutely as she wraps both hands around her mug to take a sip. I think her hands are shaking, something about seeing her so nervous bothers me. 'There's tea for you on the side.'

I glance over and see the mug, my mug, waiting by the kettle. She's never been a selfish brewer. Long summer holidays when I descended on her home, she'd always seek me out to place a tea beside me before wandering off to do her own thing.

'Let's just get this over with.' I turn my eyes back to hers, but find them too piercing. I look down at her hands.

'Your …father,' she begins falteringly, 'he did not have an easy life. I'm sorry I couldn't talk about him when you were younger and then as you got older you didn't seem interested and I felt like I'd been let off the hook.' Her voice breaks slightly as she says sorry and that sound alone causes my eyes to well up. I train my eyes down and silently inspect my fingernails. 'When I met him, it was just him and his brother. Alexei and Bendek. Their parents had died in a car accident years before. I was drawn to both of them. The three of us grew very close, but I always knew it was Alex. He was special. He was a dreamer, but he had so many brilliant ideas and plans. He was writing a book... he wouldn't let me read it. He wanted to finish it before anyone read it.'

'I did read it though in the end. They gave it to me with his things after... afterwards.' I can hear the tears now and it's excruciating. My eyes feel loaded and heavy, it's an effort to keep them open. I rarely see Mum cry. She must have been sad a lot when I was little, but hid it so well from me. 'He used to draw maps of worlds he'd dreamt up... just like you.' I look up then, surprised, and the movement causes the first gathered tear to break and fall from one eye. I didn't know she'd seen those silly maps I used to spend hours on. Naming cities and mountain ranges, shading in the oceans around the land. I think of my father doing the same thing and it feels strange, an indescribable ache. I both want the connection yet hate him for it. *I am brand new.*

'When his brother died, it was all so sudden. We got a call saying Ben had collapsed at work. He was dead before we even made it to the hospital. A brain aneurysm. Alex was never the same. I think I lost them both that day.' She wipes her eyes with her hands and takes another sip of her tea. I want to be angry with her for lying about Tristan, for keeping my father a secret until now, but I can't. Her sadness drains me.

When she is sad I am sad.

When she is lost, I am drowning.

'Alex stopped writing. He stopped drawing. He just shut me out. For a while he didn't even get out of bed. But then one day he started going out again, he wrote and drew maps again. But... I don't know, it felt different. He met a man at a bereavement group. I only ever knew his name as Tee. Alex started talking about Tee all the time and it hurt that this stranger could fix what I couldn't. I never met Tee. A whole year, all the time your father spent with him, and there was always an excuse. We always just missed each other. One of us was always busy. But from what Alex told me, Tee was charming, full of smiles.

Always knew what to say.'

I can't look away from her now. She is so vivid in her misery. 'I didn't like being excluded, but Tee was helping Alex so much that I left it alone. I'd encouraged him to join the group in the first place so I couldn't complain that it was helping.'

'Why are you telling me this now?' I don't mean to sound hostile, but I do. Why is she letting the memories and suffering back in when we both survived fine pretending nothing was wrong? Mum looks at me and we hold each other's red-rimmed eyes.

'I didn't notice right away. It took me a while to place it, but... Tristan reminds me of Tee.' My jaw tightens at Tristan's name. He feels like an intrusion in this conversation, something entirely separate. When I don't respond she continues. 'And now I see how you are and it's like watching your father all over again.'

'But, you liked Tristan...' I whisper. She nods tiredly. 'Why does it even matter if they are similar?' I press and I can almost see her retreating. She is uncomfortable, but she started this and now I'm determined she finishes it. 'What happened to my father?'

'He'd either be out with Tee, sleeping or just staring into space. I couldn't reach him. I couldn't bring him back.'

I couldn't bring him back.

Those words stick with me the most. I imagine myself face down in the river or curled up in the snow, or maybe even just sat by the fire staring blankly. Could that happen to me? I swallow the lump in my throat before I ask, 'and you think I'm the same?'

'You're not really here half the time.'

'It's got nothing to do with Tristan.'

'Tee disappeared and your father got worse. Tristan leaves and you're...' Her voice trails off. Part of me wants to demand she finish that sentence, but I already know.

'People die, people leave. Just let me deal with it my way. You don't understand.'

'Your father committed suicide.' She stands abruptly to dump her mug in the sink and stares out the window. I don't know if I'm more shocked about my father or that Mum thinks I might do the same thing. It's crossed my mind over the last few months. Never the hows or whens, never how it would affect anyone else, never with any real intent – simply the idea of not existing anymore, how much easier that sounded.

'I'm sorry.' They seem the only two words to say and as I speak them all the sorrys I've heard over the years for my dead father well up inside me. They pulse and pull until my chest feels too small for them. They aren't just empty words for the space where a father should be. They are for a man who thought it easier to take his own life. They are for a woman who lost the love of her life. They are for the struggle to raise a daughter alone while grieving. For a girl growing up not even knowing what a father was for.

'When did he do it? Did he know about me?' I feel selfish for asking. My tears feel hot and dry, burning down my face. When she doesn't answer I look up and see her indecision and grief, a pause, and then her defeat as she looks at me.

'Yes.' It is a lost little word, alone and weighed down with sadness. 'We'd just found out I was pregnant.'

I nod, taking the information in. Briefly, it threatens to swamp me, to rise up my throat and blot everything out. I grit my teeth until my face hurts. I didn't need this man before and I don't need him now – what do I care that he had no thought for me either?

'How?' Our eyes are locked and I see how she struggles. I see how much this conversation hurts.

And I hate him. I hate him for making her cry.

'In the woods. They...he– he cut himself. In the leg. They found the knife.' If I was a different person I'd go to her at this point. I'd open my arms and we'd hug each other. I'd try to make a thing that can't be made better, better. But I am physically incapable. I'm glued to my chair. The horrified silence is long and hard, until she whispers, 'it was me that found him.' This knowledge hardens inside me, if I felt nothing for him before I definitely hate him now.

She is already disappearing out the door by the time I register her quiet 'excuse me'. I watch her go, hating myself for not being able to comfort her. Part of me wants every single morbid detail, but not the awful prising conversation that goes with it. I just want to sift through her memories and know everything. If the story is dropped now, will either of us have the guts to bring it up again? I want to at least tell her how brave I think she is. I rise to follow her. I hear her bed creak as she sits down. I'm at the bottom of the stairs, my foot hovering on the first step when I see it. Out of the corner of my eye, something runs up the drive. A dark shadowy phantom, it hides in the trees that line the top of the drive. I turn instinctively and I hear it like it's inside the house and next to me.

Come closer, Liv.

Come outside.

And it's so tempting I can't resist. Mum is not forgotten, but she recedes in my mind. I follow the voices outside.

CHAPTER 9

'Come outside and play, Liv.' Tristan coaxed, his fingers danced lightly down my spine. 'It never snows, we have to enjoy it while it lasts. Please? For me?' We slipped through a small hole in the hedge at the bottom of Mum's garden. It had grown over a bit since I'd last used it God knows when. We forged our way through feeling like pioneers. The field on the other side was covered in a perfect layer of snow. Before I even knew I'd decided to, I started running in a zig-zag pattern. Snow creaked and sprayed before me, engulfing my boots with each step. I heard Tristan's laughter.

'What are you doing?' His shout cut through the stillness and I stopped to look at him from the other end of the field. Across the distance he looked small and adorable. I shrugged helplessly, spreading my arms wide and continued running. When I started to get too hot, I bounded back to him, making sure to stomp through any untouched snow.

'I don't know.' I was breathless as I reached his side. 'There's something about untouched snow... I just have to mess it up. It's all so...so *look at me*. So smug.'

Tristan tweaked the bobble on my wool hat. 'You're my favourite little destructive monster.' He laughed and used the tassels, dangling down by each ear, to pull me closer. 'Destroyer of innocent things.'

'Snow isn't innocent. You want a go?' We surveyed the churned up field. 'I think there's a bit left over there.' I pointed.

'Ok.' Tristan agreed, taking my hand. 'I like a job done well.'

We shuffled, kicked and stomped our way through the last of the perfect snow.

'Happy?' he asked as we stopped.

'Hmm I feel sorry for it now. Something about dirty snow is sad.' The cold started to leech in through my gloves and boots and I shivered. 'Destruction is fun, but the end result is kind of unsatisfying.' I flexed my fingers trying to warm them up. Tristan captured them between his own warm hands and rubbed back and forth. 'I do love you, you know.' I nodded, but then heard myself ask why.

He gave me a tiny smile. 'Because no one else sees things like you. Fresh snow is smug and dirty snow is sad.'

Sometimes it feels like my anxiety and sadness aren't even about Tristan anymore. It's just about me. Me willing and begging these feelings to go away. I hate that all it took was Tristan leaving to let them out. I am afraid I'll never be able to let someone in again. I am irreparably sad, just like dirty snow.

There is a rustle of branches and I look up to see yellow eyes watching me from a tall fir tree that stands guard over the drive. I don't even remember leaving the house and walking up the drive.

Come closer.

Do you want to play, Liv?

In a room in the house behind me, my Mum is crying, but I look at the yellow eyes and I nod.

Orla lounges across a deck chair. The sun beats down on her making the shiny material of her pastel blue bikini glisten. She stretches with eyes closed and a satisfied smile. Despite the trees, the tiny paved garden at the back of her cabin is drenched in sunlight. The simple pleasure of being in the sun, the relaxation on her face, it all washes through me. I wish I were in a bikini, so I could just lie down next to her.

'Orla.' I hear myself murmur on a smile. Everything inside me eases and loosens the longer I am in this place until I feel soft as silk.

Her eyes pop open, she unfurls like a flower and sits up. 'Livvy.' She looks so happy to see me that I laugh. She beckons me over. 'I must apologise for my behaviour the last time we met, dear. It was...' She closes her eyes a moment, her fingers twisting in the air as she tries to describe. 'It was one of those days.' She shakes her shoulders lightly before fixing those eyes back on me. Her hands reach out and my own rise to meet them. Instead of taking my hands she grasps me by the wrists. 'You'll stay this time, won't you?'

You shouldn't be here. You don't want to stay here, Rip had whispered as I'd walked back into the village searching for Orla only moments earlier.

'I need to know the truth. I want to understand.'

They're watching you for a mistake.

'I'll be careful.'

Just a tiny mistake.

'Please let me do this.'

And they will tear you apart like wolves.

'Aren't you the wolf?'

They will take everything.

'I'll stay, Orla' I confirm, 'if you answer my questions.'

'Anything.' Her voice is a soft purr. It would be so easy to follow her lead, to allow myself to just melt into her sing-song voice.

'What happened to John.' The question feels abrupt and petty, like I'm pointing out a minor flaw in a work of art. Orla's hands tighten and though her smile remains, her eyes are hard. She pulls back, but her strong grip on my wrists pulls me with her. Her face is inches from mine. This close, I can see she is trembling, but with fury or fear I can't tell.

'Don't say that name ever again.' Her eyes travel over my

shoulder and the hardness dissolves into another radiantly soft smile. 'Cillian darling, didn't I tell you she'd be back?' Her hands drop my wrists and she rises, slipping gracefully past me. I turn and see him standing in the shade of Orla's cabin. I can't see his face, until Orla drapes herself around him and guides him out into the sunlit pool of her garden.

'Liv.' He nods to acknowledge me. He is rather beautiful when he smiles. His face is sharp and masculine, but his lips look good in a smile. 'I see you're getting the hang of this,' he murmurs and his eyes travel down my body. My hands jump startled to my bare skin. I'm wearing a matching shiny bikini to Orla's, but in pale green. Normally, I'd feel self-conscious being practically naked. Instead, Cillian's appreciation feels like a magic power.

'I told you.' Orla is saying, playing with Cillian's hair. 'She needs to meet the others.'

'She will.' Cillian steps free of Orla and approaches me. He walks around me and I feel his eyes like fingers on my skin. 'Remarkable. How could I have mistaken you for anything else?'

'Orla said you'd answer my questions.'

'Yes, Liv. We will, because you belong with us.'

The Night Cafe hurts to look at. It pulses and hums like a generator. It's constantly changing, never settling on anything for long. I see ancient dark beams, glass walls, red brick, limestone, slate, pebble dash and so much more. Each glimpse of something different is only a glimmer. The words across the entrance change like letters on broken shutters going too fast. It can't make up its mind. I resist the urge to wipe my eyes, but Orla catches my expression. 'It gets easier,' she promises. 'It's just lots of different memories and moods. Everyone's memories of their favourite meeting places trying to outdo each other can get so boring. Wait until everyone's had a few drinks, then it will calm down.'

Cillian takes my hand as we step inside the building and his touch makes me realise – Tristan could be in here. I can't decide whether his presence or absence is worse. I can't decide whether I want him to see me with Cillian or whether I want to face him alone.

There are two scenarios I have run through for when I saw Tristan again (because I never accepted that I would never see him again). In one scenario I win him back and in the other, I slay him.

Either way in both versions I was strong and beautiful. In both, he saw his mistake. He rued the day he left me. I wanted him to rue. I was the girl Before Tristan. I hadn't appreciated her enough. She'd been so capable, so strong, so carefree.

My anger feels good in this world. It is courageous and powerful. It is righteous and deserved, measured and controlled. I want Tristan to tremble. I want him full of regret.

The interior of the Night Cafe has less of the frenetic energy of the outside and emits more of a gentle purr as it flips and changes around me. It is cluttered with furniture and random ornaments – nothing matches. There is a long dark wood bar that runs the entire length of one wall and a series of crooked doors leading to smaller rooms. Every inch of wall space is covered with a variety of objects - ceramic plates, copper pots, photography, paintings, posters... so much more. I see a telescope, a boomerang and even a full size harp in one corner. A second glance and they are gone, replaced with something else. We walk through old film posters, pressed flowers, maps and old newspaper articles. I see a log fire crackling in one of the smaller rooms. People look up as we go, their gazes lingering curiously.

The rooms smell like different perfumes and smoke and food, scents chasing scents. Orla sashays ahead of us, winding around people, tapping arms in greeting, whispering in ears and waving at others I can't see. She belongs here. Everyone greets her with serene smiles and soft words. When they turn to me, their eyes assess me from top to bottom. Then their lips pull into a smile at her whispered words. I don't see Tristan, but there are so many little rooms he could be in any of them. Or none of them.

'Our homes are private, but this place is for everyone.' Cillian murmurs close to my ear. 'You can relax here. We don't care much for appearances, still I don't think many would come dressed like you.' His free hand skims down my bare back and I remember I'm wearing a tiny bikini. I immediately look at Orla, but she's in a pearlescent grey shift dress. I don't remember when she changed.

Just a tiny mistake, Rip said. I look down and try to remember how I did this all those other times. Surely this is something I should be able to do if I truly belonged here. Things seem to happen when I'm not paying attention. I think of jeans, skirts, shorts and jumpers. I imagine shawls and cold days. Nothing changes. I lift one shoulder in a half shrug and try to sound confident.

'This is me relaxed. I love the sun. Let's sit outside?' After a beat, Cillian nods and leads me to the other end of the bar. People stop their conversations to speak with him, but he dismisses them gently with a smile and the smallest shake of his head.

I recognise craft ales on draught as we pass. The familiarity of it jolts me and I'm reminded of the Nectar Lounge. The smell of stale beer, clashing perfumes and sticky floors. As long as we wore the bar's tight fitted black top with its green hummingbird logo we could wear whatever else we wanted. The day Tristan walked in, I remember I was wearing my favourite most paint-splattered holey jeans. My vision stumbles and blurs a little at the memory. I grasp Cillian's arm to steady myself. *Stay, stay, stay.* I chant to myself.

'You're not disappearing on us again, are you?' Cillian asks as we enter a large leafy garden with wooden decking.

'No.' I squeeze Cillian's hand because it feels real. 'I'm staying.'

The garden is empty and still. A light breeze still ruffles the trees, the stillness is because everything looks permanent, nothing is flickering or changing in front of my eyes.

'Nice jeans.'

I look down and see my work uniform complete with my holey jeans. I'd thrown these jeans away months ago after Tristan tore them beyond repair in a silly play fight. Yet, here they are, restored to their former holey glory. I run my hands down the soft denim.

'Um yeah, the sun's gone.' There wasn't a cloud in the sky, but Cillian doesn't correct me.

When Orla joins us she is pouting because everyone else is inside. She carries a glass of white wine, which she picks up and swills a lot, but never drinks. Her entrance brings with it a flicker of mist, moss-eaten benches and cobblestones. Orla and Cillian talk around me, but their voices don't really sound like words. Wooden decking lazily switches to cobblestones and drifts back again. They are doing this, I realise. Orla and Cillian are each creating their own garden and I watch it softly battle back and forth. It is mesmerising to watch. When the sky starts to fade, dim fairy lights coat the trees and candles in coloured glass jars burn on the tables. Lights and candles change, one after the other and for the merest hint they glow together.

Cillian has a dark pint of stout, but as the sky gets darker I notice his drink barely goes down. I know neither of them went to the bar and 'ordered', but just like their clothes, whatever they want simply *is*. I'm determined to have my own drink. I want to master this art. I want to be like them. More people start to drift outside, drawn by the intimate atmosphere and traces of soft music. Orla is humming along. I like it when she does because it makes me feel solid as concrete. With the people comes the flickering melee of ideas and images. Orla is right, you do get used to it. Although, it does seem less energetic than when I first arrived. The more I watch, the more fluid it seems like a rushing tide. For an instant the air smells of the sea.

I am introduced to one person after another. New names sail through the air. Zara, Rowan, Luna, Seph. There is a sameness to these people that I can't quite describe, whether they are short or tall, dark or fair, loud or quiet. They aren't all beautiful, but they are all imminently watchable. They are interesting and striking, their voices smooth like honey. Everyone has a drink in hand, except me. My attempts vary between wishing and willing to trying not to think about it at all.

Beside me, Orla seems distracted. Her eyes fix on some middle distance for long spells until her name is actively called. I try to steal her attention as more than anyone she always makes me feel like I belong. 'Do you know everyone here?'

'Virtually. We're a small community.'

'Is this everyone?' The unasked question, *where is Tristan?*

Orla glances around, she has no idea how eager I am for her answer. 'No,' she says eventually, 'some will be on *The Otherside*.' The Otherside. I realise she means my home. Earth. I'm the 'other' entity here, not them. I am the alien.

'Have I met the people you wanted me to meet?'

Orla gives me a sidelong look and smiles. 'Are you nervous, Livvy?'

'I want to be accepted.'

Orla places her wine down and gives me her full attention. 'You're as good as in, Liv. You've already shown us that you can do things normal humans can't.' She leans in as she speaks. 'They can't wander in and out of here by themselves or master their appearance, their surroundings. Humans don't have the mental capacity.' Her voice is mildly scornful. 'You've done these things. Even if you do choose to wear rags.' She looks pointedly at my jeans. Her voice makes me want to confess. I don't know how I did these things. If you asked me to, I couldn't do them again. Will they test me? Rip's warning flits through my mind and I hate it.

Just a tiny mistake and they will take everything.

I am playing a game where I don't know the rules. Maybe, I should have listened to Rip, to Tristan. My breath hitches a little and I can sense the beginnings of anxiety tingling under my skin. The beer garden skips like a broken record. Snippets of conversation ebb and swell around me. Some words I barely catch and some feel yelled in my ear.

'I suppose she could be attractive.'

'I told him I loved him and he cried!'

' —such strange habits.'

'I hate the water, obviously, but he loves it.'

'Have you seen Celia? She's so close.'

' —exactly where I want her.'

'I don't understand it at all.'

'He's making it too easy.'

'Tristan didn't complete.'

'I know. He hasn't been back since.'

Tristan.

My heart thuds against my ribs. Tristan. My Tristan. It has to be my Tristan. Just his name across a distance causes something to expand in my chest. I whip around, but there are too many people. I don't know where it came from. I can't see him, but I can't stop looking every time someone steps near. I really wish I could make a drink appear right now. Orla has turned her back to me and is talking up to a tall man who stoops down to listen.

'I'm really am ready for another,' she is saying. 'I never like to take breaks.'

'You're an inspiration, Orla, truly,' the man laughs.

I reach out for her wine glass and take a gulp whilst she's not looking. It is not good wine, more like sour water. Possibly not even alcoholic. What I really want is gin. I'd discovered gin accidently through Tristan. It was a drink he'd ordered at the bar once, before our first date. A G and T, he'd drawled confidently like it was an old favourite. He hated it. My shift had just finished and he stopped me on my way out to offer it to me. I was so nervous around him I couldn't speak properly. I took the drink and perched at his table, wracking my brains for clever things to say. The gin had helped and I discovered I liked it. Tristan asked me out for the first time less than a week later.

'Liv,' Cillian appears in the space next to me on the bench. 'Are you finding us to your liking?' I nod automatically and smile, but my mouth feels dry. 'Ask me anything.'

The unasked question, where is Tristan?

The asked question, 'can I try some of your drink?' I sound like an idiot. Cillian frowns oddly, but slides his drink over. It tastes disgusting. I've never been a stout fan, but they made us try some of the drinks at the Nectar Lounge so we could make recommendations to customers. This is not stout. I pull a face and Cillian laughs, reaching back for this drink.

'I know. I know,' he says. 'It's not quite right. Some things are harder than others to remember.'

'Everything's stopped changing so fast.' I gesture at the beer garden, currently with decking, minimalist metal tables and coloured pillow and folded blankets. Cillian confirms our surroundings are collectively created by all of them, the more of them in one place the more it merges and blends. This village is a blank canvas and their memories the paint. Their favourite places intersperse and vie for attention. Everything they've seen and enjoyed blends and jumps in a cacophony of sights, objects and even smells and taste. Free reign is allowed in the Night Cafe. Their homes are a different matter. Homes are off limits. Homes are private.

'It is very bad etiquette to play with another Shepherds' home.' he warns me. 'Control yourself if you are invited to another's home.' I want to laugh at that, I have zero control. I have no idea what I'm doing. I wonder uneasily if I inadvertently altered anything in Orla's cabin. The picture of her and John constantly resurfacing springs to mind. Did I do that? 'The shifts always slow down in the Night Cafe once people start drinking alcohol. It subdues that part of the brain. For that reason, many of us prefer not to drink. Still enough Shepherds enjoy the effects of alcohol for the Night Cafe to generally get calmer as the night wears on.' He leans closer and our table lazily shifts to wood with a coloured lantern flickering between us. 'I prefer it like this, don't you?'

I learn that Cillian has many names for them – spirit guides, companions, guardian angels, but 'shepherd' is the one he seems to favour. He smiles slightly when he uses the word like a worn-out euphemism. Shepherds sent to the Otherside to help people. To help lost humans like lambs who've strayed from the flock.

'Help them, how exactly?' I'm curious, thinking of how Tristan 'helped' me.

He shrugs, 'it depends. Different people have different needs. People falter and struggle for all sorts of reasons. We step in and help them get back on track. In whatever way they need. We only help where we're needed.'

It's on the tip of tongue to call him a liar. I wasn't lost. I was doing just fine until Tristan showed up. I was not lost.

'If I stayed…would I go to the Otherside and help people too?'

'Yes, Liv.' Cillian grabs my hands in earnest. 'You could make such a difference. It's so rewarding.'

'And what about the wolves? Why are they here?'

Cillian looks confused.

'She sees the Shades as wolves.' Orla interrupts with a dramatic shiver as she drops down back next to us. Orla has been flitting around during our conversation, appearing and then disappearing. Cillian's mouth tightens. 'She thinks they helped her find the village.'

'Don't listen to them, Liv.' He reaches out to hold my chin gently. 'They're bitter and jealous. Any good in them died a long time ago. They blame us for being trapped here.'

But I'm fixated on Orla's words. Everything feels suspended and still. 'What did you say?'

Orla pauses, recalling her words. 'Oh? I don't know. They blame us?' She shrugs.

'No.' I'm impatient. 'Before that. What did you call them?'

'Shades?'

My face feels funny - hot and cold all at once. The creatures from Mum's bedtime story exist. Un

Cillian doesn't notice my shock. 'All we want is to help humans,' he promises earnestly. 'But some don't want to be helped. It is always the way.' Orla nods, staring at her finger as it glides around the rim of her wine glass.

'Some people,' she mutters, 'refuse to be helped.'

'They follow their Shepherd here and they refuse to leave.' Cillian's voice is angry. 'And then they blame us when they have nothing to go back to.'

'We thought you were the same at first.' Orla smiles like she's embarrassed by such a mistake. 'That you'd followed your Shepherd here and become lost.'

Did I follow Tristan here? He certainly didn't invite me. Rip (a Shade!) told me not to mention Tristan, but if I had confessed, would they not have helped me home?

I swallow uncomfortably. 'You try and help those people though? You'd send them back?'

'Yes, of course.' Cillian says after an awkward beat. 'We do our best.'

'But when you found me, you invited me back to the village.' Cillian and Orla exchange glances. I remember Orla's hypnotic voice. Trying to get back to my body, back to the Otherside was the last thing on my mind. It was the last thing it felt like they wanted.

'I suspected you were different.' Orla says almost proudly. Cillian places his hands together, almost like a prayer.

'We had to…have to–' he corrects himself. 'Make sure.'

'How do you make sure?'

'Oh, Livvy,' Orla laughs. 'Stop worrying. It's obvious!'

'You come and go by yourself.' Cillian talks seriously as if Orla never spoke. 'Normal humans can't do that. And I imagine you've seen our kind on the Otherside without even realising it. Like calls to like - humans only see the one sent to help them. A soul with the potential to join us will see any and all Shepherds.'

Instantly, I'm thinking of that bar months ago. I think of waiting and waiting for Tristan's friends. *They were there that night,* the wolves said, but I only saw Tristan.

'The final test, to truly make sure you belong with us will come with time.' Orla says, her eyes elsewhere as she smiles a greeting at someone across the garden. She looks back casually. 'If you're not meant to become like us, you'll become another Shade.' Panic washes over me. I'd be trapped here, a miserable ghost of the person I used to be.

So, not much different from how you are now then, a voice in my head points out.

'But you'd help me back before that happened, right?' So many of my childhood fears had revolved around Mum's story of Shades. Shades hidden and waiting to take me if I was too sad. I'd never even considered where they came from. My chest pounds and I really want to make a drink appear now. Something ice cold to ease my insides.

'Yes, of course, Liv.' They respond in unison like schoolchildren.

I feel cold glass against my hand. I look down and see a tumbler filled with ice and cucumber. I smell the cucumber for a moment as I lift it to my lips. It tastes perfect.

Cillian gestures for the glass and I hand it over automatically. He takes a sip and coughs. 'You made that strong, Liv!' He sounds impressed.

'See? You're perfect!' Orla laughs clinking her glass against mine.

Days pass, or maybe it's weeks? It's hard to keep track. I flit back and forth between worlds – each time is easier. Each time it's harder to remember to go back. I tell myself it's all in my head - what's the harm in dabbling with a fantasy if it makes me feel better. I've dreamt it all up in my head. I tell myself I can stop whenever I want.

None of it is real, except John.

His presence is the one niggle that I can't make up an explanation for. I try not to think about John.

Being with Orla, Cillian and their friends feels as real as anything. Realer even after the lonely stupor I've been in. I drift around the house most days, waiting for Mum to come home. I try to show my face when I can, eat a meal with her, anything to stop her worrying about me. But I'm really just killing time. Counting down minutes until I can go back to the Shepherds.

There are photos of me dotted around the house telling the story of my life, but there aren't any of Mum and me together. She took all the photos and she isn't the selfie type. It's only late afternoon, but the sun has already deserted the day and it leaves the rooms looking gloomy and grey. Often, I pretend this is the nightmare rather than the other place being the dream. I wonder how so little photographic evidence is around the house to show that my Mum lives here. I force myself to stay until I can see Mum and remind myself she's real.

We haven't spoken again about my father or the mysterious Tee. We haven't spoken about Tristan either. Occasionally, I catch her looking at me like she's about to say something. She always backs down though and retreats to her spinning wheel. If she knows that her bedtime creation has come to life she says nothing. If she knows that I spend most of my time following yellow-eyed wolf creatures called Shades to a world filled with strange and beautiful Shepherds she doesn't let on.

There are times when I want her to ask, when I want her to push, but maybe we both know we're long past that. We are passed her playing the protective parent.

Sometimes, when I slip lushly into their world I don't even look for anyone. It's like sliding behind a soft curtain. It's a hiding place. Everything feels like it can wait until I'm ready. Everything just loosens and uncoils inside of me until I feel like warm water. I wander in the meadow I first found or float in the lake staring up at the sky. When I want rain, it rains. When I want the sun, it shines. When I want to wear ripped jeans, I'm wearing them.

Best of all, when I want to be nothing, I'm nothing at all.

The Shades come and try to entice me into the village now and then, *come see Tristan*, they whisper. I still haven't seen him and each time I don't, my panic at the thought of him appearing at any moment recedes a little bit more. Sometimes, I follow them to the village and sometimes, I don't. Usually they leave me alone to my peaceful solitude. Rip is the most persistent and it always begins with the same disgust.

Why do I always find you here? I am usually in the meadow.

'I like it here.'

The way you feel here is a lie. I'd give anything to feel something out there rather than feeling nothing in here.

'I'm sorry about what happened to you.' I told her once. 'They explained it to me, about Shades.'

Did they really? Her anger is intrusive. It doesn't belong in my zen meadow.

I was lying on the thin strip of black sand between the long grass and the lake. My toes sunk into the cool wet sand and my head pillowed by the thick soft grass. I wasn't looking for Rip's confessions, old memories, truths or lies. She had followed a Shepherd here and she had refused to return. Wherever her human body lay, eventually, it had died and she became trapped here – bitter and angry. I pitied her really. I could easily understand not wanting to leave. In the end though, it was her own fault.

Did they tell you I died in this meadow? Did they tell you how I was ripped apart in this very meadow? Did they tell you that most of us die in this meadow?

'No.' I want to flick her away like an irritating fly.

Did they tell you that soon you'll die in this meadow too?

I always remain calm in the midst of her tirades. 'That won't happen to me. I'm not like you. I belong here.'

Either you're wrong and I pity you or you're right and I hate you.

CHAPTER 10

'L iv.' Mum startles as she notices me in the doorway. I blink, I hadn't seen her until she spoke, I was so preoccupied with the fresh sinking sensation in my chest. It happened every time I came back. This little grey house in the mist, waiting for failed exam results, and no idea what happens next – this is all that waits for me here.

Mum and I haven't seen each other in a while I think. I'm not sure. I feel like I don't really live in this house anymore – strange since technically I suppose I never left. She lowers the book she's reading to her lap, her ring-heavy hands fold anxiously over the top of it. 'I didn't know you were in.'

Two thoughts swarm my brain, the first is, *liar, you knew* and the second *not for long.*

'Where else would I be?'

She shrugs, looking down. 'Somewhere else.'

I continue to stand in the doorway, too restless to sit down. Why is it that when Mum's not around I want to see her, but the moment I do she irritates me?

'I'm going to use the laptop' I say as I walk out the door. I say it so she thinks I'm actually doing something and not zoning out.

'Have you started looking for a job?'

'No.' I call over my shoulder through gritted teeth. Despite not really meaning to, I go into the little box room and turn on the laptop. Looking for a job (a real job) seems too big a decision – what am I qualified for, what do I enjoy enough that I want to spend the majority of my time doing it?

I told Tristan once that I could be a student forever if they let me. I loved learning. I loved knowledge. I used to follow link after link trawling the internet from topic to topic with such curiosity. I could move from things as diverse as European history to string theory, computer programming to the renaissance, the paranormal to Shakespeare. In the beginning of my final year, a few weeks before I met Tristan, I'd decided I was going to take a gap year to travel and read lots of books, and then I'd figure my life out. I'd saved up money from working at the Nectar Lounge for air fare and then I'd work only when I needed the money to carry on travelling.

Instinctively, my email is the first thing I always check. I'm expecting only junk mail and that's what I find, except there it is hidden amongst the rubbish – an email from a pub in Edinburgh. It is short and to the point.

Dear Olivia,

I'm so sorry to tell you this, but John took his own life about 6 months ago. I'm sorry I don't have contact details for any of his family, but there is a donation page set up by this sister for a suicide awareness charity, see the link below. The charity may be able to put you in touch with her.

Yours,
Duncan Haye

I'm stunned. I sit and stare at the words, reading them and rereading them over and over as if I've missed something. For a moment it feels like I'm reading about my father.

John and my father. They have the worst thing in common.

And not only is John a real, but he's dead. Orla never mentioned him again and I kept forgetting to ask. I'd wanted to know what had happened to John and now I had my answer. Ignorance was bliss. I stumble away from the laptop and into my room. I try to switch my brain off, but it whirrs and jumps. I lie down on the bed and as my face sinks into my pillow I'm crying. Slow tears that run down the sides of my face and into my ears.

I'm crying for John McAulay and his family. I'm crying for my father.

When I close my eyes I see Orla in a pale dress, beautiful and covered in blood. She is smiling one moment and then crying the next. I see a man standing over my father's body out in the woods. The young girl Rip once was lying cold in the meadow. And most often I see myself, in those same murky woods where my father died. My blood stains the clean snow. Tristan is with me, just watching as the white snow becomes dirty with blood. When light begins to filter through the curtains and I realise it's morning. My eyelids feel scraped out with sandpaper. I force my eyes open and stare at the ceiling instead of dead bodies. John's death forces me to finally accept one thing.

It is all real.

Everything I've been through is *real*.

Shades are real.

I'd toyed with believing it was real before. In fact, I'd taken joy in believing it, believing that I was special and that maybe I belonged somewhere better than here. But some part of me had always rationalised it couldn't be real. How absurd. This fantasy was a pause button, a temporary fantasy to help me through a hard time. John's suicide ended all that.

With or without Tristan, I could imagine a forever in the village. Forever sounded right, whereas future sounded wrong – the word felt grown up and full of ambition and career plans. Forever, was dreamy and child-like. I could be happy and help people as a Shepherd…forever.

Orla tried to help John and she failed. This is what I choose to believe. I want the world she spoke of. I want to help people. Tee helped my father and he failed. How could suicide be anyone's fault? People do what they want, you can offer help and support, but ultimately the choice is theirs. Deep down even Mum must know that. She can't seriously blame Tee for my father's death. The one thing spoiling my endless thoughts is Rip. Rip believes they killed her. Rip believes they will kill me. Who do I believe? Where do I belong? I cycle through the possibilities constantly. When it comes down to it, I know this—I trust Tristan. Despite everything, I still trust him. I need to find him. I need to know the truth.

I spend the whole day with Mum for once, perhaps for the first time in years. I'm building up the courage to ask her about her bedtime story. I wonder if she knows it's real or if it's just a story she liked to shut me up when I wouldn't go to sleep.

I trail around behind her as she goes about her chores and am surprised by the amount she actually gets done for someone so easily distracted. We don't talk much, but I think she is pleased to have me along. It kind of happened by accident when I found her making soup in the kitchen this morning. I saw she'd left a knife by a pile of vegetables and I started chopping. When I was younger we used to work in sync in the kitchen with barely a word spoken between us. We'd move around the other and somehow prepare a meal. She looked up and smiled when she heard me chopping. I helped her load the vegetable soup in the car without question and followed in stunned silence as she delivered it to houses around the village. She stood on the doorsteps chatting easily with elderly people while I watched from the car. Next, we went to the library. I tried to browse books, but not a single word went in. I overheard Mum discussing books with the librarian for a book club I had no idea she went to. She stopped to talk to pretty much everyone we passed on the street. We stopped by the village hall and she talked with villagers about a craft fair, a 1940's weekend in summer, and costumes for a play they were putting on at Easter. I'd never seen this side of her or maybe I'd just never paid attention.

'I didn't know you were involved in so much.' I say when we arrive back home. The door is unlocked because she never remembers to lock it.

'I like to keep busy. I like helping people.'

Her version of helping people and Orla's strike me as so disparate that I feel a twinge of shame. Let's face it, my main reason for wanting to become a Shepherd is not to help people. I want to be like Orla because I want to be different. I want the world she lives in to be my escape, but I don't even know how Orla actually helps people.

'How long have you been doing all this?' *How did I not know this? Is the unasked question.*

'Oh, years, Liv. For years.' She looks like she's about to say more, but instead she starts humming under her breath and wanders off upstairs.

A couple of long frustrating days pass where the meadow eludes me. Agonising over John's suicide seems to have disrupted by ability to find it. Mum also seems to be avoiding me and I never find the moment to ask her about Shades. She's out all the time and now I know why. I rarely join her on her charitable trips around the village, preferring to hang around the house searching for the meadow. I think in circles and argue with myself. I try to think about a future *here*, but it feels too daunting. I have missed calls from the counselling office, but I ignore them. I feel as bad as I did when I was holed up alone in my room at school and, if anything, Mum seems pleased about this. I can tell she approves every time I drag myself out for the distraction of helping her. Every time I watch TV without zoning out to another world. She thinks I'm 'getting better', but she's wrong. This limbo feels so much worse.

There is a knock at my door, I don't look round, knowing it can only be Mum. I'm trying to read a book in bed – it's late enough in the evening that being in bed is just about acceptable, but too early to pretend to sleep.

'Liv?'

'Yes?' It comes out sounding distracted. I don't want to look away from my book. I need it to distract me and it took me long enough to get into it. I don't give up any kind of peace easily.

'I've been having a bit of a spring clean and I found this...I thought it might interest you.'

'What is it?' I still don't look around, glaring at my book with determination.

'I'll just leave it here. It belonged to your father.' *That* causes me to look. She's already left the room, but there on my bedside table is a faded brown leather notebook. Some of the pages are crumpled and it's stuffed with extra pages of loose paper. I sit up, dropping my book.

The leather is soft under my fingers. This is the closest I've ever been to my father. I feel like I'm holding him in my hands. His handwriting is small, the words slanted forward like the letters were tumbling over each other as they fell from his pen. I imagine his fingers fumbling to keep up with all the thoughts he wanted to spread on the page. They are the plans of his novel, notes about characters, scenes and places. I turn a page and stop short. It's a map – painstakingly intricate, coloured and labelled. There is a lump in my throat making it hard to breathe. It looks like one of my maps.

Just like me. Like me. Like me. He was like me. This is me.

He's been dead for more than twenty years and suddenly I can't believe it. How can the man who drew these, who was full of such creativity be gone? How can so much just suddenly stop existing? We had something in common. We could've been close. The three of us could have been a normal family. Tears are welling in my eyes and I wipe them angrily away. This doesn't change what he did. He still left us. I continue to skim through his notes. There are so many beginnings. So many paragraphs that are never continued and half formed thoughts. I stop when I see a name I recognise.

> *Today, Tee suggested we go somewhere special. He wanted to get out of the city, so we skipped the group session and just jumped on a train and left. As simple as that. It's been ages since I spent a day hiking. It's strange – I don't really remember the journey. I only remember the place. A beautiful wildflower meadow. And for the first time in months I felt at peace. We found a lake, it was so calm we decided to stay and sit a while. We didn't talk much, but it was a good silence. For the first time, I didn't think about Bendek. I felt like I could breathe again.*

My heart thuds so hard it feels like it's going to burst through my chest. My father went to the meadow – my meadow. My father has been there and just like me he loved it. *Just like me.* Mum said Tee and Tristan were alike and here is the proof. Yet, Tee took my father to the meadow and Tristan never took me. That hurts. Then I remember that Rip said the meadow is where humans go to die.

Mum drops her car keys in front of my breakfast. My 'breakfast' consists of cold peppermint and nettle tea and a dry ryvita. Outside is another miserable drizzly February day.

'Liv, I need a favour.' When she pauses, I gesture for her to continue. 'I promised I'd volunteer today at the library, but I'm supposed to be picking up my friend's dog to look after while she's away for the weekend. You remember Abbie? She has a collie called Sky. Can you take my car and pick up Sky?' She looks at the clock on the kitchen wall. 'I have to be at the library in half an hour.' The old me loved driving and loved dogs even more. Now, I hesitate and try to think up excuses. She sees my reluctance. 'I can probably get out of the library shift.' She's half muttering to herself. 'Never mind, I'll sort something. Just a thought.' I can see the disappointment and frustration in the sag of her shoulders. She picks up the keys and turns away looking busy as she drifts about the kitchen looking for her phone.

'Wait.' I grab her arm as she passes me to leave. 'I'll do it.'

I haven't driven a car in months, not since the last time I was home. Tristan was with me and I was both proud and coolly dismissive as I drove us around. Tristan was such a tourist. I fed him stories and we meandered through quaint villages and fields and sat in autumnal beer gardens. It felt like I rediscovered my home as the summer turned red with autumn.

My Mum's friend, Abbie, lives in a neighbouring village so it's an easy mindless drive. I'm always surprised that I can still drive. It feels like one of those complex and important skills that you should forget without practice. Yet, every time I get behind the wheel it is instinctive. Lost in my thoughts, whole stretches of road pass and I don't remember driving them. It scares me, a little. It scares me how easily a small twist of my hands could smash me into a tree.

Today the fog renders the sky white and makes the landscape look sad and neglected. I drive past faded homemade signs for ancient tearooms and free-range eggs. I feel a twinge of sadness as I imagine interminably empty tearooms, cobwebs and everyone buying their eggs from supermarkets. Tristan wanted to stop and get eggs one time – although he'd thought the sign was for 'free' range eggs. I almost smile at the stupid memory. What are range eggs and why are they free, Liv?

When I see the yellow eyes in the verge I'm going too fast to stop. They blur past me. More appear.

Liv.

Liv.

Liv.

Liv.

It's a hum that rises in my ears and grows until it thunders through my bones like a plane taking off. Black dots squirm into my vision. Against the drab colours of winter, the yellow eyes glow intensely, more real than anything around them ... The village is dappled in sunlight. Against my bare arms the sun feels like a caress. I am wearing an ancient T-Shirt with Scooby Doo on the front and my indecent denim shorts. My feet are bare and I curl my toes into the squishy moss that carpets the forest. I'm on the edge of the village. Behind me I can hear the scuffle and playful yips of wolves.

Liv's back. Come closer. Liv's back. Time to play.

Their silliness feels infectious. I step out from the trees onto the road that winds through the sprawl of houses. The wolves don't follow me into the village, but looking back I recognise Rip sitting apart from them and watching me. I shrug off her disapproval. It's hard to worry in such a chaotic and beautiful place. I pass a thatched cottage pressed up against a spindly Victorian redbrick terrace and further on an ivy-eaten wooden chalet with window boxes bursting with flowers. I keep a look out for Orla's cabin or the Night Cafe, but really I'm happy to wander, just happy to be back. A few unfamiliar people pass me, sometimes they smile in greeting, but others look at me with a frown and when I check over my shoulder they're staring after me. Their eyes feel like cold fingers. They feel like whispered words, you don't belong here.

A week after Tristan left me my housemates staged an intervention. They'd figured out something had changed, that my bubble had burst.

'You'll get over this Liv!'

'Boys are rubbish.'

'We're here for you.'

'We love you.' They nodded, patting my shoulder, my hand, any part of me they could reach, apart from Beth. Her eyes told me to get over it already. She tended to move through guys with minimal fuss. I thanked them, but I didn't share any details. I left the room and I never sought their help.

'She's her own private pity party.' I heard Beth mutter to one of the others before I was out of earshot. Stupid kitchen door that doesn't shut properly. The words came back to me weeks later in a counselling session with Miss Salter.

'You can't allow yourself to feel this forever.' The words were spoken around the pen she periodically poked in and out of her mouth. *Private pity party.*

Did some masochistic part of me actually enjoy torturing myself? Sometimes, I'd give anything to switch it off. Other times, I admit, I cling to it like it's the only thing about me that's left.

But I feel real when I'm here, real without the mess Tristan left behind.

The Night Cafe is crowded tonight. I've never come here alone before. I'd turned corner after corner and street after winding street, but then glancing back, it was behind me all along. I'm not alone for long, Orla finds me quickly. We wear matching peach backless chiffon dresses. Orla wears it first and then I notice I am too.

'You flatter me, dear,' she smiles. Cillian, Zara and a few others I'm beginning to recognise from their circle join us. Unlike the Shepherds I passed earlier they all accept me and I relish the sense of belonging. I can be one of the beautiful people. Their laughter and talk spills over each other as they tell stories about cities they've visited. Their voices are musical water rushing around me. Submerging me. They ask me questions about humans like I'm not quite human myself.

'Why say sorry if they don't mean it?'

To make an awkward situation feel less awkward

'What does it mean when they say they need space?'

Probably that they never want to see you again

'Why do they cry so easily?'

We have a lot of feelings. We're basically just water and hormones.

I struggle to keep up and they laugh loudly at my answers like I'm completely hilarious. They are mesmerising when they laugh. The joy that bubbles up from entertaining them is so addictive. There is something different about each of them that draws me in; Orla's voice, Cillian's charm, Rowan's kind eyes, Zara's infectious energy, Seph's sarcastic wit and Luna's calm strength. They love all my tales of working behind the bar. They adore talking about human food, drink and music – all things light hearted….and then.

Tristan.

I see Tristan and time slows, stretching taut.

Time slows while my heart wants to escape through my mouth, nose and eyes all at once. His back is to me, but I recognise that dark hair and faded denim jacket. His hair is longer than I remember and starting to curl – just like I knew it would if he ever grew it. Turn around so I can dismiss you, so I can continue with my day. Orla is talking to me, her fingers play with the ends of my hair. I barely notice her. Tristan is like an inkblot obscuring everything. All I see is the back of a boy who may or may not be him.

He turns. Everything rises within me.

There is a mischievous curve to his lips. I used to press my lips to that jaw. Tristan had the best jawline. I swallow. I feel trapped, elated, and terrified all at once. I'm not ready. Panic rises like bile and vicious excitement courses through me. It's Tristan. It's really him. Tristan smiling. Tristan talking. Tristan happy. My Tristan.

My Tristan with his arm casually draped around another girl's shoulders.

CHAPTER 11

These are the things I've learnt about love.

Love is cruel. Love is beautiful. Love is fleeting. Love is a gamble. Some love is constant and some love is fickle. It can creep up on you or hit you like lightning. Regardless of how it starts, it can wither away. Love can leak through the cracks until you don't even realise it's gone. Until you look at the person across from you and think … I can't do this anymore.

And there he is. Perfectly happy. Perfectly able to *do this* with someone else and it hurts to see it. I feel like someone's punching my throat, determined to stop me from breathing.

'Livvy?' Orla's fingers dance across my neck, her sing-song voice pulling me back. She follows my gaze and despite all the laughing people milling around she hones in on Tristan. I see her eyes narrow and I shiver. 'Do you know him?' Her eyes are calculating, her voice so soft and carefree.

Yes, I know him. He's my soulmate and my jailor. He holds my heart and refuses to give it back. I love him. I hate him. He's my partner in crime, my best friend and my greatest enemy.

'No.' I reply so quietly that Orla has to lean closer. I can't look away. It's a special kind of torture loving and hating someone this much.

'Are you sure, dear?' Orla's fingers move down my spine lightly. 'You seem a little put out?' Her voice does that thing where it wraps around me making me want to share my every thought. Why shouldn't I tell Orla everything? She's my friend. She'll understand. She loved John. She misses him. She'll understand.

'I-' I'm shoved forward suddenly and Orla has to grab me to keep us both from toppling over. I hear a shriek and angry voices.

'Get that thing out of here,' a man snarls.

A woman shudders. 'Disgusting.'

I see a flash of yellow eyes and then Rip is gone, disappearing between legs. She leaps up to an open windowsill. Her eyes meet mine briefly and then she is gone. Tension runs through the crowd, Rip has upset them all. Orla leans against me for support and without thinking I put an arm around her shoulders.

'Oh, they make me feel ill,' she whispers dramatically.

Cillian moves closer to us, 'It's gone, darling.' He smooths the hair away from her face and gathers us both up in his arms for a hug.

Get out. Get out. Get out now. My thoughts are like a physical touch on the back of my neck. I shiver as I step out of Cillian's arms. I look around and my gaze crashes.

Tristan.

His eyes stare me down. I have never in my life wanted so much to read someone's thoughts. His dark eyes give nothing away. Everything inside me rises and falls and all I can hear is the thud thud thud of my heart. There is no softening, no smile, no look of love quickly hidden by grim resolve. Nothing.

Just this agonising endless moment.

Words of power and anger desert me and I stare like an idiot. The girl by his side is laughing at something her friend is saying, but holding Tristan's hand loosely. Seeing the touch seems so intimate and it makes my face burn. I hate her. I hate him. His eyes skip down a second and I know he sees, but he doesn't drop her hand. Instead, he leans slowly towards her, his eyes back on mine, and whispers something in her ear. His lips curve, almost like he's smiling at me. I see her dark hair move as his breath ruffles it. She nods and he squeezes her shoulder before finally looking away and disappearing in the crowd. I shift, craning my neck, but he's gone.

People spend their whole lives searching for this feeling. They crave the rush, the burning, the fire, this sickening bloom in the pit of their stomach. Before Tristan, I thought I wanted this. Desire, overwhelming desire. At uni, my housemates and I, we wanted to be worshipped and treated like princesses. We wanted to be seen and *deserved.*

I want to leave, but Orla is clinging to my arm. Rip has really unsettled her. Her eyes seem lost somewhere far away. They glisten with unshed tears. Cillian is on my other side and he is telling me another stupid story about human antics. I nod, I smile, but I'm not listening. I look through him and around him. I don't see Tristan anywhere. Now that I've had a glimpse, every cell in my body wants to fall toward Tristan. I want us to go back to before any of this happened. Back when he looked at me like I was the only thing that mattered. Like I was the best thing he'd ever tasted.

'Cillian, I'll be right back.' I don't wait for his response. I don't even look at his face as I walk away. My eyes rest on Tristan's girl. I get closer to her. I have no idea what I'll do when I reach her. I want to pull her hair and all manner of other pathetic scorned ex things. I want to ask her how she makes him happy. I study her. Why would Tristan want me when he had this? Her hair is dark like his, but long, straight and shining. As soon as I see them, I know it's her eyes he fell in love with. They are amber, a liquid brown that sparkles golden and bottomless. If I had those eyes... and then she sees me. Her smile remains, but a small frown creases her forehead. She's tiny and beneath all that beautiful hair confusion becomes her. I should look away, but I can't. A hand grabs mine gently and turns me away. I'm irritated until I am confronted by a man with dark onyx eyes. He emanates power. He's tall, with strict hard features, but his eyes smile at me.

'You're new.' His deep voice thrums through my entire body. I feel warm, like his voice is sunlight. 'And yet...' he pauses, and his free hand grazes across my cheek, 'you look familiar.'

I open my mouth to speak, but no words come out. I'm mute. Words. Could I ever speak? I don't remember how. He laughs gently at my open mouth. 'I don't think Tal desires the interruption.' He nods over my shoulder towards the girl. Tal. A new space forms within me. A space to hate. I hate Tal. 'But, I do. Walk with me?' It's a question, but before I even manage a nod we are gliding towards the doors and the fairy lit garden outside. I glance back. Tal is watching us, but her smile no longer seems real.

Outside it is just as busy, but the darkness makes it feel more intimate. The conversations are quieter. Secrets are being shared. I feel like we're alone when he looks at me. 'Your name?' Olivia. I must say it out loud because he nods.

'Why are you here, Olivia?'

Tristan, I think. 'I belong here.' I say. And it's the truth. I'm happier here than I've been in months. As strange as this place is, I make sense here.

'Maybe, you do,' he murmurs and leans in closer, 'and then again maybe, you don't.' I'm not even sure if I'm breathing. 'Such lovely eyes,' he whispers. 'They remind me of an old friend.' He likes my eyes, I almost laugh out loud. Go back inside and check out Tal's. I close my eyes for what I'm sure is only a moment, but when I open them he's gone.

Suddenly, there is a sound in my head, like a headache made out of metal screeching as it crunches and scrapes. Then silence.

A crystal glass is in my hand. I drink and taste the cool bite of neat vodka. For a moment I think I see blood splattered across the glass in my hand.

'Livvy?' Orla and Zara are in front of me. They're smiling excitedly. 'How did that go?' Orla asks. 'Did Tobias like you? He's the one you need to impress.'

'I'm not sure.'

'You're still here so I imagine it went well.' Cillian speaks from behind Orla.

'Yes!' Zara claps her hands. 'Yes. Yes. I knew it! You'll be an awesome Shepherd.'

I'm nodding even though I don't really know what that means. Yes, I'll be a Shepherd. I'll herd humans.

I drift with them a while longer. We talk, we mill, and we simply exist in a state of beautiful shimmering surroundings. But I don't feel safe anymore. How can I feel both happy and unsafe? Both exhilarated and terrified? Everything is right and then wrong.

I move away from Orla while she's preoccupied. She's telling some sad story or another. Another man who is hopelessly in love with her. These creatures live for love. They live to be cherished and adored. Finally, I am outside the front of the Night Cafe. The streets are cobbled and smooth and behind me the Night Cafe flickers like a broken light between cosy country, dive bar and city chic.

I walk away with no destination in mind, only solitude. However, the moment I see the quiet lane hidden between the streets I know it belongs to Tristan. A single-track lane with fruit trees and autumn colours, it twists so you can't see too far along. There is a little red post box almost engulfed by ivy and the house name, *The Refuge*.

'I don't want a house number, let's give our dream house a name.'

I rolled over to my front so I could see Tristan through my sunglasses. He didn't open his eyes, but smiled and lifted a hand faintly to find me.

'Hmm ok. How about The Refuge? Because that's how I feel when I'm with you.'

'I love it.' I replied.

Moss casts a greenish tint to the stone-etched letters. I stare at them for too long as if the letters might change. My heart aches in a way that makes me wish I didn't have a heart. I follow the lane. It is exactly as I imagined. It curves until I can't see where it began and I am entirely alone. The rustle of leaves is gentle and there is the hammer of a woodpecker nearby. I know what I'll find at the end of this lane, but seeing it outside of my mind's eye is something else.

Our dream house. Nestled at the end of the lane as if it's been waiting for me all along. I run forward, a choked laugh escaping me. The lane opens into a little clearing. A stream meanders down one side and off behind the house. It is all the things I ever wanted, but realised ever so slightly differently. A twin, with the indefinable stamp of Tristan where he'd added parts and interpreted my words. It's the barn I wanted, but looking close to collapse. It's rustic and ivy eaten with giant wooden doors and faded beams. Tristan may have taken 'ramshackled' a touch too far, but it makes me smile. Tristan probably didn't even know what a barn conversion was.

Despite Tristan's additions, it's still my fairytale house bathed in an orange sunglow. Bluebells and honeysuckle are haphazard around the clearing and more bluebells spill and wander off into the trees. Flower boxes in the windows bloom brightly. I even see smooth solar panels gleaming in the sun on the precarious roof. The giant doors are locked, but there is an ornate metal knocker shaped into an ugly face. It reminds me of a film about a goblin king that I loved as a kid. Looking at the knocker, I wonder if I made Tristan watch that film or am I already influencing the appearance of this house.

Running along the stream is a wooden pathway beckoning me around the side of the house. I follow, peeking in through the windows as I pass. There are glimpses of the modern, but also the cosy finishes I'd talked about and even more beams. Again, maybe, he'd gone too far with all the beams but the quirks were all so Tristan. I loved it.

Around the back is a little patio area sheltered by blossoming cherry trees. A wooden stable door leads back inside. The top door is open like an invitation. Even though I really want to see inside, there is something more important I want to see first. The wooden path and stream continue on, veering away from the patio and garden and disappearing through the forest. The path winds to a little red bridge and crosses the stream. There is something sparkling through the trees. I already know it is Tristan's lake, his morbid reminder of death. One of the only things he told me he wanted. I see glimmers where the sun hits the water through the trees and then the full picture-perfect beauty opens up. The path runs to a veranda with two wicker chairs turned toward the lake. A wooden pier strides out into the calm water. Green and brown mountains frame the lake. Their hazy reflection casts the far corner of the lake dark. I know this lake.

'Where is this place?' Tristan asked.

I glanced up from my revision. I smiled seeing the framed canvas he meant.

'It's somewhere in the Lake District. North of here. I don't remember which exact lake it is. I love that photo though.'

'Me too,' he murmured.

His fingers lightly touch the canvas, skimming over the water.

'When your exams are over, can we go there?'

'Most definitely.' I closed my notebook and kissed him instead.

Derwent Water. I don't forget the name of the lake anymore. We never went in the end.

I walk along the pier until my bare toes tip over the edge. The wood is warm beneath my feet. I can feel every grain through my toes. I can feel the wind skim across my skin. I close my eyes. I almost think I could fly. Or at least my spirit can fly. My mind can fly. I can be anything here.

'I thought I'd find you here.' Tristan's voice. I can't face him. He doesn't want me here. For a second I am powerless. I'm the wreck he left behind. The caramel and moss-coloured mountains shudder.

No. I will not leave. I open my eyes with a deep breath. I summon my courage and the words I've honed and practised for so long. *Give back what you stole from me.*

But as I turn and see him properly for the first time in months, the words dry up in my mouth. His familiar face. So dear to me. My breath bunches up in my chest. He's so close, so real, I could reach out and touch him.

'Hi Tris.'

'Liv.' His eyes are sad. I hate it.

'I love what you've done with the place.' I try to smile, but it's impossible.

Tristan sighs. 'You're making this hard, Liv. Why couldn't you just let it go?'

It hurts to hear, but it kindles an anger too. 'Let it go? And you? This house. This is *my* house. Our house! Is this you letting it go?'

'You don't understand.' Tristan looks uncomfortable and that only makes me angrier.

'Then why don't you explain, Tris! Why didn't you tell me about any of this? I would have understood. You never let me in.' My voice breaks over the last words and I fall silent, unable to say more.

Let me in. Those words reverberate in my head. I lowered a drawbridge. I let him in. I gave him everything. *Give back what you stole from me.*
'You could have told me your secret,' I finally continue.
'Letting you in was the problem.' Tristan snaps. His hands clench at his sides. They rise and they fall, but they don't reach for me like they used to. I've never really seen him angry before.
'You should have been the one to bring me here.' I'm so full of regret. Did the last few months even have to happen if Tristan had just shared his secrets? I turn my back on him and look back to the water.
'How did you even get here?' I hear him move closer. He stands beside me. We aren't touching, but I feel his closeness all along my left side. The air feels charged.
'I found the way on my own.'
'And where are you, Liv?' His eyes are suddenly intent on mine. He leans towards me. I can see where the darkest browns thread with gold and meet the iris. 'Right now. Think.'
I swallow, he won't send me away. 'I'm where I belong. I'm where I want to be. You should have brought me here.'
His lip curls in disgust and he laughs coldly. 'Really?' He looks away. When he looks back, I think he'll grab me in his anger, but he doesn't. Go on. I dare you, I think. Touch me, Tristan. I want his hands on me both so I can feel them and so I can rip them off. Instead the air hisses out through his teeth and he takes a step back throwing his hands up as if to shield himself from me. 'No, Liv.' And suddenly he is calm again. 'Think. Where are you? Where *are* you really? If this part of you is here, what's left behind? Where is your mother?'
Everything shimmers around me. Mum? The lake and the mountains try to disappear and I hear a faint wailing sound. But,

no. I'm better at this now. He can't push me out.

'I belong here.' My voice is low and measured and I smile when everything settles around me.

'Trust me. You don't.'

I thought Tristan had hurt me before. But he'd never spoken to me like this. His voice a snarl and ice in his eyes.

And everything flickers violently around me. Trees, soft brown mountains, the gentle lake, blood splatters across glass, a sun-soaked pier and a sky grey with rain. Tristan zooms in and out of focus. He doesn't want me. Time has changed nothing. Tristan didn't want me then and he still doesn't want me now.

I can't do this anymore.

There is a deafening wail in my head. My ears feel like they're bleeding. I don't know where I am. All I see is Tristan and his angry eyes. But then they aren't angry anymore. No. Tristan looks horrified. Something trickles down my face. I feel dizzy. I sway, but catch myself before Tristan can. My lungs are burning.

'Liv!'

His face is faint like he's yelling from down a well. Hands grab my shoulders. Tristan's hands. Hands in blue medical gloves. He shakes me hard. They're gentle as they move me. 'Where are you? You need to go back.' Tristan's hands are on my shoulders and I don't shake them off. They are warm and solid. The blue hands are warm and solid too.

He pushes me away. 'Go back!'

I touch my fingers to my forehead and they come back slick with blood.

'What's happening?' I frown and it sends shards of hot pain spiralling through my skull. I've never seen Tristan look so scared.

Liv! Please,' he begs, 'please go back right now.'

'I was driving.' I finally remember. Flashing blue lights reflect in a broken wing mirror.

Tristan grabs me. 'You idiot!' He shoves me away hard. It feels like my body snaps in two as I fall away from him. I miss the

edge of the pier and feel myself falling. My bloody hands scrabble desperately for sometime to hold on to. Anything. I reach out toward Tristan, but he just watches me fall and fall and fall.
The wailing won't stop and I see flashes of blue light reflected in his eyes. I taste metal between my teeth. And I fall, until Tristan is nothing and pain is everything.

CHAPTER 12

'Turn this car around, right now. We're going back for the free eggs.'

'Tristan!' I took my eyes off the road for a moment to reach for his hand. 'You don't even like eggs. Remember that drink I made you with the egg white?' I looked back at the road, but squeezed his hand as I spoke.

'Range eggs might be nicer.'

'Trust me. They're the same as regular eggs.'

'Liv, what are range eggs and why are they free?'

'You idiot.' I shook my head, amused.

'Please? Let's go back right now. Me and you.' I glanced over and those dark eyes stared into mine.

'You know, you remind me of him. And sometimes, I,' her voice caught in her throat. 'Sometimes, I can't stand to even look at you.'

The front door opened and I ran to the top of the stairs, still in my long socks and school skirt. There Mum was laden with bags and I imagined she looked happy. My foot hovered on the top step, but when she looked up and saw me her face fell.

❖ ❖ ❖

'I always see his eyes. The look in his eyes when they told him about Ben. His eyes when he wasn't really here. His eyes were open when I found him.'

❖ ❖ ❖

The light is white and it hurts my eyes. Even when I close them everything is burning white.

❖ ❖ ❖

Somewhere a cuckoo won't stop calling. Over and over she calls. Stop, I want to tell her. She carries on calling. *Cuckoo cuckoo.*

❖ ❖ ❖

At some point the cuckoo morphs to machine. A rhythmic and regular beeping that never ends. Her cry starts to sound like words. I was. I was. I was. I was. The next thing I'm aware of is pain. Pain like an itch, irritating me back to life. There are collections of noises above the endless cuckoo call.

'I can't go through this again.' Mum.

'I'm sorry.' A soft voice replies.

'Are you?' There is silence and then Mum again. 'I know what you are.'

'I know.'

'You… You're a call to the rocks, you're a dead end and she's only at the beginning. She's-'

'I know.' He interrupts. A sigh. Footsteps. Silence, and then 'Why do you think I left?'

'Then stay away, Siren.'

'I'm trying. But she found her own way through.'
'What does that mean?'
'I don't know.'

'Is this him?' Tristan wandered into the kitchen holding a picture frame.
'What?' I was distracted as I leaned over a huge soup pot on the stove. I was cooking dinner for us and Mum. She'd offered to go out and buy wine. It was our first weekend visiting her and so far they were getting on surprisingly well.
'He looks familiar to me.' Tristan continued quieter.
'Who? Can you pass me the lemon juice? The cupboard on your left.' My style of cooking always deviated from the recipe. Tristan handed me the lemon juice and I finally looked up to see what he was talking about. He held a photo of my father in a homemade frame decorated with dry pasta spray painted gold. 'Where did you get that?"
'It was in one of the bedrooms upstairs.'
I knew immediately it was from Mum's room. I never went in there.
'I remember making that frame at primary school. I haven't seen it in years.' I turned back to my soup and poured in too much lemon juice. 'That's my father,' I added. It was a photo of him I'd never seen before. Sitting and smiling on a garden bench, squinting slightly against the sun.
'What was he like?' Tristan asked.
'Never met him,' I shrugged.
'But your mother must have told you stories about him?'
'Talking about him was always really hard for her. I stopped asking.' Normally, at this point people's faces turn into a soft kind of pity. It was automatic that I pressed on. 'But I honestly don't care anymore. I barely think about him now.'
There was no pity from Tristan, only curiosity. 'He looks happy. I

wish I knew why he looked familiar.'

'You better put that back where you found it before my mum gets home.' I think I might have spoken more sharply than I intended. The familiarity I saw when I looked at his face bothered me too.

I am brand new. I'm not him. I'm not you. I can find my own way through. No one listens to me. Life bustles around me. Even the cuckoo ignores me. Her beeps are an unanswered question. *Was I? Was I? Was I?*

'What's next after school?' Tristan asked, almost idly. The way he rubbed his thumb along my knuckles as we held hands was surprisingly distracting.

'University I guess, assuming I get in.' I looked at our interlaced fingers. 'I can't believe my final year has started.' His thumb moved back and forth and across the top of my hand to the inside of my wrist. I was so aware of every part of his thumb as it skimmed my hand leaving a tingling in its wake.

'My housemates spent their summers travelling or in apprenticeship placements. And me?' I sighed.

'You spent it working in a dirty little bar?' Tristan finished and I laughed.

'At least I met you.'

'Best summer ever,' Tristan said, his thumb running up the inside of my arm.

'Best summer ever,' I agreed.

There was so much more I wanted to do. So many ideas and dreams. The potential of it all was terrifyingly exhilarating. Exhilaratingly terrifying. It was everything. The blank slate of my future could feel so ominous and at once so golden.

'What is it?' It was like he could read my mind.

'Just thinking about all the things I want to do with my life.' His fingers joined his thumb as they ran up and down my bare arm. It was difficult to remember what I was thinking when he did that. 'I want to learn a language and I want to travel. I want to make music. I want to leave a mark. I want to write a book and play an instrument. I want to make memories I'll love to relive when I'm old. I want to tell stories. I want a house in the woods with a stable door. I want a family with stupid in jokes and traditions at Christmas.' Tristan's fingers left my arm and I shivered.

'I never knew you wanted all that.' He looked unusually grave. 'You never talk about the future. But it sounds right. It sounds like what you deserve.' For a moment I thought he was joking.

'You know I hate that word!' I poked him in the ribs, but he remained serious.

'But you do, Liv. You deserve so much. More than I can give you.' And I could tell he really meant it. 'You deserve better than me.'

I grabbed his hand and wrapped my fingers around it. 'Don't you think that's my choice?'

I am disorientated. Caught between fog, dreams and memories. Something squeezes my hand. I can't move.

'Hey.' Her voice is so gentle and tired. 'Can you hear me?'

I don't think I move at all, but she carries on talking. 'Stay with me, Olivia. Please. Please just don't go.'

Orla is singing and I think it's become one of my favourite sounds. She's absorbed in her garden, resting on her knees and bent over flowers. I don't think I've ever seen her so peaceful. I lean against the side of her cabin as I watch her work. How can this place be bad? How can something so pure be wrong?

'Don't stop.' I whisper as her voice dies away at the end of her song.

'Liv!' She's startled and I see the happy scene is less than I'd thought. There are faint tear tracks running down her face, but her composure is always so quick and she smiles. 'How nice to see you.'

'Why are you sad?' I move closer.

'Me sad?' she laughs. 'I'm not sad. I'm marvellous. Look at my flowers! They're growing so well. Aren't they beautiful?'

'Everything's beautiful here.'

'True.' she nods. 'But, nothing's as beautiful as something you build yourself. John used to...' she stops abruptly.

'Did John say that?' Orla doesn't move. 'Is John the reason you're sad?'

Orla purses her lips, she looks down, but eventually she nods.

'Will you tell me what happened to him?' I rush over and drop to my knees beside her. 'Before you say no. Maybe I can help you.' I reach for her hand. Despite the gardening, they're pristine with mint-coloured nails and a diamond ring on her left hand.

'It's such bad form,' she murmurs, looking over my shoulder, but she allows me to hold her hand. 'I shouldn't speak of him. I should be clean by now and ready for the next. If anyone heard...'

'You can trust me.'

She doesn't like that word. Trust. I see her eyes narrow and she pulls her hand away. 'Tell me how you help them. Humans. Tell me how you pick them.' It's a safer topic and I see her relax a little.

She smiles. 'Oh Liv, that's the best part.' All traces of sadness are gone. She's giddy. Her cheeks flush and I wonder what memories she recalls. 'Have you ever been in love?'

I nod. I don't think I can reliably speak as Tristen suddenly clouds my mind. I feel my face burn. Orla laughs at my face. 'Yes,' she says. 'It's just like that. Love at first sight. You spot them in the crowd and something just burns up. It takes over and you'll do anything to have them. To help them. It's a calling so strong.

So undeniable. You'll know when you find your person. When they look up and see you for the first time…' Orla closes her eyes. She doesn't need to say anything more. I remember that moment with Tristan. I remember the first time I spoke to him and the slow smile as he replied.

I swallow. 'But, why that person? How do you know they need help?'

'That's what we're drawn to,' she shrugs as if that's the least important part. 'The lonely. Only those who are lost can see the help they need. We're the light at the end of a dark tunnel.'

An uneasy feeling steals across me. No, no, no. This is not right. Maybe John was lost, and my father too. But I was not lost. I was not lost. Was I? I'm on my feet instantly, the garden is shaking. Orla doesn't notice, her mint nails have gone back to her flowers. Even they look different now. Did they grow from seeds? Did she nurture them? Or did she dream the finished product into existence? Was I lost when Tristen found me? I back away, but already I can barely see a thing. Everything is melting and bleeding into one dark murky colour.

Was I? Was I? Was I?

'Oliva, I'm so sorry.' A broken sigh and the rustle of clothes. 'I know this is all my fault. I haven't been a good mother.' Her voice is small, barely louder than a whisper. I have to concentrate to hear the words over the beeping and the effort hurts. 'Maybe if you'd known more about him….and me.. If I had spoken of him.' There is a broken exhale. 'Maybe you'd be on a different path.'

I am aware of pain in my wrist. My throat is dry and sore. My head starts to pound. This feels real. My eyes feel glued shut as I fight to open them. I fight to remember what happened. Mum's friend and her dog. I was driving. The accident. Had I already picked up the dog when I crashed?

'Dog?' I don't think a sound actually comes out, but Mum

notices.

'Olivia? Can you hear me?' Her hand squeezes mine and I try to squeeze back. I feel something strapped to my face and I reach up to pull it away. 'No, Olivia. Just rest. There's no need to talk.'

I shake my head slowly. My fingers feel along the edge of a mask and I manage to pull it down slightly.

'Dog?' I repeat. Finally my eyes open, but the light is so bright I close them again. Mum leans in.

'Dog? Oh, the dog! Oh Olivia, the dog is fine. You never made it to Abbie's house. Don't think about that now. '

I slump back, my hand dropping away and I feel her place the mask back over my mouth. 'It's so good to see you awake!' I open my eyes and manage to focus on her. Dark circles, red-rimmed eyes and papery skin. She looks exhausted. She looks old. I've never thought of her as old before.

I'm in a small plain hospital room. I see the machine, the cuckoo that has been torturing me, still beeping away. Then the pain starts to steal over me stronger than before. My chest burns and the pounding in my head gets louder.

There was no pain with Orla. The memories of her flower garden feel faint like a dissolving dream. Orla talking about love. A pier overlooking a lake. I'd give anything to be there again and away from this pain. Is this how my father felt?

'Olivia?' Mum stands and calls a nurse for help.

'It hurts,' I croak.

'I wish I could feel it for you.' It feels so unnatural to see her cry. I hate it.

'I can help with the pain,' the nurse promises when she arrives. Yes, I think, please help me. I close my eyes. I don't know what she does, but when it comes it's like a wave rushing in. It grabs me and pulls me out beyond the shore. I'm pulled to deep gentle waters.

'Mum?' I struggle and she pulls my mask down. I can feel myself going under, but the question feels important to be asked. 'My father. What did Tee do to him?' I'm floating deeper and I see her agonised eyes before I'm gone.

I could float face down in this lake all day and I would be happy.

◆ ◆ ◆

I could float in this lake all day if you let me. I could just watch the skies and let the gentle water lap over me. I'm content with birds and dragonflies for company.

'Why Olivia,' a voice says, 'Fancy finding you here at the lake. I wondered when we'd get the chance to speak again.'

I tilt my head back, chin to the sky and there he is standing over me. He obscures the sun, a face hidden in shadow, but I know his voice.

'Hello Tobias.' I don't feel nervous like last time. Maybe it is the lake and the meadow that make me relaxed. 'How can I help you?'

He wades closer through the water and out of the sun's eye. I see his face. If I squint it's almost like looking at Tristan.

'A better question is, how can I help you?' I feel his palm move gently beneath me as if he's keeping me afloat. His other hand glides softly down my arm and he leans in close. 'What do you want, Olivia?' His eyes are like Tristan's, but his mouth is different. I want to erase Tristan. Some reckless instinct makes me lift my arm up around his neck and pull his lips to mine. The palm beneath me grabs and pulls me up as he kisses me hard. I didn't know I'd missed this until now. I press against him and revel in the feeling of wanting. Of being wanted. It's addictive. In that moment I feel something I'd thought Tristan had killed when he left. After seeing Tristan with Tal, kissing Tobias feels good, it feels like a fuck you to Tristan. We pull part, both breathing heavily. He's so close his smiling mouth is all I see. I rest my forehead against his throat.

'I think you'll do well here,' he breathes. 'I can help you stay, if that's what you want.'

Stay? There's no contest. I can barely remember what there is to go back to. Just pain and a drab little room. With Tobias' warm and reassuring presence, it's the easiest decision I ever made. I nod. 'Yes. I want to stay.'

His other arm reaches under me and he scoops me up and wades out of the lake. He lowers my feet to the ground and then runs his fingers over my forehead, pushing the wet hair back. 'Olivia,' he smiles again. 'You really do remind me of someone.'

I stare out the window at the miserable grey day. It rains and then it stops and then it comes back harder than before. The wind rattles the windows. The hospital room is chilly and the blanket feels stiff and itchy. If I focus, I realise every part of me either itches or hurts. I don't know which is worse. I'm lucky I didn't break any bones and yet I feel so uncomfortable in this body. My body. Apparently I'm lucky I only fractured some ribs, punctured a lung, and sprained a wrist. Yet every breath feels forced.

Mum keeps me company. I might be able to go home soon. At this point, home feels like an abstract concept rather than an actual place. Mum reads stories from the newspaper or talks aloud as she works through the puzzle section. She likes the cryptic crosswords.

'Dances quietly, held by leader mostly. Four letters. What do you think?' Now that I'm lucid, she doesn't want to talk about my father.

Do you blame Tee for what happened to my father? And the new question that now crosses my mind. *What if my father isn't really dead? What if he's living his life in another place?* He could be a Shepherd and maybe I could find him…

And if I tell the doctors it hurts? The pain relief they give makes it all so much easier to slide on over to the meadow.

◆ ◆ ◆

Walking through the long rope-like grass, hiking up my long skirt and running until my heart beats hard against my ribs. It's a feeling of freedom, just being able to breathe deep and full and easy. Being able to run and run and run is worth everything. More often than not, Tobias joins me. It's hard to remember what I found scary about him. Sometimes, he runs after me and I let him catch me just to feel strong hands around my waist. Sometimes, I see yellow eyes watching, but they always keep their distance.

'Why is there a statue fallen in the lake? I ask him.

He looks grave as he replies. 'I'm afraid to say that not all of my kind honour their responsibilities.' He glances over to the lake briefly. We're at the far side of the meadow, enjoying the shade of trees. The lake is a distant slice of silver between the grass. 'A fate of stone is what happens to Shepherds who break the rules. It is the only way we can die.'

'He used to be alive?' I'm horrified, but not as much as I expected. I recall the details of that sunken face. So resigned and life-like. A man who accepted his fate. 'How did he break the rules?'

'Depends which face you saw.' Tobias shrugs. 'A few have fallen there over the years. They're all the same though. They all abused their power.' Tobias turns his full attention back to me. He sees my questions before I ask them and speaks firmly. 'Being a Shepherd is a gift, but also a responsibility. You don't need to worry. That fate would never await you so long as your heart stays true.' He flashes one of his devastating smiles and leans down to me until his black eyes are all I can see. Eyes like Tristan that have me hooked. His breath flutters against my cheek and I shiver. A wall of anticipation builds around us, pulsing and ready to break. 'Is your heart true, Olivia?' he asks in a low voice that curls around me. I sway slightly and feel my heart racing. Am I true?

'Always for you.' I breathe aloud. *I am always true for you, Tristan.* Tobias straightens with a chuckle. I blink suddenly seeing him in focus again. Not Tristan.

'I love humans,' Tobias murmurs. 'So much feeling contained in such a tiny vessel.' He runs his fingers across my forehead lightly and down the side of my face to rest under my chin. His gaze is so intent I almost imagine he can see right inside.

'What does immortality feel like?' I ask.

Tobias pauses like it's a question he's never considered. His fingers travel down my neck and along my collarbone. 'It can blur. I treasure all the moments that ripple the surface of the blue. The moments and people that make themselves memorable. I take delight in all the poor souls I've helped. You'll understand soon enough.'

Another time, we stand side by side at the edge of the lake. "I see you. You love to be chased.' Tobias says. Our fingers brush every now and again. I step away to break the connection, but he follows. 'You will love chasing even more. You'll discover a whole new side of yourself.'

Thoughts of my father, John, and even Rip, never completely leave me. 'The humans. You don't ever...hurt them, do you?' I ask cautiously. I want the reassurance desperately that Tee didn't kill my father and Orla didn't kill John...that Tristan hadn't planned to kill me.

'We have no power over humans. We provide comfort and solace. We encourage and advise, but a person's fate is their own. We are just a friend in the dark.'

'Do many humans become Shepherds?' *Did my father become a Shepherd?* Is the question I hold back.

Tobias shrugs. 'Some. It is not common. We've not had one such as you for a long time. You have so much potential. It's remarkable. '

'When can I start?' Tobias is pleased with my answer. I want to stop drifting back to that painful grey place.

'Soon. A few little loose ends to tie up first. For example, you must be voted in by the village to be confirmed.'

I pull his forehead down to mine. 'Everyone loves me.' I think of Orla, Cillian and the others at the Night Cafe.

'Yes. Your light shines so strong.' Tobias agrees, running his hand down my hair.

'Do I need everyone to vote for me?' Could Tristan vote against me? Could his friends? Except for Tal, I'd still yet to meet anyone who claimed to be one of Tristan's friends. No one seemed to recognise me from that night in the bar.

'Yes, you feel the full vote, but fear not with my endorsement it's a formality. No one disagrees with me.' He takes hold of my face between his hands, his thumbs stroking my cheeks. We stare at each other for a long moment. It feels like my last chance to object, my last chance to run away. I don't move an inch and he smiles. 'Come on, no time like the present, let's seal your fate.'

The Night Cafe is heaving when we arrive. Tobias leads the way, holding me by the hand. I hear whispers around us and watching eyes. I wonder if my father could really be among them. Would he recognise me? Would I want him to? This changes nothing - he still left my mother alone in the worst way possible.

Like father, like daughter. A small voice in my head remarks and I try to ignore the guilt it brings.

I see understanding smiles from the faces I recognise and curiosity from the others. 'Friends!' Tobias calls out when he reaches the bar. He doesn't shout and yet he gets everyone's attention. The conversations die away. More fill the bar, entering from other rooms and outside. 'It is not often we welcome newcomers to our little family. Not many have the strength to do what we do.' The room agrees by raising their glasses. 'Strength of mind. Of spirit. And especially strength of heart. But here, I introduce you to Olivia.' Tobias looks at me. His eyes defy me to look away. The moment feels locked in time. His magnetism holds everyone and they wait for him to speak again. 'Many of you already have the pleasure of her acquaintance and those that haven't can take my word for it. More than just a lost lamb, Olivia is a keeper. Olivia has proved herself to me. Not only does she have the strength, she wants to belong here, she longs to do what we do.' He raises our joined hands. 'You can cast your votes at my door and I will deliver the verdict in three days' time.'

Three days. My fate will be sealed in three days. Tobias continues and I see the power he holds by the way he commands the room. 'However, I trust I'm not being too hasty when I ask you all to please join me in making her feel welcome.' There is a moment of silence and then applause that builds and even some whoops. I laugh when I see the source is Orla, Zara and Rowan. Beside them, Luna smiles encouragingly and Seph smirks. I catch familiar eyes at the back of the room and see Tristan push out of the room. I want to follow him, for so many reasons, but most pressing on my mind at this moment is begging him not to vote against me. Tobias seems pretty sure no one would vote against me with his endorsement, but the Tristan I know always had a stubborn streak. Around me the rest of the Shepherds are full of cheer and in the mood for celebration. New faces come up to me to shake my hand and offer their assistance for anything I might need. I notice the quick glances at Tobias though, almost as though to confirm if he's witnessing their magnanimity. I'm pulled away from Tobias and into the dancing embrace of Orla and Zara.

'Oh, Liv! I knew you'd do it!' Orla sings as they both jump around me excitedly. 'You're one of us.'

I'm a Shepherd, or as good as. Good or bad, I belong. Finally, good or bad, I have a family. I relax amidst them and the happy vibe. It's all so infectious. I find a drink in my hand and this time it's prosecco - a drink I've always associated with celebrations.

'Marvellous news kid.' Rowan winks and squeezes my shoulder
'I have complete faith that you'll serve well.' Luna says, slightly
out of place with a mug of steaming tea. So many warm hands
touch me as they pass with kind words and well wishes.
'Almost there, little lamb.' Seph says. 'Shepherd or Shade. Which
one will you be?'
'Shut up Seph!' Zara admonishes and playfully pushes his face
away. He holds his hands up in surrender and saunters away.
'Don't listen to him. You're no Shade.' I smile gratefully, but
Seph's words ring in my ears.
Shepherd or Shade?
I slip away once I'm no longer the centre of attention. It's
dark outside and I wander the gardens watching the lights and
only half listening to the conversations around me. The garden
flickers in a way I'm still growing used to. Fairy lights, lanterns,
candles, torches made of fire. Sometimes, they go out completely
and we're plunged in darkness, but only for a moment.
Shifting patterns of light reflect and flash across the planes of
faces. We're all hidden in the semi-darkness and then starkly
illuminated. A hand gently touches my wrist.
'Congratulations Liv,' he says from behind me.
Tristan.
'I told you I belonged.' I reply quietly as I face him.
'Congratulations,' he repeats with a half smile, but it's hard to
tell in the changing light. 'You got what you wanted.'
'Not everything.'
Tristan looks like he's about to say something else, but changes
course last minute. 'I've seen you in the meadow with Tobias,' he
says mildly instead. I feel my face burn and hope the night hides
it. I didn't feel like I was doing anything wrong with Tobias,
but now with Tristan's fingers still curled around my wrist and
his thumb tracing my pulse... now it feels like betrayal. But no,
Tristan does not deserve my loyalty. I'm angry that he has the
power to make me feel ashamed.
I'm staring at this thumb against my pulse. 'Jealous?' I finally say,
looking up.

Tristan looks aside. 'Jealousy.' A flash of light across the garden illuminates the amusement in his face. 'That's a human thing.'

'I was human.' I don't notice I've used the past tense until Tristan's hand tightens about my wrist and he corrects me.

'You still are.' I feel my anger growing. How dare he turn up and immediately make me feel worthless.

'Will you vote against me then?' I pull my arm away sharply.

'Made a new friend, Liv?' A voice from the dark asks, before Tristan can respond. For a second, I think it's Tobias and I'm afraid without knowing why. Instead, Cillian slides his arm around my shoulders.

'Oh, Cillian.' I look up at him with a relieved smile, wondering how much he overheard. 'Yes. It's nice to meet so many new faces tonight.'

'Of course, and Tristan here is one of the best. Best company that is.' Cillian laughs before continuing, 'don't take any advice off this one though!' he reaches out and shakes Tristan's shoulder good naturedly. 'His last foray was a bit of a disaster I hear.'

Tristan's face darkens. I think you have to know him really well to see his veiled anger. Cillian obviously doesn't and carries on. 'I say his *last*. I should say his first. His only!'

'Really?' That revelation gets my full attention.

Cillian nods. 'Very unlucky. Quite embarrassing to lose your human. I hope your confidence is not knocked too hard to get back out there, Tris.'

'Of course not.' Tristan bristles. The tension coiled in his fists is so apparent I'm amazed Cillian doesn't notice.

'Come inside, Liv.' Cillian coaxes, giving my shoulder a squeeze. 'I can introduce you to some more experienced Shepherds.' He tries to guide me away, but I duck out from under his arm.

'Go ahead without me. I'll be in shortly. I'm just enjoying the air.' Cillian lingers a moment with narrowed eyes, but then gives the smallest of bows and walks away.

'I was your first?' I blurt as soon as he's gone. Tristan looks around, there are a handful of people still in the garden laughing and talking. He grabs my arm and pulls me a step closer to him.

A step away from the flickering lights.

'No one knows you're the human I failed to catch. You must keep it that way.' His voice is low and urgent. The urgency reminds me of Rip and her warnings. He smiles politely at a passing girl as she wanders by us with curious eyes. 'We can't talk here. Come with me.'

CHAPTER 13

The Refuge feels eerily still after the buzz and flicker of the Night Cafe. The constant vie for attention of every object and every surface is becoming familiar, although it takes leaving to remind me that I prefer the stillness.

It's difficult not to get distracted by the home Tristan has created. He leads me through a pristine unused kitchen to a small sitting room. It's familiar and foreign all at once. An orange cushion on the sofa with a grazing pig and Chinese characters catches my eye. I pick it up absently, it's as soft as mine. But mine sits far away from here in the easy chair in my room at school. The woven rug beneath my feet is the same one that lies in Mum's living room. There is an old coffee grinder on a side table. I never made coffee with it, but I used to play with it when I was little, turning the handle around and around. It had a faded green and blue logo on the front and one word in yellowed white text. This one says *Jasmine*. I frown, that isn't the right word. Tristan must have remembered it wrong from its place inside a glass cabinet at my Mum's.

'You know it's considered bad form to edit someone's home.' Tristan observes from behind me. I jump at the intrusion. The coffee grinder is in my hands and the text now reads *Jaded* the way I remember. 'You'll have to learn to control that if you stay here.' I put the grinder down carefully and face him.

'Does that mean you finally believe I actually belong here?'

'No.' He doesn't expand. His face gives nothing away and all my unspent anguish turns to anger. All my nervous exhilaration at seeing him snaps and wanes. How has Tristan got so good at making me angry?

Give back what you stole from me.

'Why don't you believe in me?' I snap. 'Tobias, Orla, Cillian, Zara and the others. They all see me. They all accept me.' My voice catches and breaks. I swallow and take a deep breath to calm the shuddering around me. I breathe to calm the moving shapes and it brings Tristan back into focus. 'And you. You of all people.' A tear slides down my face. Tristan watches it a moment before looking away. He always hated it when I cried. 'Look at me!'

'Liv! You're crying.' Tristan strode over from the doorway and crouched before me, running his hands over me gently. 'Are you hurt?'
'Tris!' I gave him a watery smile and laid my book down on my chest. 'I'm fine. It's just a sad part in my book.'
'The book did this?' He picked it up and threw it across the room. 'Then it's gone.'
'Hey! I was reading that, it's one of my favourites.'
'You've read it before?' Tristan was horrified. 'Why would you read something you knew would make you sad?'
My face felt itchy with the tears I'd been crying, but I laughed. I sat up in my seat and hugged him. 'Sometimes it feels good to be sad, you know?'

'Well,' I demand Tristan after the silence stretches. 'Say something!'
'What can I say?' he sighs. He's keeping his distance. He paces the

room, picking up objects and putting them down again. I'm not used to seeing him upset. I want to hold him. I want to tell him it's alright. I want him to tell me it'll be alright.

Another part of me wants to prod, needle and stab. 'It's like you never knew me at all,' I whisper.

'I saw you, Liv,' he snarls, suddenly rushing up to me. His face is so close to mine. I remember the amber bolts running through his dark eyes. I remember the look in those eyes right before he would kiss me. They never used to look so angry. His eyes drop to my mouth. Go on, I dare you.

For an electric moment we're trapped. One of us will close the distance I think. We're both breathing hard, but neither of us moves. When it finally matters, why can't I move? His breath against my face is like a gentle touch.

Then Tristan backs away, resuming control. 'Do you remember when you were supposed to meet my friends?' he asks.

'I remember.'

Tristan nods with a pained expression. 'They were there.' *They were there.* The wolves already told me that. 'If you truly belonged here, you should have been able to see them.'

'I don't understand.'

'It's always the first test. To know if a human really has the strength. You see us. All of us, not just the Shepherd who selected you. '

'I failed? But Tobias says I can-'

'I saw you,' interrupts Tristan. 'I thought you could be one of us. I would have done anything to help you.' The way he stresses the word *anything* reminds me of the old Tristan that loved me.

'There must be another way. Tobias wouldn't-'

'No human gets a chance once they fail,' Tristan interrupts me again.

I shake my head. 'You're wrong. Yes!' I point at him, 'Cillian said you're new at this. There must be things you don't know.'

'I know Tobias likes to play games, especially with humans.' All Tobias and I have done is play games. He's the hunter and I am the hunted. Racing through the meadow, letting myself be captured. 'You're lucky none of my friends have recognised you from that night at the bar,' he continues, talking more to himself. 'Yet at least. You're lucky Tobias didn't join us that night. He never forgets a face.'

'Look, I don't know. I don't have the answers. Maybe I wasn't ready then and now I am. I came here without you. Tobias believes in me.'

'Liv!' Tristan's voice is sharp. 'Nothing you can say will make me accept that you belong here. You're making a mistake.'

'I guess I can't count on your vote.' I hate the sound of my own bitter voice.

Tristan sighs. 'I can't vote against you. It would raise too many questions. But you shouldn't be here. Do you realise what you're giving up?'

'I do.' I feel the emotion welling up and I have to steel myself to push it down, to not let him push me out. 'Tris, I came here. I found you. Don't push me out.'

And finally he reaches for me, just a gentle touch. Fingers against my cheek. He wipes away a tear with his thumb and his hand remains there.

'Liv.'

No time could have passed since he walked away. I love him just the same. And this time I *can* move. I step closer. I lift my hand and run my fingers down his face. It's the same as it always was. His brows, smooth cheekbones, chin, lips. I never thought I'd want another person so badly. Let me in.

Tristan watches me guardedly, but he doesn't move away. I lean closer, rising to my tip toes and steadying myself against his chest. When our lips finally touch it's the softest of kisses. He shifts and I'm afraid he'll pull away. Maybe I've just thrown myself at him and he's desperate to escape. Instead, his arms slide around me, they pull me closer, and then we're both holding on to each other so tightly.

The room is dark and cosy. A dying fire glows in the corner, but most of the light creeps in through the window. The moon, I think. I stretch feeling deliciously at ease and comfy in this warm bed with all the time in the world.

Tristan is still asleep. I could watch him sleep forever. I remember other nights just like this. Nights where I memorised every contour of his face and wondered how much time I'd have before he disappeared again. Anxiety and happiness warring madly through my body. At this moment though, I am calm. There is just acceptance and love here.

We'd moved easily to the bedroom with no need for words and fallen into each other. Clothes no longer existed and my overriding memory is of skin. Tristan's skin under my hands. My skin against his. Sweat, tingling, glowing fire-lit limbs. My favourite part of his collar bone. The taste of his neck. His fingers tightening and leaving marks on my hips.

The light outside seems brighter than before. I ignore it for as long as I can, preferring to curl up and make myself a little spoon in Tristan's arms. But a gap between the curtain flutters and the light winks and flashes. Eventually, I leave the bed and pad over to pull it closed.

The moon is a fluorescent white ball of light, like a torch held to interrogate me. I squint using my hand as a shield. It's not the forest I see behind the light, but grey walls and faded blue hospital curtains.

Was I? Was I? Was I?

I back away slowly as if I might get caught. I crawl back into the lovely soft bed and fold myself into Tristan's warm body. I close my eyes and pull his heavy arm over me like I'm willing myself back into a dream … I don't leave *The Refuge* for a time after that. Tristan and I have so much time to make up for. I don't miss anything or anyone. For a time, there is only us. He's almost back to his old self. The one that loved me.

◆ ◆ ◆

I haven't seen Tobias, but I know there is only one day left of voting. Tristan left The Refuge briefly to cast his vote and returned with the news. One more day of limbo before my fate is sealed. We cuddle up underneath a blanket on the pier on my last night of not knowing. The sky is turning from amber to sapphire and the first stars appear winking. We don't talk about us or about why he left. Instead, Tristan asks after Mum, my exams and my friends. We talk of easy things and stupid things and it's nice. And then I go and ruin it.

'Who was that girl I saw you with?'

'Hmm?' he murmurs, staring out across the lake. 'Oh, you mean Tal?' A smile. 'She's a sister.'

'You seemed very close in the Night Cafe.'

'Yeah,' he agreed. 'She's one of the only ones who stood by me after … everything.'

"Everything" I gather is some failure to do with me. I was his first human and he failed me. Maybe he failed by picking me at all? Someone who is not lost has no need for his kind. I'm still having trouble understanding what about me suggested I was 'lost'.

'She wasn't one of your friends in the bar that night though?'

'No, thankfully she wasn't. I don't think any of them will remember your face. You look …different here, but we need to be careful that we aren't seen together too often.'

I nod, but I'm wondering who his friends are. Other than Tal I haven't seen him hang out with other Shepherds. He and Cillian were clearly not friends.

'You may have noticed that we're all loners here.' Tristan continues his hand absently playing with the hair at the nape of my neck. 'We live alone, we work alone. We only really meet to share our stories and gloat. Isn't that what friends are for?'

I suppress a smile. He's right, the Night Cafe is all a performance.

An immersive theatre experience with everybody believing they were the star.

'So Tal is family?' I press a moment later.

'As good as. I'd do anything for her. But our only true connections are with humans.'

It was only later that I wondered about this. *Our only true connections are with humans.* Where did that leave us? Finally reunited, but not allowed to be together.

'I want to show you something.'

I see Tristan's bare feet on the pier as I emerge from the lake. I look up, he's wearing sunglasses and smiling as he holds out a hand to help me out of the water. My main non-Tristan activity involves floating in his Derwent water inspired lake. Meditating I call it. I know later today I will have to face Tobias at the Night Cafe and hear the verdict from the vote. I know I should have been schmoozing people in the Night Cafe to ensure no one voted against me, but *The Refuge* feels like home. I am reluctant to leave and even when Tristan isn't around I stay here alone. I change things subtly to bring the house closer to my dream. I don't ask Tristan where he goes when he isn't with me and it's like falling back into an easy old routine.

Sometimes I'm vaguely aware of my body in stiff hospital sheets, but I'm not ready to focus on that. I'm not ready to let it go either.

'Sure. Where are we going?' I ask as we walk back to the veranda.

'For a walk.' Seeing Tristan so casual in a t-shirt and sunglasses reminds of all the days we spent enjoying the sun last summer. So many afternoons sprawled in the botanical gardens. The memories inspire a high-waisted red maxi skirt and black crop top that I often wore. Tristan smiles at the change, his fingers skim the skin at the small of my back as he leads me through the woods. 'It was a good summer wasn't it?' I nod and we both lapse into our memories. There is something so untouchable about that time, like museum objects we observe behind glass. 'Do you remember all those plans you had?' I look up at him and startle at our surroundings. Lost in the perfection of the past I hadn't even realised we'd left the wood and now walked along a leafy tree-lined suburban street. The leaves were red and brown and yellow and crunch beneath our feet. It was a familiar street, but I couldn't remember ever being here before in any of my village wanders. 'You were going to see the world, remember?'

'I can still do that as a Shepherd. People all over the world need help.' We pass a couple of pubs standing opposite each other. One has a red sign with gold letters. *The Closed Shop.* I've been here before. 'Is this still part of *The Refuge?*'

'No, Liv. You know where we are.' Tristan moves his arm to rest across my shoulders. 'Such a great time. I remember passing here so many times on my way to see you. Do you remember you wanted to write a book?'

I stare around me at the tall red brick houses, the streets lined with wheelie bins with faded house numbers painted to their sides. Parked cars squeeze back to back along the street on both sides. Nothing flickers.

It's all still and very real.

'No,' I whisper. 'How are we here? Is this real? This can't be.'

'You loved this city, Liv. You told me you could imagine settling down here with a family after all your adventures.'

'Yes, I remember.' We turn onto the street I've lived on for the last two years. It's a typical terrace street full of unloved student houses, second-hand cars and patches of weeds masquerading as gardens. There's even the same old abandoned leather sofa outside number 473. 'I never meant this part of town though.'

Tristan laughs. 'I like it here. Good memories.'

'Are we really here?' I grab his hand tightly. We turn a corner and suddenly we're in front of the gates to the botanical gardens.

'No, Liv.' He leads me into the gardens and to a bench lining the main promenade. 'We're still in the village, at *The Refuge.*' He pulls me to sit beside him. I'm stunned into silence. A mix of relief, confusion, nostalgia and God knows what else swells up inside me. 'I brought you here because I wanted to remind you. I couldn't forgive myself if I didn't try.'

'Remind me of what?'

'Of what you're giving up if you stay.'

'Tristan.' There is a hint of warning in my voice.

'Hear me out.' He holds up his hands. 'All those dreams you had. The writing. Travel. Your friends. Your mother.' He emphasises my mum and it takes me a split second to recall her face. 'What you get in return is not equal. Not-'

'No, it's better,' I interrupt. 'And I can still visit. I'll still see the world. Tobias told me I could go anywhere to find people. I can still write.'

I'm startled by a man passing by us as he walks through the garden. The man nods at us and says good morning. I see a dog racing across the grass to catch up. I thought we were alone in this creation of Tristan's. Looking harder I notice an old man reading a newspaper at a bench far across the park from us near the Italian gardens.

'Tobias is economical with the truth.' Tristan looks away. 'You *can* go anywhere, but whether you will is another matter. You won't be able to just stop by and visit your mother.'

'Why not?'

'She won't be able to see you.' That thought sinks in a moment before I shake my head.

'I don't expect you to understand, Tris, but Mum would want me to be happy no matter what. Even if we couldn't see each other. She'd be happy to know I was helping people.' Tristan stifles a laugh. I look at him sharply and he's anything but amused. What is more noble than sacrificing a life to help others? How can Tristan not understand that? There's so little left for me beyond that hospital bed.

'Who are these people?' I ask, changing the subject. Tristan frowns a moment before seeing where I indicate.

'Oh, them. Also, not real. Part of what you can create in the village with a bit of practice. Whole worlds - all of it fake.' He stands. 'Come on, we can go now.' The streets outside the gardens are quiet, but not empty. We walk in silence passing made up people and their fake conversations.

'Liv,' Tristan says eventually. 'I'm not trying to get rid of you. I just want you to truly consider everything you're giving up.' A couple pushing a pram pass and I look back to watch them. 'Including that.' Tristan follows my gaze. 'There are no children in the village. No future. No family.'

Children are such an abstract concept. Yes, I'd always imagined having a family. And recently all those dreams had included Tristan. But the details of when and what our life would look like was too far in the future to even think about properly.

I stop in the middle of the street still watching the young couple. It's the one thing I haven't thought about since I started rationalising my life here. But then who are these unborn future children if they're not mine and Tristan's? A little boy with Tristan's big dark eyes is what it feels like I'm giving up.

But that dream is already dead. Tristan can't have children.

All of a sudden, I don't know what to do. I feel frozen with indecision. I feel like I'm running out of time. Tristan's hand takes mine, but I barely notice until his thumb strokes my palm. 'Liv?' When I turn back to him, we're back in the forest by *The Refuge*. 'It's gone, Liv.' Tristan confirms.

I spin and all around me is forest.

'Can you hear me?' a soft voice asks. There is desperation in that voice. There is sadness. In my hand is a button. I can feel it between my fingers. 'You are not alone. I'm sorry you ever felt that way. But, this is not the answer.' A warm hand briefly rests over mine. 'Please come home.' The hand moves away and leaves my hand colder than before.

But the button is still there. So easy to press. So easy to stop the fog and drilling pain in my head. I open my eyes and even that feels hard. The light is harsh and bright. As my eyes adjust I see

her grey face. My fingers tighten on the button.
The last thing I hear is her voice. 'Liv, don't go!'

CHAPTER 14

'She will blame me for the choice you're making.' I know Tristan is talking about Mum, even though the statement comes out of nowhere. Words out of the easy silence between us, our warm bodies curled up, awake but drifting in and out of a half sleep in the dark.

'She doesn't understand. This reminds her of my father. She thinks I'm choosing some kind of catatonic state I guess, like choosing nothingness.'

'You are choosing nothingness.'

'Don't say that.' I bury my head into the bed. I hate it when he says things like this.

'Here is nothing without the humans that have shaped us.'

Thinking too much about the differences between *here* and *there* makes my hold start to slip. It's easier to only live in the now.

'Do you know any Shepherds who used to be human like me? Maybe, I could talk to them about it? How they coped with the transition.'

Tristan frowns. 'None that I know. This doesn't happen a lot. Although I sometimes wonder if we were all human once, but so long ago that we've forgotten.'

'None that you've heard of?' I push, suddenly thinking of my father.

'None that I remember.' He looks unsure though. 'Speaking of humans. I need to go back to the Otherside. It's time for me to start again.'

'Start again?'

'After you,' he says quietly, running his hand slowly down my side. 'I feel ready. You taught me a lot.'

'Like how to drink?' I smile.

He pinches me lightly. 'Yes that. And other things.' He's silent for a moment. 'You should start thinking about your home here. What it'll look like. How it will feel.'

'Can't I just stay here?' I mutter curling up tighter and pulling him around me.

'No. We can't live together. Everyone needs their private space. There would be too many questions from the others. They might find out who you are...were.'

'Does it really matter if they know?'

'Liv,' Tristan warns. 'We've talked about this before. The girl I met failed. She doesn't belong here. If you want to stay, you can't be her.'

'Are we allowed to be friends?'

'Of course. In the Night Cafe.' Tristan affirms. I feel alone all of a sudden - choosing *here* is not choosing Tristan. We can't be together. He'll just be a guy I see around the village sometimes. As if he can read my mind his lips touch the back of my shoulder and I shiver. 'And here, Liv,' he whispers. 'As long as we're careful, you're always welcome in my home.'

I feel less alone than the moment before.

Tristan is gone when I wake up. I can tell he's *gone* gone. The house feels too big without him. I wander around trying not to change things. A feeling of emptiness grows through the quiet house as I roam around like a spirit unable to let go. The hollow feeling grows until I finally have to leave his house. I can't be here without him.

I need to figure out how to build my own refuge. I weave through the tumble of cottages, houses and apartment blocks. Even though the village is a calming place, I want more isolation.

I head up the mountain side. And the higher I go, the fewer and far between the homes. But I want to be higher. The highest.

What are you doing? Rip joins me in an easy lope as I start running. It's steep and I have to use my hands to climb some parts. Rip jumps the rocks like they're nothing.

'I'm finding a place to live. I can't keep running around the meadow.'

So, you are one of them.

'Yes. But I won't let anyone end up like you. I promise.' There is no real path through the trees, but I stop when I find a rocky clearing. Pine trees block the view over the valley and down to the village. Could I cut down the trees or just imagine them gone to open up the view? They shudder. Because of me or the wind? I concentrate harder, envisioning the perfect view. This time the way they tremor and blur is definitely me. The idea of such power is intoxicating, I almost forget about Rip until her sour snarl speaks again.

How noble. You think you can be better than them.

The trees snap solid. 'Argh!' I wave my hands irritatedly and motion her away. She dances back, but doesn't leave.

You'll forget about me once you start playing their games.

It's impossible to think with her fuzzy frame skulking around my clearing. Maybe the village would have been a better place to build, away from Shades. Maybe that's why the Shepherds all live so close together. But here would be the perfect spot for Tristan and I to keep our relationship secret. The view would be spectacular too.

Here, we could relax and just be.

And just like that the trees are parted and it's as if they'd always grown that way. For a moment we stand side by side taking in the breathtaking view of the valley; the rows and rows of pine trees and then sky

You really are one of them. Rip's voice sounds small and afraid. From here, the only signs of the village are a few thin trails of smoke rising up and mingling with the gentle mist that hangs in the air. Knowing that I made this happen is so amazing that I laugh out loud. Once I've started creating, it gets easier. It's not concentration that is required, it's almost the opposite. Nothing comes easily when it is forced. It's imagination, but it's also calm and it's a willingness to just be.

There is a leafy pond with a small red bridge crossing it and log slices as stepping stones lead to a bench perfectly positioned to sit and enjoy my view. All suddenly just here in a moment and yet it feels so right - like it's always been this way. I'm barely aware of Rip as she backs away, but I hear her last words before she's gone through the trees.

Tristan will forget you too once he's back on the chase.

It makes me pause. But I won't let a jealous Shade destroy my happiness. I take a seat on my bench and start dreaming up a house.

The Night Cafe is quiet, but I'm sure it's nearing the end of day three so Tobias must be around somewhere. It's hard to keep count of the days sometimes. It also felt like the perfect place to go to celebrate the creation of my new home. It's the perfect proof that I have what it takes to live as a Shepherd. I take a seat by a burning log fire in a cosy side room, it reminds me of a country pub I've visited before and my chair is a cosy leather wingback. In front of me is whiskey on ice. I'm content to sit alone and enjoy my drink. Happy thinking of the home I'll return to tonight. I wonder when Tristan will be back. I can't wait to show him. It was hard at times to create something that didn't copy *The Refuge* completely since Tristan's home feels pretty perfect to me

'Olivia. I've missed you.' A warm voice purrs against my ear and two hands appear on either side of the chair's wings.

For a second I think *Tristan*. 'Hey.' I bring a hand up to his wrist, but it's Tobias who moves into view and takes a seat on the coffee table in front of me. 'Tobias.'

'I think you've been busy making friends.' He is so amiable and relaxed, but I wonder if he knows about Tristan.

'Every vote counts.' I joke weakly. 'Do you have the verdict?'

'Nervous?' He rests his hands on my bare knees and squeezes gently, with an indulgent smile. His hands slide up the outside of my legs. I'm wearing a knee length skirt and it pushes up to mid-thigh with his hands. I take a sip of whiskey to hide my discomfort. His hands on me feel unwelcome now. 'No need, Olivia. You're one of us.'

'What now?' I can't believe it's so easy. 'When do I start?' I consider telling him about the house I built, but I really want Tristan to be the first to see it.

'Soon Olivia.' Tobias smiles. 'There are a few loose ends to tie up first. We want to make sure you're all settled in and hopefully you'll be able to witness one of your fellow Shepherds complete. Usually this happens in the meadow.'

Complete what? I wonder, but I just nod along. After the day I've had, I already feel very settled in. 'But the most important thing,' Tobias continues, dancing a finger across my skin, 'you have to die first.'

I choke on my drink.

Tobias presses his fingers into my legs. 'You'll barely feel it, Olivia.' He snaps his fingers. 'All it takes is a moment. You need to break that final string between here and there.' I have a fleeting image of *there* - a hospital bed and tired machines. It feels like the fading memory of a dream.

'That final string being ...my body?'

'Exactly. They're pesky things. Prone to disease, injury and ageing. You don't need it to visit or to help people. You'll be so much happier without its weight holding you down.'

I swallow and close my eyes. I knew this was coming so why does it suddenly terrify me? Did I really think my body was going to lie comatose waiting for my return? Did I expect to bring it with me?

'Will it hurt?'

'Not in the slightest,' Tobias reassures me. 'It really is just like taking scissors to a thread.'

'And if I don't belong here-'

'You'd become a Shade.' he interrupts calmly. 'Trust me, Olivia. I wouldn't let you make the final cut if I didn't know that you belonged here.' He places a hand on my cheek in an almost fatherly gesture, except the intensity in his eyes and the hand on my thigh are anything but fatherly.

The atmosphere at the Night Cafe slides from intimate to hectic in a matter of moments. At least that's how it feels. Tobias and I are alone one minute and I'm wondering how to escape his interest and the next we're surrounded by voices as Shepherds start to pour in. He's soon drawn away by acquaintances. I think maybe I've misinterpreted our previous flirting as I watch him move between groups with ease. He treats everyone the way he treats me. He makes people feel special, his small touches are in equal parts friendly, commanding and teasing. He leans in and whispers something in a girl's ear, her cheeks colour but she continues sipping her drink and nodding along to another conversation. He rests a hand on the small of a man's back as he joins a new group and immediately dominates their attention. His is the sun and they lap him up until he decides to cast them back in shadow. I am just one of many to him and it's a relief.

'He's good, isn't he?' I jump at the voice, but relax when it's only Orla. 'He can teach you so much.' She has a martini in her hand but it seems more like an accessory the way she uses it to indicate Tobias, stabbing her hand to make her point. 'I only wish I was half as good.'

'Orla,' I gently admonish. 'I'm sure you're twice as good.'

She laughs, but it sounds wobbly. 'Anyway, tell me about you Livvy. Why haven't I seen you?' Her voice begs for the truth and I really want to tell her about Tristan. At the last moment I close my eyes a moment, breathe, and play it safe.

'Oh, I've been around. Here, the meadow, the woods. I've spent some time with Tobias.' It's only half a lie.

'It's different here, isn't it?' she says quietly, turning to watch Tobias again. 'Not quite how it is *there*.' *There* is a gesture with a small flick of her martini towards the door and the sense that here lacks in comparison. There is no question that she means the Otherside.

'Are you alright, Orla?' It takes a moment before her eyes focus on me. She looks nervous. I lean in feeling like her eyes are reeling me in 'Liv,'

'Ah my two favourite ladies.' Cillian's voice interrupts behind us before Orla can speak. She pauses to muster a smile. And just like that she's back. Composed, flirtatious and smiling.

'Cillian!' She slips her free hand through his arm to link him to her and rests her head a moment on his shoulder in greeting. He grins down at her affectionately and then winks at me.

'How are we?'

'We're excellent, of course,' Orla simpers. 'Aren't we, Livvy?' She sips her drink finally and it's like I imagined the vulnerable girl from a moment ago. But Cillian isn't really interested in an answer from us as he launches straight into his own tales.

'Have either of you ever been to Galway?' he asks, but doesn't pause for an answer. 'I've come from there just now.' The usual faces appear as Cillian regales us with his stories. I drift in and out of the story, but manage to catch the gist. Cillian has met a new boy. His next lamb. He's never been to Ireland before, but is already full of stories and a smooth Irish accent which he puts on to exaggerate them. He makes us all laugh and starts a debate on all things Irish now that he's the resident expert.

I glance up and see Tristan enter the Night Cafe. He scans the room and when he finds me, his eyes rest a moment with a secret smile and then he continues scanning. My face burns. How can he do so much to me with so little?

He's drawn into a different group and talking so much I wish I could read lips. Knowing he's in the same room makes it hard to concentrate on Cillian and the others as they now compete with tales of the complexities of humans. They all enjoy trying on different accents and repeating phrases they've heard. I follow the faces of those talking, absently nodding, but inside I'm planning how soon before I can get to Tristan. I look around more often than I should to reassure myself where Tristan is.

Sometimes we catch eyes and it's hard to look away.

Tobias briefly joins my group. People look to him for advice and he offers it kindly, making everyone he sets his eyes on feel like the centre of the universe, including me. He brushes a strand of hair behind my ear, his fingers lingering on my neck. The strength of my feeling for Tristan obliterates everything I thought I felt for Tobias and I only tolerate his hand on my neck. 'We'll catch up again very soon, Olivia.' He says before moving away. I'm sure our catch up will involve cutting that final string and I shiver. Orla speaks to me quietly, her head turned to one side so it's separate from the group. 'You know, you can have fun with him if you want. But that's all it will ever be.' I nod thinking of Tristan's words that we couldn't live here together. 'We don't have real relationships here. No one belongs to anyone and everyone is free to play.'
'I understand,' I assure her.
She bumps my shoulder with hers in a friendly gesture. 'I'll let you off with a little bit of infatuation since you're new. And it is Tobias. He's the best.' Her tone is light, but her eyes feel cold. Without missing a beat, she turns and interjects into the group conversation. 'Cillian, you have to stop with that awful accent. It's more American than Irish!'
I start at a gentle touch across my lower back. Tristan. He's facing away from me talking to some girls, but hidden from view his fingers graze against me. I lift my hand subtly and the tips of our fingers meet. It's simple, almost nothing, and yet it feels like everything. I feel the pads of his fingers, the shape of his fingernails, his knuckles, the hairs on the back of his hand. His thumb traces little circles in my palm. Every circle winds me tighter.

I am just a hand. I am just a circle of skin.

The terror of cutting that final tie fades away as I remember why

I'm doing this. It's all for Tristan. I love him. He loves me. If this is the only way we can be together, stolen moments and secret meetings, then so be it.

'Tris!' Tristan's hand suddenly pulls away as a girl shouts his name launching herself into him for a hug and his arms come up to catch her. I'm forced to step closer to Cillian as Tristan and the girl stumble into me.

'Tal.' I hear the warmth in his voice. I hate the jealousy that lurks, it is ugly and fierce. I remember Tal, the girl I saw draped all over him that first time. It's not fair that she doesn't have to hide her affection.

'Tell me everything,' she orders. 'How was it?'

'It went really well.' His voice is soft. 'Better than I expected actually.'

'And did you find the one?'

'Yes, I did. A girl. A bit older I think.'

'Oh.' Tal claps her hands together with a squeal. 'That's good. They're easier to work with when they're older. More desperate. Did you talk?

'Only briefly. But it was-'

'Liv!' Cillian pulls me under his arm as he steers me away. 'We're going outside. Where were you?' He says in response to my vacant expression and taps my forehead.

'Oh, I was just thinking. About... the future.'

'Slightly overwhelming?"

I nod, but twist to look over my shoulder. Tristan is still talking with Tal, they've slid away from the rest of their group and it's just the two of them. Tal is practically on her tiptoes leaning up to Tristan with excitement.

But it was ... but it was *what*?

He hasn't noticed I'm no longer there, he dips his head down closer to Tal as he speaks.

'No need to fret, my dear,' Cillian murmurs. 'That's why you have us. We're all friends here. I won't let you go astray.' We rejoin the others outside. The slide between colours and shapes are replaced by buzzing patio heaters every now and then. It's quieter so the shift is gentle and almost soothing, more so as people bid us goodnight and start to leave. Eventually, it's just me, Orla, Cillian, Zara and Seph. I still feel uneasy around Seph after he suggested I might end up as a Shade.

'So Liv, where are you staying now?' Orla asks. 'There's still room at the inn if you want to stay with me.' She strokes my arm softly. 'More time for girl talk,' she adds. Orla could have me telling her everything if she tried. It's a dangerous place to stay.

'Thanks. But I actually have my own home now.'

They all look stunned. 'You created a house here? By yourself?' Cillian asks after a beat. I nod and Orla bursts into laughter. 'This is brilliant, Liv!'

'And here I thought you were having second thoughts,' Cillian grins. 'You're practically a native.'

'I bet you're hardly on the Otherside anymore. Not long left now.' Seph adds, but I only see the white of his teeth as the garden goes dark a moment. *Not long left now.* Multicoloured Christmas lights flicker briefly and then I notice Seph is watching me with a strange expression.

'Party at Liv's house!' declares Zara with a giggle. 'Can we have a tour?' Cillian nods in agreement. Seph just watches me, a slight tilt to his head.

Torn, I don't know how to respond. I wanted to show Tristan my new home.

'I know you.' Seph announces suddenly and the Christmas lights flick back.

'No, you don't.' I shift uneasily. The others look between me and Seph with confusion.

'Yes!' Seph says. 'I've got it.' He snaps his fingers and points at me. 'I do know you. We've met before, haven't we? At least,' he amends. '*I* met you … on the Otherside.'

CHAPTER 15

The colour drains from my face. Not from his words, spoken in his mild easy going voice, but from the cold predatory expression that transforms his face.

'I don't think so.' I smile tightly. Tristan said no one could know I'd followed him here. But maybe it would be ok? I'm one of them now. But Seph's eyes send a chill through me as he looks at me as though I'm less than I was the moment before.

'Yes. I think so,' Seph continues calmly. 'You didn't see me, but I remember you. We have a friend in common.'

Tristan's hands come down on Seph's shoulders. 'Seph,' he says softly. 'It's been awhile.' He barely acknowledges me as he surveys us all with a curt nod. Seph laughs, throwing his hands up. 'Of course, Tristan is here. I think we have some catching up to do, old friend. I'm dying to hear what you've been up to.'

'Let's talk.' Tristan looks resigned. Seph stands and walks away, heading inside, without even checking if Tristan follows.

'Well, what was that all about?' Cillian asks after Tristan disappears inside after Seph, but I have a bad feeling he already knows.

'I have no idea.'

Orla shrugs. 'It happens.' She pats my hand kindly. 'We start to confuse all the faces. So many humans on the Otherside.' I'm so grateful to Orla at that moment for believing me. 'I might have to have my own catch up with young Tristan.' She grins at Cillian, 'Did you hear? He's back on the Otherside. *Finally.*'

'About time.' Cillian mutters.

'I think Tobias had words with him.' Zara adds.

'He shouldn't have to. Tristan's a joke. He should have known better than to-' Cillian stops as fat raindrops start to fall. Scattered at first and then stronger. 'This is me. Sorry ladies. Irish weather.' Cillian stands up, pushing wet hair back from his face. 'I'll take this with me. Rain check on the house party, Liv?' he laughs at his own joke. I nod and he leaves out the back of the garden, taking the rain with him.

'What did Cillian mean?'

'Hmm?' Orla is preoccupied staring into space like she hasn't just been soaked by a very localised rain storm.

'Tristan's a joke? He should have known better?'

'Oh,' she draws it out. 'Tristan fell in love with his first human and then he let her escape. It was a complete disaster. He's an embarrassment to Tobias.'

I hold up a hand to stop her. 'He let a human escape what?'

'Liv.' Orla is impatient all of a sudden and rises from the table. 'You'll understand when you experience the completion.' She's angry all of a sudden. 'The last thing you ever do is let them go,' she snarls and walks away without another word.

'Orla and her moods!' Zara shrugs helplessly. "I'll go check on her.' She slips away leaving me alone in the garden.

The last thing you ever do is let them go. Those words. They don't sound like the kind words of a Shepherd helping a lost lamb through the dark. Why did Tristan 'let me go'? Rip's warnings suddenly feel less like bitterness and more like the truth.

I jump when a hand clamps down on my shoulder

'Liv.' Tristan says. 'Come on, we should get out of here.' I follow him out the beer garden to the street.

'What happened with Seph?'

'I corrected him. Don't worry about it.' Tristan stops short suddenly, he grabs my hand and pulls me quickly into the darkness between two buildings. He holds a finger to my lips, issuing a warning with his eyes. We watch as two men appear out of the shadows, deep in conversation. I can't hear their hushed conversation, but as they pass I think I catch a few words as they pass, *let's see what Tristan says.* Tristan stiffens and I feel a chill in the air before rain starts to fall. The men pass under the shifting lights of the Night Cafe sign and I finally see their faces before they disappear back inside. Cillian and Tobias.

◆ ◆ ◆

It's that quiet part of the night. Beyond late, but before morning. We're twisted up limbs and sheets. Our breathing is steady, but I can't sleep.

'Are you awake?' I say to the darkness.

'Yeah baby, I'm here.'

I half smile at the *baby,* but it's short lived. 'What will happen if everyone finds out about us?' There is silence in the darkness and I wonder what he's thinking. 'Cillian suspects. Maybe he already told Tobias.'

'Once you're one of us it won't matter what Cillian or Seph say.' Tristan eventually replies. 'They'll take it out on me, not you.'

'What will they do to you?'

'Don't worry about that. I'll fix it.'

I remember Tobias' words. *A fate of stone awaits Shepherds who break the rules.* I can't stop the image of him with vacant stone eyes flooding my mind. I can't stand the thought of everything that makes Tristan *Tristan* no longer existing, just a stone relic at the bottom of a lake.

'It's getting harder to go back, Tris.' I whisper. 'I can't remember the last time I was really there.'

'It's the transition. Once the connection between you and your body is broken you won't be able to go back. The transition will be complete.'

'How much time do I have left?'

'I don't know. But you're strong Liv, you can still stop this and go back if you want. I can help you.'

I feel a tear slip down my cheek. 'No, I want this. I want you. This is the only way for us to be together then it's worth it. Besides there's nothing left for me back there.'

'That isn't true. Your mother never wanted this for you.'

'She doesn't know what *this* is.'

There is silence on the other side of the bed. 'Tris?'

'Yeah?'

'There is no other way, is there? You couldn't live as a human on the Otherside?'

Tristan lets out a shaky sigh before answering. 'Liv, I promise you there is no other way. If there was anything I could have done to stay with you I would have done it.'

'Ok, ok.' I wipe away my tears. 'I guess I'm just feeling a bit desperate. It's starting to feel real.'

'Liv, you know I would choose the Otherside for you. You're giving up so much-'

'I choose you.' I'm firm and in the dark his fingers find mine and we hold tight. A dim memory of Mum's voice surfaces from some time and memory I can't place.

You're a call to the rocks, you're a dead end. Stay away, Siren.

When I sleep I don't go back *there* anymore. To the Otherside. That's how it feels now, alien and *other*. Sometimes I have a dream-like misty memory of a hospital bed, stiff sheets and tears cried over me. There are words spoken through the tears.

You're making the wrong choice. Come back.

Haven't I already been punished enough?

And like a dream, the more I chase the details the more they dance out of reach.

I've taken up running. Running never really held much appeal to me before. I'd nod along to how amazing it was when Nina and Stef returned sweaty and beaming from a run. I might promise to go with them next time and maybe even I did go once or twice. But, I never really got it. Not until I experienced running here, in the meadow and through the woods and hills around the village. Even running with the Shades nipping at my heels, never quite able to reach me. Sometimes I'm running towards something. A destination, my future. A life with Tristan. A life as a Shepherd, a higher purpose. A calling. And other times I'm running away. Running away from this strange place, from Shepherds and Shades, from cryptic conversations, paranoia and sidelong glances. Either way, it feels good to run.

Today, I'm running away.

The last few days I've avoided the Night Cafe and Shepherds. I'm afraid Seph has spoken and told them all I'm a fraud. A lost little human who wandered into their village pining for Tristan. Tristan and I never had the fun house tour I was hoping for either. We were both so on edge that when Tristan wandered through my home, he was quiet except for the odd suggestion of changes so it didn't copy *The Refuge* quite so much.

'You stole *The Refuge* from me!' I'd complain.

'But I was here first.'

Tristan and I have already fallen back into how our relationship was before. Tristan disappears a lot and I'm always waiting for him when he comes back. Except now I know where he's going. To the Otherside. To see *her*. His new project. I preferred to call her that. Tristan said I shouldn't feel jealous. He said it was a human emotion I'd soon outgrow once the transition was complete.

'Tell me about her.'

Tristan pulls a face. 'There's not much to tell. She's sad and kind of boring.'

'What's her name?'

'Sara. Don't ask me for details. I don't know anything. It's hard to get her to open up.'

'Jeez, I hope you weren't this enthusiastic when you spoke about me!' But I liked that he was uninterested in Sara.

'Liv,' he smiles. 'You were different.'

'I'm sure that's what you tell all the girls.'

'You'll find this easier to talk about once your human side is gone.'

Once your human side is gone.

It's eerie to think about and sends my head spiralling with questions. Isn't it my human side that makes me who I am? Who did Tristan fall in love with? Who am I without it?

And so I run to forget the questions. To try and block out the answers.

I don't want to lose my human side. What are my feelings for Tristan without human emotions?

The day starts nice, just like all the others. Sun and clear skies stretch across the sky. The days are actually starting to blur together, like spending too long on holiday or that weird time between Christmas and New Year. Tristan is away again so I'd decided to go for a run. There isn't much else to do.

After breakfast an empty feeling had started gnawing away inside of me. Everything came so easily. It was beginning to feel unsatisfying. Getting dressed, cooking, eating, even running. It all just was. There was no planning, no thought, no preparation, no hard work. No disappointments, just results.

Tristan and my feelings for him are the only real thing is this paradise and even that will change soon. Orla said Shepherds didn't have relationships with each other and maybe this was why. Without the human element, they are all just superficial acquaintances. It's all fake.

Siren.

Ever since the word surfaced in my thoughts, it kept returning. I'd read enough about sirens in folklore during a phase when I was fifteen where I'd become obsessed with Greek mythology. Sirens were not a good thing, but they were always female and hung around rocks in the sea luring sailors to their doom. Sirens were definitely not dark-eyed boys frequenting bars and sampling drinks.

My feet pound the ground as I run. With every negative thought they hit harder like I am grounding out all the bad and crushing it beneath me.

If you want Tristan, this is how it will be.

If you want to help people, you have to make sacrifices.

But what if it's too much? Giving up a body, a life, Mum, my future. Is it worth it? And around and around my thoughts go. Fighting, reconciling and back again. When I reach the summit of the mountain, I stop to take in the view. My lungs don't ache the way they would after a hill when I ran with Nina and Steph. My legs don't feel like jelly, they feel strong and ready to go again. I lower to my knees and sit back on my heels, eyes closed. I take deep breaths to clear my thoughts. I'm pretty good now at mastering my surroundings and my appearance. The scenery no longer shudders when I focus on the differences between here and home. But going back to that hospital bed feels so hard. It's like I'm slipping further and further down a hole. It is such an effort to remember, so tiring to grab hold and pull myself back up.

I'd tried to go back and failed a lot recently. I remember wandering Mum's house willing myself here and failing so many times. I remember the tiniest thing could shatter this world and send me falling back into my body. And now, nothing can shake me. Maybe I'm already dead.

I try to stay calm as I feel nothing from the Otherside.

'Liv?'

I'm too deep in my frustrated calm to jump. 'Hi Orla,' I reply without opening my eyes. I try to compose my face before Orla asks questions.

'I like it up here too,' she sighs and I hear her take a seat beside me. We're both silent for a while. I try to ignore Orla and focus on finding my way home, but when I hear her shuddering indrawn breath I give up. Opening my eyes I see her battle to get herself under control. All the times she'd used her silky melodic voice and nearly got me to tell her all my deepest secrets and yet it is seeing her like this that releases them.

'Have you ever wanted children, Orla?' I ask quietly. I can't face her so I stare at the horizon. I'm surprised when she answers.

'Once, I did.'

'With John?'

A pause. 'Yes. He made me want a lot of things I never thought possible.' I don't know what to say. I'd expected her to turn the question around on me. 'There were so many before him,' she continues, wrapping her arms about her knees. 'Men, women, friends, lovers, but none of them made me want things I couldn't have. Why did John?'

'Love does that.'

'I wasn't in love with him,' Orla snaps. 'You're so human sometimes it's sickening.' Her eyes suddenly meet mine and they're not kind. 'I told you never to say his name to me.' Her hand shoots out and grabs my wrist. 'You always bring him up. Are you trying to torture me?' Her eyes flash angrily and her hand tightens, reminding me she's a lot stronger than she looks. A trickle of fear passes down my spine, no one knows where I am. In fact, apart from Tristan, no one cares where I am. I can't believe I ever thought Orla was my friend.

For a moment, I miss Nina intensely.

Orla smiles widely at the fear in my eyes and it turns her angelic features savage. Siren, I think looking into her gleaming eyes. This is what I always imagined a Siren's face to look like. I lean away, but a second later her face crumbles and she drops my wrist. It's only fear that she'll chase me that keeps me from running away.

'I close my eyes and still see his face,' she whispers. 'I can't stand it.' The venom in her voice is bitter and harsh. 'Some days, I just want to sink in the lake until I stop breathing.' She takes a shuddering breath. 'I should have stopped it. I should have tried. I should have run away with him when I had the chance.'

'Run away?' I interrupt.

She shakes her head. 'It doesn't happen though. No Shepherd runs away with their lamb. How pathetic,' she laughs coldly, wiping at her eyes. 'I couldn't do it. I couldn't. I only heard about one Siren who ran away. She couldn't let her human go. And she was punished.' Orla is talking so fast, slightly delirious and I'm sure she's forgotten I'm there. 'She ran away to the Otherside. She thought she'd live happily ever after. But it all went wrong. The lamb, the man, he left her. After she gave up everything for him. He left her. Humans can be so fickle. She wanted to come back, but she couldn't, she was trapped. She grew old.' Orla shudders like it is the worst thing she can imagine. So a Shepherd has run away and lived as a human before. If it happened once, it can happen again.

And that possibility instantly crystalizes everything. My mind stops jumping back and forth. It is finally clear. I don't want to be here. I want to go home. With Tristan. I want a real life.

'Growing old doesn't sound so bad,' I murmur, suddenly seeing a future before me where previously I'd seen nothing.

Orla recoils. 'When you've witnessed it for as many years as I have you might feel differently. Ageing is cruel and ugly. Although,' she smiles slightly. 'I always wondered how John would look older. I think it should suit him.'

'Shepherds don't grow old?'

'Not really,' Orla responds, staring far off through the trees. Her smile is gone. 'We only age on the Otherside and no one spends enough time there."

'You could have grown old with John.' Just saying his name aloud feels like playing with fire with Orla and her mood swings, but I don't care. I'm only thinking about Tristan and the life that now seems possible.

'And then what?' Orla angrily jumps up. She stalks away a few steps before spinning back to where I'm still crouched on the ground. 'Then we die? Who would choose that when they could live forever?'

'You're right,' I say carefully, looking up at her. Her face is on the edge of something that scares me. 'If Shepherds can't die, then I'd choose forever too.' Can she tell that I'm lying?

'Shepherds can die.' Her eyes glow and she turns away again. 'Dying is difficult, but we can certainly die.' Her face changes again, turning vulnerable. 'You know, I think about it sometimes,' she confesses, playing with her hair like a child. She pulls it tight atop her head and lets it fall over and over.

Some days I just want to sink in the lake until I stop breathing. Her tragic words from earlier creep up unbidden. Tristan wanted a lake in his dream home, a reminder of his own mortality. Now I understand why. I straighten to stretch my legs and consider running away while Orla's lost in her thoughts. I want to ask her more questions about the girl who escaped, but I think I've pushed her enough for one day. She's not as strong as she first appeared ...or as nice. 'There's a completion today.' Orla says abruptly, pacing back to me. 'Have you seen one yet?' I shake my head. She considers me for a moment and I see the remaining energy drain out of her body. 'Go watch,' she whispers. 'And then tell me that I loved John.' She presses her hands hard against her face, curling her fingers until they claw her face. Her body shakes. 'I didn't. I didn't. I didn't love him. We don't love. We can't.'

'Orla, it's ok that you loved John. Just because you didn't run away with him doesn't mean you didn't love him.' Despite my reassurances, I take a step back. I want to get away from her before her mood snaps again. I need to find Tristan and tell him that a way out for us exists. Now that my mind is set, every moment longer is a moment my body could die and I'd be stuck here. We'll find out how and then we'll leave this place.

'No.' Orla shakes her head viciously. 'No. no. If I loved him I should have kept him safe.' She pulls her hands away and looks up at me distraught. Her nails have left angry red lines down her face. 'If I loved him, I shouldn't have helped them kill him.'

We stare at each in horror for a long second.

And then I run.

CHAPTER 16

The Refuge stands dark and empty by the time I get back. Orla didn't chase me, but I didn't stop running the whole way. I'm breathing so hard, I bend to rest my hands on my knees. But I can't keep still for long, I'm full of so much pent up energy. I'm ready to leave.

I want to scream. I want answers. I want Tristan. But like so many times before when I need him he is nowhere to be found.

The Night Cafe is deserted and I realise that everyone must be at the completion Orla mentioned.

'Tristan, where are you?' I mutter under my breath as I burst through checking all the rooms. Do I join the completion? I suspect it's in the meadow, but the thought of finding out the truth of what happens there twists my stomach in knots. I hear muted voices as I enter the beer garden. I see no one, but hear the faint conversation from the far end of the garden hidden by a trellis blurring between sprawling jasmine and lush ivy. I edge up not wanting to be seen, but close enough to check if either voice belongs to Tristan.

'It's good to see you like this again.' A girl's voice.

A soft laugh that I would know anywhere replies. 'Thanks, Tal. It's good to feel like this again! I didn't think I could.' Tristan's smiling voice. My immediate thought is he's told Tal about us.

'Oh, I know! The first is the hardest. I couldn't imagine

developing feelings like that again, but I did. We just need to make sure you complete this one.'

'Don't worry about me. My connection with Sara feels solid. I really like her.'

Oh. *Sara.* Not me. I hate listening to this. I hate wondering what Tristan is doing with Sara. Smiling at her in bars, shyly asking her out for dinner.

Jealousy feels like something rotting in my stomach.

I must make a noise or change something in their surroundings, as they both stop, alerted to a presence. I step forward even though my legs beg to go backward. They smile when they see me. Really? Smiles? It's hard to look away from Tristan. He seems genuinely happy to see me, no trace of guilt. There is nothing of betrayal on his face. Nothing of *Sara.*

'Hey!' he says with friendly warmth.

'Hi ... Liv, isn't it?' Tal blinks up at me with wide-eyed kindness. I bet that's how she gets them on the Otherside, with her giant innocent eyes. She shuffles along the bench in a silent invitation to sit beside her, but I can't move. I stare at them and their friendliness doesn't waver.

'I heard there's a completion today,' I say eventually because they're both still looking at me expectantly.

'Oh yes!' Tal jumps up. 'I forgot. Explains why no one is here! I really want to see this one through.' She stretches, like she's preparing for a run. 'Let's go together. If we hurry we'll still catch most of it.'

Tristan's hand reaches out and grabs mine. 'You go ahead Tal, we'll catch up. I'd like a word with Liv.'

'Sure.' Tal shrugs and surprises me with a quick hug. She pats Tristan's head playfully as she passes, skipping out of the beer garden.

'Hey,' His smile is broad and warm once we're alone. 'I've missed you.' Against his easy charm, I struggle with my lingering jealousy. I push it aside remembering why I was looking for him. 'I've found a way out. For both of us.' My voice is low and calm. Inside, I'm anything but calm. Inside, I am racing.

Tristan drops my hand, his smile fades. 'What are you talking about?'

'There's a way we can be together on the Otherside. It's happened before. We can go home. Both of us.' He stares at me, aloof and unreadable. I rush on. 'We could be happy there. We could be a real couple. We could be a family. I know you'd be happy.' Tristan looks down at the table. I slide onto the bench opposite him and take both his hands excitedly. 'Tris? You said you didn't want me to have to make this choice, but don't you see? I don't have to. We can still have the future we used to dream about, remember?'

'Liv.'

'I don't know yet exactly how it works or where we need to go, but we can figure that out. It's real! Orla told me.'

'Liv.'

'You could have a real life. The highs and lows of real life are better than this empty high feeling, better than losing our emotions.' I can't believe it's me saying these words after so many weeks of wanting to feel nothing at all, of wanting the peace of the meadow. It all comes bubbling rushing up from somewhere deep and real inside me. 'I don't want to lose my humanity. I want a real life. With you. I want a future.'

'Liv, will you stop!' Tristan finally snaps. He pulls his hands away and looks around us like he's afraid someone will hear. I stare at him in stunned silence. 'Forget what you heard. There is no way out.'

'But Tris-'

'No! I won't open that door.' He stands and stalks away, his hands absently reaching out and ripping the jasmine from its trellis and throwing it angrily to the ground as he passes. I jump up after him and grab his arm.

'What door Tristan?' I demand. He stops uncomfortably, his eyes sliding past mine and his anger dwindling. 'Tristan. What door?' I repeat.

'Liv, you don't understand-'

'No,' I interrupt. 'You said there was no other way. You said you would have done anything to be with me.'

'I've also been encouraging you to go home, remember? This is exactly why I didn't bring you here in the first place. I didn't want you to choose between your life and this place. This choice isn't worth it. I've been telling you this all along. I'm not worth it.'

I feel tears build in my eyes. My dreams for our future crack open, vulnerable and full of flaws. Here or there, it didn't really matter because all I'd wanted was Tristan, but now neither are starting to feel possible. My best friend looks wrong. I look at him and it's like looking at a stranger. Everything feels ruined. I feel so stupid.

'You already knew there was a way out,' I breathe shakily. 'You chose not to take it back then. You're choosing not to take it now. Clearly, it's me who's not worth it.'

'It's not like that! This is the world I know. I don't want to grow old. I don't want to watch you grow old. I don't want sickness or, or flu.' I think we both latch on to the same memory of our days spent in bed with the flu. I didn't think it was so bad, but maybe that was another beginning of the end for Tristan. Another strike against me and the Otherside.

'Tristan, that's just life!' I'm suddenly so angry that we're not together because Tristan is afraid of growing up. 'You said yourself, the Otherside is a better life than here. Than this nothingness.' I gesture around the beautiful leafy garden and the perfect blue sky.

'I don't want to die, Liv.' His words are solemn and quiet and so firm I know there is nothing I can do to change them.

'But I love you,' I whisper, staring at him aghast.

'Liv,' he sighs. 'You know, I love you too.'

Even the words feel ruined. They feel past tense already. I'm backing away from him. I only realise when he reaches for me, misses, and has to step forward. Stay away, Siren. That name I heard, it sounds very fitting all of a sudden. I shake my head, raising my fists out of reach.

'No! You lied to me.'

And just like that I'm running away again.

From the last person I ever expected to run from.

The air smells like the sky before rain and the scent of the flowers rolls in humid waves through the trees. I thought about escaping to my new home or even *The Refuge,* but the mountain had other ideas and it's the calm and shiny surface of the lake I see through the trees.

The meadow feels like where it all began, maybe this is where it ends. I feel like it's time to finally end this dream and face reality. It's time to go home.

Another warm wash of air rushes through and this time the flowers carry a sickly rotten edge to their sweetness.

You're just in time.

I can't see Rip at first, until I look up and find her curled into a tight fuzzy ball in a tree. Her yellow eyes stand out from the black mass of her body. Uneasiness washes through me. Before I can reply I hear whoops and whistles cry out from further up the mountain. Moments later their fast footsteps and the rustle of bodies through the forest are all around me. I fall back against a tree trunk to keep out of their way. Shepherds, glorious mesmerising Sirens, come striking the ground and laughing as they race to the meadow. Rip isn't paying attention to me anymore. She curls into an even tighter ball with raised hackles. Everything about her is agonisingly alert and miserable.

This is the completion.

Every part of me wants to run in the opposite direction. The Shepherds nearest to me are all whispering excitedly as they pass. Their cheers would be infectious if I hadn't just had my heart broken. Their cheer might be infectious if I could forget the things I'd heard.

Did they tell you how I was hunted down and ripped apart in this very meadow?

◆ ◆ ◆

If I loved him, I shouldn't have helped them kill him.

◆ ◆ ◆

Did they tell you that most of us die in this meadow?

◆ ◆ ◆

They will take everything.

◆ ◆ ◆

Do you want to play?

◆ ◆ ◆

'Liv! You came. Come and play.' Cillian's voice pulls me from my thoughts. His words are eerily similar to those spoken by the Shades as they'd lured me here. He runs by me with a wink and wades straight into the lake until it's deep enough to dive in. Others are ready swimming across. When they emerge on the far side they melt into the tall grass.

This will be my only chance to know once and for all what it means to be a Shepherd and what a completion truly is. But I don't move. I feel paralysed with a sense of dread. I look for Rip, but can't see her anymore. She was in a tree for a reason. It feels safer than the ground, am I more Shade than Shepherd to feel this way? I turn to face the tree I've been hiding behind and climb. The higher I climb, the more invisible I feel and my anxiety eases.

Just when I think I'm alone, two more Shepherds race past my tree, talking easily despite their speed.

'Come on, he'll be back any minute!'

'At least we haven't missed the ending.' The second voice belongs to Tal. 'I'm always late.'

'Don't worry, Seph will take his time with this one.'

'I hope so.' Tal grins as they reach the lake. She turns with arms outstretched to fall backwards, but then she spots me. Her friend is already in the water. Tal pauses with a frown and lifts a hand in greeting. I stare back at her and I'm already planning how I'll escape. The jump from the tree, the direction I'll run, even how I'll kick her face if she tries to climb the tree to get me. Eventually, her face relaxes like she understands something. She falls back into the water without a word and gracefully swims away with powerful back strokes. I breathe a huge sigh of relief feeling like I've dodged a bullet.

I climb higher as the relaxing quiet sounds of the forest take. I stop only when I'm high enough for a decent view across the lake to the meadow. The sun is setting and it's all grown quiet. Almost as if a raucous bunch of inhuman creatures hadn't just raced through. I start to feel slightly stupid for hiding up a tree. Maybe, I should have followed them. Then I see movement in the meadow.

A lone couple walking hand in hand. At first they're just a silhouette moving at an easy pace picking their way aimlessly through the tall grass. The sun is sinking further and it casts the meadow in a dusky golden light filled with long shadows and floating dandelion seeds. The man is tall and leans protectively down to his companion, he says something to her and I faintly hear her laughter. He pulls her gently to a stop and they face each other, lacing their fingers together with both hands. I see his face now.

Seph. Tristan's friend from the other night.

I can't see the girl's face. She's slight with light brown hair pulled back in a messy bun. They resume their walk and her head rests against his shoulder. Seph's arm comes up around her. When she tilts her face to him I see her for the first time. I don't recognise her, but I know that expression. That look of trust, safety, and utter devotion.

It's how I looked at Tristan.

Even across the distance, I know in an instant that this girl would do anything for Seph. She will do anything to keep him near to her. She loves him. She's human.

Seph leans down and must be whispering something close to her ear. The girl suddenly stiffens and steps back. Seph is talking, but all I see is his smiling mouth as he talks. Her hand whips out and slaps him hard across the face.

She's braver than me. I'd never stood up to Tristan.

Seph's hand comes up to his cheek. And then it all happens so fast. One moment she's standing and the next she's flung to the ground by the force of Seph's backhand as he returns the slap.

Seph stands over her casually. He offers a hand to help her up, but she scrabbles away. She climbs shakily to her feet, looking dazed. Seph's talking as he stalks towards her. She backs away before finally turning to run. As soon as she runs, Seph laughs and looks around. He raises one hand in the air and makes a signal.

I see the grass shivering and then they emerge running with speed and stealth. Seph waits for them to reach him before joining them. As a pack they take chase.

My body starts shaking and I grip the branch beneath me tightly to stop myself from falling. I feel sick and close my eyes until I hear her scream seconds later.

More Shepherds appear from the far side of the meadow —the direction the girl runs. She swerves to the side, but I can see from my vantage point that they have her surrounded. It's only a matter of moments before they close in.

Adrenaline courses through me. It feels like it's me they're chasing. I hear their laughter. I hear their howls. They've never looked so inhuman.

They're monsters.

The circle tightens around her and I see the moment she realises it's over. She stops running. She cries and drops to her knees. She begs and still the circle tightens.

Seph breaks away from the circle to face her. Despite everything that has just happened she latches onto him with the remnants of that love she felt less than a minute earlier. He pushes her away and then he strikes, knocking her down and jumping on her like a lion pulling down prey.

CHAPTER 17

A nd they will tear you apart like wolves.

It's the strike of a predator. Fast and lethal. I can't see her as the circle moves in, but I hear them clapping, congratulating and howling their approval. I see a thin skein of pure light pulled and passed between them until all in the crowd touch a section, I follow its twisting path through fingers and bodies and find its source hidden in the centre. This pulsing curling thread of light has been pulled from the girl. At first I hear her screams amidst their cheers and then abruptly the screaming stops.

'The girls are trying to convince me to go running with them,' I moaned, referring to my housemates, and flopped down to the grass. Tristan's lips curved, but his eyes were hidden behind his sunglasses. There was something extra hot about Tristan in sunglasses. He lay resting with head on his hands. I'd spotted him almost immediately as I'd entered the botanical gardens. I touched his arm and slid my hand up to rest on his chest. I loved that he was mine to touch whenever I wanted. I still couldn't believe that of all the girls out there, he'd actually chosen me.

'Maybe the exercise would be good for you?' Tristan suggested and ducked to the side as I swatted him.

'Hey! I'm not that unfit. Besides, when am I ever going to need the skill of being able to run fast?'

Tristan shrugs. 'You never know when you'll be chased by a pack of blood-thirsty monsters and wishing you'd practised running more often.'

I laughed. 'Like a zombie apocalypse or something?'

'Or something,' he said as he pulled me down to kiss him.

I think glimpses of the completion will stay etched to my eyelids forever. Seph stretching and cracking his shoulders, his top drenched in blood. His face, neck and hands all smeared with it and his hair sticky and slick to his skull. Sirens dancing around a fire in the beautiful green meadow. Cillian and Zara with bloody hands raised above their heads and threads of light in their hands like glow sticks as they danced. Tal tucked under Seph's arm with a cute little smile. Seph running his finger down her forehead to leave a trail of blood and her sticking her tongue out playfully in return. Tobias surveying the scene with satisfaction, perfect except for a small drop of blood under his mouth. At some point the thread of light flickered and went out.

I stay shivering in shock in my tree, unable to look away. I don't see Tristan. But he's not innocent. He's one of them. This is his life. They are no longer Shepherds in my eyes, they are Sirens now. A name that seems to suit them so much better than Shepherds, I wonder why it didn't come to me sooner.

The other absence I notice is Orla, but finally, I know for sure how John died.

Just like Rip had died.

Probably, just like my father had died.

I am alive because Tristan left me. I was the lamb who'd escaped. *Like a lamb to the slaughter.* The phrase resurfaces in my mind and is almost funny in its accuracy. Tristan left me. He left to protect me. But I'd come running after him like a stupid pet lamb. What an idiot. I deserve this fate.

Deserve. Deserve. Deserve. I really deserved it.

I must have existed in some half waking, half sleep state for a long time. The sun had disappeared and eventually even the fires from the celebration had died away. The last remaining Sirens dwindled to low murmured conversations and finally they too had left. The forest was still and silent for longer after that. And only then did I move.

Only then did I ease my way down from the tree feeling like I'd aged years rather than hours.

Every sound makes me jump. I've never wished for my mum so badly. I just want to be in bed being looked after. I wonder if the dead girl's mother is somewhere missing her daughter.

I slide into the lake and swim silently across. I'm not sure what I hope to find in the meadow. There can be no chance that the girl is still alive, but I can't just leave her here. Can I take us both back home?

Without daylight the meadow feels ominous. I pass through the grass in a daze. This was a killing field and now it's empty and quiet. The wind rustling the grass is the only sound. As I get closer I see the trampled grass. Several abandoned fires still smoke in small clearings. Soon, I see blood. A rusty footprint in the ground, splatters across the waving grass. Soon, I smell the blood and I find the place. The centre of it all where Seph took her down.

She's gone. There is no body, no remnants of her clothes. Only torn and flattened grass and an ugly seeping stain that spreads over the ground. The shape of a star. Of course, in this incorporeal place there would not be a body. Her body will be somewhere on the Otherside waiting to be found. That final string so brutally and unwillingly cut.

I hear a thin keening wail. My immediate thought is the Sirens are back and I panic falling to the ground to hide in the grass. The wail is soft and sometimes dies away completely before returning with renewed force. It reminds me of the time a girl hit a cat with her car outside Mum's house. She came knocking on our door in tears and shock. Mum told me to stay with her while she went to check on the cat. But I didn't listen. I made the girl a cup of tea and then I went outside. I found Mum softly whispering and shushing a crumpled heap by the pavement. The sound was one of pure pain. It was a sound I wished I'd never heard and knew I could never erase.

Keeping low I follow the sound. It's dark with only the moonlight to see by, but I find it. A small huddled form lies shivering, darker than the shadows around it. It's the girl. I drop to my knees by her side.

'Hey, I got you.' I lift my hand to touch her, but up close I realise this is no human girl. The mass shivers and recoils as it wails again. I stare in horror as two yellow eyes appear one at a time blinking slowly. I fall back and the Shades rush in. They move so quickly, I didn't notice them until their shifting black shadows swarm around us.

Don't be afraid, little one. Stay with us.

It hurts to let go.

We'll hold you until you're quiet.

I crawl back as they crowd what's left of the girl. Their new Shade.

She's ours now.

Your time is done.

You should leave. Several pairs of eyes watch me and I belatedly realise I am a Siren to them. They're no longer the friendly creatures who helped me here. They're hostile. I climb to my feet and back away slowly. 'I'm not a Siren. I just want to go home.'

They advance. *You are home.*

'No! Home is the Otherside.'

Not anymore, they snap at me. *Tristan. You followed him here.*

More Shades join those stalking me. Behind them, I see the new Shade is carried away. *You're not one of us.* They curl their lips and despite their intangible appearance, their sharp teeth look real and solid.

Rip appears by my side, hackles raised. Still the only Shade I recognise.

Run, she says to me and dives in to intercept the first Shade as it jumps at me. My new found favourite thing, I run.

Tobias steps out of the trees blocking my path.

'What are you running from now Olivia?' His eyes are intense and his smile is full. I stop abruptly before I crash into him. I'm breathing hard, but he seems to suck up all the oxygen and I can't catch my breath. 'I think you did not enjoy the completion.'

'I'm leaving,' I manage to whisper. 'I've made my decision.'

'I thought you wanted to help people? Don't you want a higher purpose?'

'Helping people? You're killing them. You're monsters.'

'There are two sides to every coin.'

'You lied to me. Shepherds. Guardian angels. It's all fake.'

'I just showed you the side you wanted to see.' Tobias says gently like I'm an unruly child. 'Some people are better off finished. They're only suffering in life. We help them and they help us.'

'I wasn't suffering! I was fine until you monsters tried to drag me under! ' I yell before I can stop myself. His eyes light up and I realise my mistake.

No one can know you followed your Shepherd here.

'Yes.' His smile vanishes and his eyes are cold. 'Tristan really did make a mess of things.' I feel the blood drain from my face. He knows about Tristan. Tobias must enjoy the expression on my face as he laughs quietly behind his hand.

In that moment I know it's all over. I've just witnessed what they do to humans like me. Humans too lost and too trusting.

Humans too weak to fight back. Humans like that end up dead. Worse they end up like Rip, bitter remnants of the unique and brilliant person they once were.

'You don't want to be here?' Tobias smirks. 'Let me follow the thread and see where you've come from.' His eyes glaze over a moment, but I only have a split second to debate running before he's back. His eyes are now full of excitement and he laughs loudly. It takes a moment for him to gather himself. 'Of course.' he finally breathes, staring at me, until I take a step back. 'You don't want to be here?' Tobias suddenly speaks, all traces of humour gone. He steps closer to me. 'Fine. I won't force you to stay.' His face is inches from mine and he brings his hand up and rests his fingers lightly on my cheek a moment. I shiver with a strange mix of revulsion and yearning. 'You want to go back?' He drags his index finger up until it's pressed against my forehead, 'then go.' He flicks his finger against my forehead like I'm a bug on his sleeve.

Everything shatters. The last thing I see are his cruel eyes and the mocking smile.

CHAPTER 18

T he sun blasts through the hospital window. It looks like a beautiful day is starting. A bouquet of pink and yellow flowers sits on a side table and masks the sterile hospital smell. Mum will be here soon. Today is the day the doctors say I can go home. I can't wait. I stretch under the sheets before sitting up and testing my feet on the floor. I look out the window again and imagine sitting outside in the garden at home with a cold drink and a book.

Mum said I'd been sleeping for over a week. I've been awake forty eight hours and the completion feels like an old nightmare. The more I think about it the more fantastical and ridiculous it sounds. I blame the power of opioids. I barely feel like I've been in an accident. The doctors said I was recovering especially well and they reduced my pain medication. Even my lungs feel like they can breathe deeply again.

'Olivia!' Mum beams as she walks in. She takes my hand in hers and kisses my cheek. 'You look so well. Are you excited to come home?'

'I am so ready.'

There is not a moment of doubt over my decision. I miss Tristan, but I know that staying here was the right decision. Just seeing Mum's happiness at having me back is proof enough. I'm actually grateful to Tobias for sending me home. Assuming he did send me home and all my memories of him and Sirens aren't just drug-induced hallucinations. Sometimes, it's hard to know for sure what was real and what wasn't.

'I made you a drink, dear.' A glass of shandy is placed beside me. I smile up in thanks before she disappears back inside. I try to get back into my book, but it's hard to not simply stare and take in my surroundings. The last few days have been unusually warm for early spring so I've been able to sit outside all day until the sun disappears behind the hills. I move my chair along the patio following the sun as it glides across the garden.

For long stretches at a time my eyes get caught on things. A cloud. A bumblebee, the way a flower bobs in the breeze. Once the birds are used to me, they get brave and return to the birdfeeder.

How could I have taken this place for granted? The Otherside is so beautiful and complex and perfect and ...real. The Otherside? I sound stupid. The only side. Home.

Mum and I have settled into a routine again, except this time she hovers a lot more. Her frequent wanders into the village, committee meetings, and library volunteering are all put on hold to take care of me. I didn't think I'd like so much of her attention, but for once it's really nice to have a mother who acts like one.

It's nice to be able to stare lost in thoughtless moments with a peaceful mind. It's nice to not have phantoms gnawing at my subconscious. It's nice to be able to stare and not get drawn away.

'Thought I'd come join you out here.' Mum settles on the patio step beside my chair.

'I don't remember a March this warm.' I murmur, my eyes fixed on a butterfly hanging heavily on a flower that can't handle its weight. My book is already resting on my chest. I want to ask her about my father. I watch the butterfly awkwardly manoeuvre and don't know where to start. I'm not sure if anything's changed. Maybe, nothing.

'Do you blame Tee for what happened to my father?' I finally ask. The flower droops so low the butterfly's wings almost touch the ground.

'Of course not,' she replies calmly. 'Tee was a good friend to your father. He helped him when I couldn't. Some people just can't be saved.' I've never heard her speak so matter of factly about my father.

'So, you don't blame Tristan either?'

'I blame him for being weak. For always taking the easy way.' The butterfly either gets what it wants or gives up as it finally flutters away. The flower head springs back up.

'What do you mean?' I glance at her. She's wearing a pair of sunglasses I've never seen before and a thin silk shirt. She leans back to rest on her elbows, her face turned up to the sun. Chasing memories is like chasing my own tail, but sometimes I look at her and think she knows everything.

'Tristan never deserved you.'

She knows I hate that word. 'I remember you calling him a Siren.'

'Did I?' She smiles widely.

Sometimes everything still feels like the dying remnants of a dream. Mum says that brain fog is caused by the pain relief I'm still taking.

I search for my father's journal in my room, but I can't find it. In fact, lots of things in the house seem missing.

'You know you can go back to all your friends and other stuff, right?' I say as Mum is trying to french braid my hair. She hasn't attempted this since I was little.

'Oh, they can all wait. You know I'd rather be here with my darling daughter.' Her hands in my hair pull tight as she speaks and I grimace. 'Making up for lost time. Living life etcetera.' Suddenly, she places both hands under my arms and pulls me up. 'There now. Done.' She steers me towards a mirror. 'Don't you look absolutely perfect?' Our eyes meet in the mirror and for a moment I don't recognise her.

Some nondescript game show is playing on the TV. Mum is quietly spinning her wheel and rhythmically feeding in the wool. It's almost hypnotic to watch her hands and more entertaining than following the rules of the game show. I'm curled up on the easy chair next to the fire, which is lit despite the warm weather. Mum normally only lights the fire when it's really cold outside. But I don't question her behaviour as I like the cosiness of a crackling fire.

I keep thinking about my father and all the possibilities for him. Did Tee try to help him or not? Did my father die in the meadow or not? I imagine a mental flower as I go, picking off the petals with each thought. Did he become a Shade or not? 'Did my father become a Siren or not?' I don't realise I mutter the last thought out loud until Mum gives an abrupt laugh.

'Not,' she snorts, not even looking up from the wool in her hands. 'Alexei could never be a Siren. He was too gentle.' I can only stare as I try to process her words. 'Darling!' Mum calls, looking up from her spinning now. She's watching me calmly, but her voice is for someone else. 'You can come out now. I think I've put my foot in it.'

Tobias appears in the doorway with a debonair smile. He walks in and places his hand on my mum's shoulder. She smiles placidly up at him. He laughs at my expression. 'Olivia, really!' He shakes his head at me with a tsk. 'You didn't really think I'd let you go, did you? I'm not weak like Tristan and Alexei. I'm not weak like your mother.' The sight of Tobias and my mum together before me makes no sense. Tobias is grinning, full of mischief. But Mum just continues to smile vacantly.

'Mum? No...I don't understand.'

'So much for the unbreakable bond between parent and child.' Tobias chides, his excitement barely contained. 'I thought you'd figure it out so much quicker. It's like you barely know her!'

'What is happening?' Bile rises up my throat.

'Stop playing with my daughter.' Mum reprimands Tobias.

'Fine. But you know how I like my games.' Before me, Mum's face and shape bubble and morph until she's gone. In her place is a young man I recognise from only photos.

My father.

'Yeah I remember Tee.' The stranger's mouth moves and he looks adoringly up at Tobias. I think somehow I'd already known. Tobias is my father's 'Tee'. Tee is Tobias. My father's murderer.

My father smiles at me and stands. He looks too big behind the spinning wheel and he steps around it with his arms outstretched. He's the same age as the man in the photos, probably only ten years older than me. 'Come and give your old man a hug.'

'This can't be real. This is not real.' I stare past my father into Tobias' delighted eyes.

'Well, finally!'

'Make him go away.' I say through gritted teeth, unable to look at the phantom of my father, still smiling with his arms ready to embrace me.

'As you wish.' With a dismissive flick of his fingers my father is gone and I let out the breath I've been holding and close my eyes.

I can't believe I was so stupid to think Tobias would let me go. I'd ignored Mum's weird behaviour because I'd wanted so badly to believe she was real. I'd ignored the missing things in the house because I desperately wanted to be home. 'You missed me, Olivia.' Tobias is right beside me, his lips brush my neck. 'Admit it.'

I open my eyes and we're back in the meadow. Just as I knew we would be.

'It was all a lie? I'm still just lying in a hospital bed.'

'Lucky for you, I'm here to help you.' His voice is silky smooth and inviting as he strokes my hair. 'You do make the days more memorable. I said you were a favourite of mine, didn't I?'

'Because of my father.'

He considers this. 'I knew there was something the moment I saw you. Now I realise, it's Alexei that I see in your face. Alexei was special to me. Helping him was personal. I always hoped I'd get to meet his child.'

'You knew about me?'

'I made it my business to know everything about Alexei. It was hard enough convincing him to leave your mother. I knew once he found out about you I'd lose him for good. I had to move quickly.'

'Mum said he knew about me.'

'In fairness to your dear mother, it certainly looked like he did. I took her pregnancy test out of the bin and left it by their bed.' I'm horrified as I imagine Mum finding the test and then finding my father dead.

The knowledge that my father didn't commit suicide rattles down and settles inside me. He never wanted to leave me. He never even knew I existed.

Tobias circles, looking me up and down. 'You know you shouldn't be here, don't you? Yet, you came here all the same.' His smile is carnal. As he leans in I notice how perfect his lips are. 'I will enjoy you.' His cheek grazes mine as he whispers in my ear. I shiver with an awful mix of exhilaration and disgust. Some tiny part of me still anticipates his touch, but at the same time he repulses me. I want to claw his eyes out, but my body is a traitor. 'And do you know what's the best part, Olivia?' His voice, barely a breath, is raspy with excitement. My heart drums so loud I feel weak. 'When I'm done with you,' he moves back so I can see his hungry eyes. He stares at me and his mouth moves a fraction closer. 'Next, I'll have your mother.'

CHAPTER 19

How could I believe that the mirage Tobias had created was real? There is a vibrance to the sky, an alien-like otherness to the blue wrapping itself around the meadow. There is a pearlescent quality to the gentle clouds. It's almost painful in its perfection. I only had to look up to know that I'd never left. Since when had my Mum ever called me Darling?

❖ ❖ ❖

'Olivia, I'm giving you a choice. I have never been so generous before.' Tobias' voice is silky smooth. His words coax and infiltrate, his voice encourages me to forget everything else.

One more step. Then another. Just take another step and follow me over the edge.

I steel myself. I have to repeat my purpose over and over in my head for fear of forgetting and losing myself in his eyes. 'I want to go home.' It sounds childish out loud.

'Maybe, you still can go,' Tobias muses. 'But you'll end up back here. One way or another you'll end up right back here.' He grabs my wrists and pulls us both down to sit in the grass. He places my hands flat on the ground and covers them with his own. The earth is warm beneath my fingers. 'You will be reborn here or you will die here. Your choice.'

I feel a tear slide down my face. 'Why are you doing this?'

He smiles, almost kindly. 'It's in my blood.' He leans closer.

'You've come so far now, don't stop. You think we disgust you. But once you make the final cut. Once you're one of us, you'll relish it. If you're truly honest with yourself, Olivia, you want to be a Shepherd.' My fingers dig into the earth and feel the cooler soil below.

'I want to go home.'

'The thrill is undeniable.' he continues as if I haven't spoken. 'The chase can be so deliciously satisfying. The power you feel coursing through you is pure magic. The perfection of our world and how it smooths around and complements the Otherside is a special balance. I don't lightly offer anyone a second chance.' I make the mistake of meeting his eyes. 'But you're special.

'Like my father was special?'

Tobias' eyes grow fond. 'Even Alexei did not get this choice.' He moves to a crouch before me. 'Olivia, Shade or Shepherd?'

'Why me?'

He cups my face, his thumbs wiping away the tears gently. 'It's in your blood, my dear.' Tobias rises and walks away. My face feels cold as his hands fall away.

It's not in my blood, I want to argue. I am not a monster. Except, I don't say a word.

It feels like all my energy is needed just to focus on breathing. It feels like I could stop at any moment and never be able to start again.

'Oh, Olivia dear?' Tobias calls, turning to walk backwards a couple of steps. 'I promise to leave your mother alone if you make the right choice.' As he turns away, I hear his laughter.

Rip finds me wandering the forest. I'm trudging uphill vaguely headed for where I think the house I created must be. It doesn't feel like home anymore. I know it's still far to go as the humidity still clings near to the lake.

You're close now. I can tell. Rip whispers. Close to death. Close to

that final cut. I can feel it too. *Did you enjoy the completion?*
'No. I could never-'
I've watched many of them, she interrupts quietly, scanning the forest as she trots by my side. *I never get to speak to the humans… before the completion. For whatever reason I can speak with you. I don't know why. But if I make you leave… if you return safely home, then I was able to make a difference. It means I am more than this nothing they left me with.*
'What's it like being a Shade?'
When they tear your soul from your body, that is the worst pain imaginable. After, there's nothing for a time but confusion and disbelief that this could ever happen to you. Soon you forget your old life, your name, most things. I think of that girl in the meadow. She'd been so happy. I don't think I'll ever forget the sound of her screams. That she'd trusted Seph made it so much worse. He'd betrayed her. And that had been his intention from the moment he'd laid eyes on her. This was the 'help' he and all the Sirens desired to bestow.
I remember the moment Tristen first saw me. I believed our relationship was real, even if it didn't start out that way. Still knowing his true intentions in that first smile across the bar ripped away so much of the good. We were born from lies.
All that's left now is rotten and old. I am nothing.
'You're not nothing,' I argue.
I would not wish this existence on anyone.
'The other Shades aren't like you. They enticed me here as much as Tristan did. They tricked me. It's like they hate me.'
They do hate you. They're angry. They feel cheated. They want everyone to feel as awful and empty as they do.
'Is that how you feel?'
Yes. She is blunt. I pause in the forest feeling lost. Rip must sense my doubt. *I know where your house is.* She turns and runs through the trees leaving me no choice but to follow. We climb higher, shedding the humidity like an old skin. Rip slows as we approach a familiar part of the forest. *There is another part of me though…* The wolf's voice is unsure and full of wonder. *A part I thought was*

destroyed. A part that feels... protective of you. After so much pain. It's a good feeling.

I suddenly feel so intensely grateful to her for all the times she's helped me. Maybe being a Shade wouldn't be so bad if I became like Rip.

But Tobias wants me to become a Siren.

I'd rather die.

I see my house through the trees. It wasn't too long ago that I created this place. Everything felt so different then.

Rip stops abruptly. *There's one of them inside.* And in the next instant she's gone.

It has to be Tristan looking for me. I run to the front door desperate to see him, but stop with my hand on the handle. What am I running to? Tristan can't help me. Tristan is a liar. He is a Siren. He is a monster, just like Tobias. He is not mine anymore. That last thought feels the worst. I wish I could feel the truth in my heart and not just in my head. He doesn't feel like a liar or a monster. My heart still races at the thought of seeing him. I just want to be held in his arms and hear that everything will be alright.

I open the door and step inside. The hallway is long and dark. I wander around, but all the rooms are empty. Rip must have been wrong about someone being here. I pass a window and I see a figure sitting outside on the bench I created to take in the view. Orla.

'Did you enjoy the completion?' she asks as I approach, unknowingly echoing Rip's question.

'I think you knew I wouldn't.'

'It's the natural order of things,' she states, surprising me with her defensive tone. 'You don't blame the cat for hunting the mouse, so why are we any different?' She doesn't meet my eyes, but she seems more composed than the last time I saw her. 'You'll be one of us very soon. You'll feel differently then.'

'I can still refuse.'

Orla laughs gently. 'Oh Liv, you can't refuse. Tobias has his eyes on you. He always gets what he wants. Would you rather become a Shade?'

I sigh. Everything inside me is so at odds with our surroundings. The clear warm day and the birdsong. The rustle of leaves and occasional distant sounds of village life rising up like smoke.

'You know,' Orla continues as if she's picking up an old conversation. 'I've always preferred the name Siren. It feels much more real. Terrifying and beautiful.'

'And honest,' I add.

Orla nods, finally looking directly at me. 'And honest.' Her voice is quiet. 'Siren's aren't good creatures in human stories so the name fell out of favour. Now, shepherd's on the other hand.' She starts to sing softly.

> *My Shepherd will supply my need. In the meadow fresh, he makes me feed, Beside the living stream. He brings my wandering spirit back.When I walk through the shades of death. His presence is my stay. One word of his supporting grace Drives all my fears away.*

Her voice wraps around me like a warm and tangible thing and I am powerless. Her eyes gleam like liquid jade as she sings. 'You'll make a good Siren, Livvy.' Orla reaches out to stroke my face. Her expression reminds me of Tobias and I recall his words.

Next, I'll have your mother.

Do I trust Tobias to leave Mum alone if I become a Siren? No, the answer is easy. But as a Shade, I lose everything and will be powerless to protect her.

Tobias wants me to become a Siren. What choice do I really have?

I lie as still as possible, as if stillness could make me part of the landscape. I think I'd like that.

'You haven't got long now before the final cut.' Tobias rests his head down on the ground beside me. 'And you know, I'll find you if you do wander home?' His voice is soft with the intimacy of a lover. He shifts to his side and rests his head on his arm to get a better look at me. 'I'll be angry if I have to come and get you.' His fingers lightly play with my hair. 'Ask your mother, she knows how I get when I'm angry.'

Why do I want to curl up in his arms? Into a tight little ball until all the light can no longer find me and everything is warm and dark. A never ending darkness, isn't that what I'd once longed for?

My choices are limited. The distant cuckoo bleep of the machine has been like a secret soundtrack that resurfaces every now and again, sometimes stronger than others. It reminds me of the Otherside, of home.

It reminds me that, for now at least, I'm still alive.

I was. I was. I was. I was.

Shut up is what I'd say if my mouth worked. I have that groggy sensation that feels like waking up from an unplanned overlong nap. It's followed by mild panic that I've missed or forgotten something.

I feel uncomfortable, itchy and misplaced. I feel bruised and broken and like I can't catch my breath. My eyes are crusty with sleep, but I force them open. I try to bring my arm up to wipe my eyes but my arm is stiff and sore. The hospital room is as grey and stark as I remember. The pink curtains are drawn so I can't judge the perfection of the sky, but I don't think I need to. This is real. There's an irritating prickly rawness to everything.

I don't know how. But somehow, and typically without even trying, I am back. I sigh and it hurts. My body feels battered and old. It has taken me too long to realise this reality, no matter how painful, is the truth I want. And the irony, that now I have to give it up for good to protect my mum.

The door opens and Mum walks in. For a moment, I've never been so happy to see her. The reality of her soon catches up. 'Liv!' she exclaims, seeing me awake. She hesitates and comes closer slowly like she's afraid I'll disappear. She looks smaller than I remember. I just want her to hug me, but she lingers at the end of the bed. I lift my unbandaged hand weakly. She grabs it before it falls.

'I want to go home.'

'Soon Olivia,' the doctor says. 'How is your pain?'

'It's fine.' I raise my voice. 'I don't want any more drugs.' My chest hurts. A lot. Pain is preferable to the alternative. I need to stay in control if I don't want to slip back immediately.

'That's good. Let the nurse know if the pain gets worse.'

'I feel fine.'

'Recovery can be a slow process. You woke up less than 24 hours ago. You need to be patient with your body.'

I've read every word in this room. Twice. A couple of magazines, charts, instructions on how to use the bed, emergency exits, a lone get well soon card. I've tried pacing the room until my legs feel too heavy. I've counted the cars I can see from the window. I've watched the hospital car park fill up and then empty as the day stretches.

I should get back to the meadow. I should ask for drugs and sleep and get back before Tobias comes for me. Becoming a Siren is the only way to protect my mum. Yet every time I close my eyes I am filled with dread. I try to keep it contained in a ball beneath my ribs, but it expands and spills and consumes me until I'm back pacing the floor and reading the magazines.

How long before Tobias comes for me?

I am released from the hospital. I hate hospitals. The doctor doesn't seem happy with me. I'm sure my bloodshot eyes, semi-vacant expression and random bouts of crying are not endearing. But I'm someone else's problem now and there's no need for me to take up a bed.

The doctor gives me instructions on pain relief and the light cast on my wrist. She also recommends a counsellor but her eyes are already glazed over, and she's looking down at paperwork, so I don't tell her I already have one of those. Her mind has skipped ahead to the next task. I don't blame her. Mine has too.

I inspect the entire house before I'm willing to sit and accept the cup of tea Mum offers as she follows me from room to room. I look for the tiny imperfections that I know. Things that Tobias can't know. I won't be fooled again. The time I'd burnt a patch of carpet with my hair straighteners. A chunk of missing wall hidden behind a painting in the living room from a botched DIY attempt. A dent in the laminate floor in the kitchen that can only be felt with fingers that know where to touch. A chest of drawers where the fourth drawer down refuses to close completely.

'Liv, you're home. You're safe.' Mum says.

'Let me just check one more thing,' I mutter as I think of things Tobias can't know. A creak on the stair, the loose screw on the swivel chair in the box room. Everything passes. This is real. It's real. The aches wracking my body feel real. The house looks real. It must be real.

'Of course this is real,' Mum says and I realise I've been talking aloud. 'You need to rest. Come and sit down.'

She brings me turmeric tea and sits opposite, watching me with concern. I'm sure she's wrestling with how best to deal with me.

The taste of the tea fills me with so much nostalgia. My eyes well up as I sip the tea using my good hand.

'Liv,' Mum notices. 'I don't want to see your glass eyes.' She hands me a handkerchief from up her sleeve. 'It's clean.'

'I want to tell you something.' And I want to tell her everything. Even if she doesn't believe me, I just want her to hear it. To hear me.

'That can wait,' she soothes. 'You're exhausted. Finish your tea. I'll run you a bath and then you need to sleep. We can talk after you sleep.'

I recoil when she mentions sleep. At the same time the thought of crawling into my bed is enticing. But there is no hiding from Tobias. I don't know how much time I have left. I need her to know everything, I need to say goodbye.

'No.' I put the tea down. 'This is important. It can't wait.'

Mum sighs and moves to sit behind her spinning wheel as if it might offer protection from me. 'Ok, what is so important?'

'Alexei didn't kill himself.' Her hands freeze on the skein of wool she's been playing with. 'I've met Tee. He's called Tobias and he killed Alexei.'

'Oh, Liv,' she whispers without looking up.

'Please just listen,' I interrupt. 'There's more. Tobias, he's - he … isn't human. He's coming after me.' The tears pour down my face. 'I'm afraid he'll come for you too.'

I expect confusion. I expect sadness and shock.

I do not expect pure rage.

Her eyes meet mine and something in them scares me. 'Trust me, I am not afraid of Tobias.'

We stare at each in silence and slowly I realise nothing I have just told her is new information.

'You already know?' I am accusing.

Her face is grim. 'As far as the Otherside is concerned Alexei died from suicide. But yes, I always suspected Tobias was the knife. I was stupid to think he wouldn't come back eventually. He didn't manage to take everything from me the first time.' She shakes her head with frustration. 'Of course, he'd remember about you.'

I stare at her horrified. 'I don't understand. Why have you never told me any of this before? Tobias is dangerous. He's a monster. He's been out there and you knew?'

'Liv, I'm sorry.' She shoves the skein, stretched and taut, in her hands back in her kit box. 'It's hard to explain. I thought I had more time. I made sure we were hidden. We were safe. I thought that would be enough. I thought taking Alexei from me was enough for him. I never thought he'd find us. But…' she stops and sighs. She looks away.

'But what?'

'Tristan.' She looks at me with resignation. 'Tristan led you straight to Tobias.' Her face turns bitter. 'I'm sure Tobias couldn't believe his luck when he figured out who you were.'

'I still don't understand.' I look at this woman, my mother, and hardly recognise her. Her calmness, her flighty thoughts and gentle smile are all replaced by fierceness, by anger, hate and regrets burned dark. 'How do you know all this? Why is Tobias after us?'

'Liv,' she smiles humourlessly. 'You've met them. Do Sirens need a reason to be cruel?'

Do Sirens need a reason to be cruel?

I think she finally notices my confusion as she makes her voice more gentle, more like the Mum I remember. 'I'm a Siren, Liv. Tobias hates me because I'm the Siren that escaped.'

CHAPTER 20

'The first time I saw you, I thought to myself, this girl is not for me.' Tristan smiled across the table at me like he'd just paid me the greatest compliment. This was only dinner on our third date.

'At the bar? Oh, thanks!' I pulled a face at him.

Tristan didn't react. 'No, I saw you before that night in the bar.'

'When?'

'I saw you on campus with some friends. A few times actually. I always noticed you.'

'You never told me this!' Secretly, I was delighted to have been noticed and singled out.

'You shone so bright. Your kindness was beautiful. Your aura was so strong and resilient. You always looked so self-reliant.'

Sometimes, he really took my breath away.

'You see auras?" I teased lamely. 'What colour is mine?'

'Yellow,' Tristan said without a pause.

'Yet despite my strong yellow aura and beautiful kindness, you still thought, nope not for me?'

'You were out of reach.' Tristan brushed his fingers against mine. 'You didn't need me. You didn't need anybody, but you were still kind enough to grant people your company.'

'I'm not so kind.' I pouted. I know it's wrong, but I'd have preferred to hear it was my beautiful face rather than beautiful kindness that he'd noticed.

'Don't underestimate kindness.' Tristan replied, almost as if he had read my thoughts. 'I was so surprised when…' He trailed off and took a sip of his wine.

'When what?' I pressed when he didn't finish the sentence.

'Oh?' he muttered like he'd been lost in thought. 'I meant, I was surprised to find you weren't out of reach after all.' He wrapped his fingers around my hand. Despite the noise of the restaurant around us, it felt like there was no one else there.

I finally slept. Except, it was curled up with Mum in her bed like I was a little kid.

'Liv, you're safe here. You can sleep, Tobias can't touch you here,' she reassured me.

'I have no control when I slip over to the meadow. I'm scared I'll wake up back there.'

'I'll watch over you,' she promised. I fell asleep to her soft voice repeating words in my ear.

You are safe. You can sleep. Finally, I sleep. It is a long, deep and dreamless sleep.

When I wake up I can tell from her breathing that she's asleep. Instead of feeling panic that she left me unguarded, I just feel gratitude to have this time to spend with her. To finally know everything. Her face is still the face of my mum. I see no trace of the Siren's cruelness, of the Siren's cunning and lure. I wonder how many humans she's 'completed'. I imagine how much she must have loved my father to leave it all behind to be with him. She was so brave.

So much braver than Tristan, a little voice in my head reminds me. And that hurts.

'Mum,' I whisper. It's half-hearted as I don't know how to tell her what I'm going to do. Her eyes open immediately. 'I need to go back.'

'No. Liv, you-'

'Wait. There's more I haven't told you.' She frowns unhappily. 'Tobias promised me he'd force me back. He promised me he'd destroy you next. But he gave me a choice.'

'Tobias gives no choices unless both outcomes benefit him.'

I feel a tear slip out and soak into the pillow under my face. 'Either he makes me a Shade and then comes for you, or he'll leave you alone if I become a Siren.'

'No!' She bolts upright. 'You can't do that! I don't care how tempting it seems or what he promised you. He's lying. He'll still make a Shade of you. And if by some chance there is enough in you to become a Siren, that's no life either.'

'You think I don't have enough in me?' I sit up beside her.

It's in your blood Tobias had told me once.

'Liv,' she sighs. 'Don't take this personally. It's so rare for humans to become Sirens.'

'Even the daughter of a Siren?' I challenge.

'This isn't the point. Siren or Shade the answer is no.'

'Mum,' I say sadly. 'I'm not asking for permission. Tobias will come here if I don't go back. At least as a Siren I have some power to protect you, as a Shade I am nothing. I have no other choice.'

'You do. Tobias can't touch you here. I can help protect you.'

'Mum. I can't live the rest of my life afraid to sleep. You can't watch over me forever. He's already won.' We're silent as the thought echoes between us, *you can't watch over me forever*. 'There's something else.' I whisper eventually. 'Alexei didn't know about me. Tobias wanted you to think he knew, but he didn't.' She closes her eyes and a shudder wracks through her. This is new information for her. When Mum opens her eyes they're wet and shining.

'Listen to me, Liv. I know I haven't been the best mother. I know I have no right to tell you what to do now you're an adult. But, you will see sense.' I'm silent, she has never spoken to me like this. We could almost be a mother and daughter arguing about something normal like getting a tattoo. I almost laugh. 'Do you think it was easy for me to protect myself from him? Do you think he didn't try and drag me back when I left? Do you think I wasn't at my most exhausted with a newborn baby when he came for me? He never succeeded and eventually I hid.'

'I don't know how you coped. You're amazing,' I say honestly.

'And so are you, Liv. You're so much stronger than you realise.'

We reach a quiet stalemate. Am I being brave by going back to face Tobias or am I taking the easy way out?

Eventually, sensing she might have won me around, Mum climbs off the bed. 'I can train you to build your mental defences and stand up to Tobias here on your own turf. You never have to go back there.'

I lean my head against the headboard and give her a sideways glance. 'Really? You could teach me?'

'Yes, I've done it before.' I give her a questioning look and she continues. 'I trained Abbie. I saved her life.'

Mum drives us to Abbie's house in silence. The roads are quiet, I remember almost the exact spot where I lost control of the car. Seconds later we pass the site of my car crash without a word from either of us. There is not much left to tell the story of what happened. Tire marks on the verge and a broken wooden fence. Yet, I stare all the same.

When we reach Abbie's village, Mum pulls over on a leafy side street opposite a pub and a playground. She points to a sign further up for a dead-end lane and insists I go ahead without her.

'Do I really have to speak to her? You're the one doing the training.' I say again for probably the tenth time since she told me.

'You'll only believe it's possible after you meet her.'

A siren tried to lure Abbie away once, years ago now. Mum noticed the signs and intervened quietly, first by befriending Abbie and then by teaching her everything she knew to improve her control and resist the Siren's lure.

'It was the first time I'd ever seen evidence of the Sirens since escaping.' She'd told me that morning. 'Still playing their games and still taking vulnerable and lonely people. Leaving it all behind me didn't seem enough anymore. I had to stop it.'

'Ok, fine. I'll talk to her.' I say as I climb out of the car. It's only when I start down the single-track lane and the sounds of life around me fade away that I hear my heart pounding again. Grass grows up through old tarmac and the hedges press in from each side. Habit forces me to scan for the yellow eyes. I haven't really been alone since I returned to the Otherside.

I almost miss the rusty gate hiding amongst the gnarly hedgerow. Beyond it, an overgrown garden with broken paving leads to a small cottage with grey pebble-dashed walls and cracked blue paint around the windows. The windows are dark and dusty like the place has been abandoned. Trusting my Mum, I make my way through the garden to the front door to knock. When the door finally opens a crack, Abbie does not look surprised to see me. She closes the door to release the chain and then opens it wide indicating I should follow her inside.

'I'm glad you came by,' she says as she leads us down a dark hallway. My eyes take a moment to adjust after the bright daylight. Every surface is covered with objects, those both familiar and strange. It feels like being in a Victorian museum and I touch nothing, even though I want to dance my fingers across the objects we pass. 'Your mum has told me a lot about you over the years. I think we're much alike.' I want to shake my head and argue. I'm nothing like her. I'm brand new. I'm half Siren. Mum never told Abbie that she was a Siren for fear of scaring her, instead she lied. She was just another victim of the Sirens who'd escaped. Perhaps partly true.

Abbie leads me straight through an ancient kitchen and into a warm sun room. Judging by all the plants and seedlings crowding the shelves and the soil across the floor this serves more as a greenhouse than anything else. 'You caught me tending to my plants. I hope you don't mind if I continue while we talk.' She sits down onto a low stool and resumes tending to a tray of seedlings.

'Of course not.' Glancing around me, I find there is nowhere to sit in the small room so I stand awkwardly watching her work.

I push away the tiredness that steals up too easily after my accident. Outside, I see an old brown dog lounging in the only square of light where the sun catches the ground. I see all of Abbie's gardening efforts are spent on the back garden. While the front of the house looks broken and overgrown, the back is lush, green and impressive. 'I'm sorry I didn't pick up Sky that day. I hope your plans weren't ruined.' I add.

'Accidents happen,' Abbie replies matter of factly.

'I'm still sorry. I want to make sure that kind of accident never happens again. Actually, that's why I'm here. My mum thought it would be good for me to meet you.'

'Really?' Abbie's eyes lift with interest to meet mine.

'I need to learn control. I need to make sure I can never be dragged back to that ...place. If that's possible.' In the silence that follows, I don't know if I've said enough or if Abbie will even know what I'm talking about.

'It's possible,' she smiles. 'I wouldn't be here if it weren't.' Abbie settles back into the rhythm of methodically repotting baby plants. 'It took me a long time to hold the amount of discipline and self-control I have now,' she says mostly distractedly as she carefully moves another seedling. 'But, the greatest thing that will help you is *knowing* that you have more power than them.' My heart sinks, one word to describe how Tobias makes me feel would be powerless. 'Trust me, I know it's hard to believe, but it makes all the difference.' Abbie's voice is grim. 'They may be masters in their world, but here they are nothing.' She must sense my doubt as finally she stands, wiping her hands on her trousers. I'm not tall, but as she faces me fiercely she has to look up. 'Olivia. Your mum taught me everything, she's been through so much. I can't even imagine how she escaped those monsters. I used to live in fear, now they're just a fading memory. They still come looking for me from time to time. But they can't have me. You can do this too.' I study her small frame and firm stance differently now. I see her in the meadow. I see another me, another Rip, another lost girl. It doesn't seem possible, but Abbie's the proof that finally filters through my fear. As I leave, I don't scan the shadows for the first time in months.

The front door slammed loudly, but typically in our student house, it still didn't close properly. It creaked back open slowly almost like a taunt.

'Argh.' I heard Nina growl and then a bang as she must have returned to kick it closed.

'Bad day?' I asked looking up from my phone when she barged into the kitchen.

'The worst.' She banged around the cupboards.

'Want to talk about it?'

'Yes. No. I can't right now.' She sighed and eventually settled for pouring a glass of water.

'I'm here whenever you're ready. How about we go do something fun?' I put my phone down and focussed on her. 'I've been reading about the extraordinary powers of distraction to relieve your brain.'

'Really?' she replied half heartedly and I could tell she was still thinking about her day.

'Fool your brain, reduce your pain.' I quoted, although I forgot where it had come from now.

'What?' That got her full attention.

'Want to go for a run and fool your brain?'

'You hate running.'

'You don't though.'

Nina finally smiled. 'Thanks, Liv.' she said sincerely. 'But I just need to be alone for a bit.'

'Phew,' I joked. 'Thought I might actually have to dig out my running shoes.'

Nina laughed briefly. 'I still might take you up on the run offer later.' She refilled her glass and turned to leave.

'Anything you need, Neen. Remember, you're not alone.'

After a few days practising with Mum, I feel ready to give up. She's endlessly patient and calm, but it only adds to my frustration. Half the things she talks about are intangible concepts that I struggle to grasp and take seriously. I fail to see how breathing right can really protect me.

'Did you do the mindfulness exercises?'

'Yes.'

'And you've been meditating?'

'Yes'

'Hmm.' What does that mean I want to yell? A happy hmm or an 'I think you're lying' hmm? I don't think either of us are happy with my progress. I do all the exercises she gives me, mainly to avoid having to lie. They feel pointless though. It feels like wasting time. When she spoke of building my mental defences, I'd imagined swords and shields not breathing exercises. I don't want to feel cheated, but I do.

And then thoughts of Tobias creep in.

'Focus.' Mum says quietly, tapping my hand. I scowl, but think better of responding. 'You need to stop over thinking, stop worrying. A good night's sleep will make a big difference.'

Easier said than done I think. She's starting to remind me of Miss Salter. Mum ends each of our practices with the same reminder. 'Remember Liv, he has no power over you.'

'Tell me how you did it.' I ask Mum. It's late one night and I'm reluctant to go to bed. I find any excuse to prolong conversations. Any excuse to avoid being alone in the dark. 'How does a Siren escape?' I can see her thinking before she answers, deciding what to tell me and what to withhold. I think she is worried my thoughts lie with Tristan.

'There is a lot more to their world than you realise. It's more than Sirens, more than just a meadow.'

'I know,' I interrupt. 'I've been across the lake, to the village and the Night Cafe.' She looks surprised, but covers it up quickly to continue.

'There is more beyond all that. Other lands and places beyond the maps. Other creatures that reside there.' It is my turn to be surprised. I'd never considered there was more to Tristan's world than Sirens and Shades.

'Some of the other creatures can not move easily between worlds the way Sirens do so they created doorways to pass between the folds. I found out that such doorways held a lot of power. They are a one way passage for Siren's because their power strips away the Siren's abilities. Effectively they leave a human behind.'

Over the past months, I feel like my mind has been broken and rebuilt to accept the knowledge that other creatures exist, that another world alongside ours exists. Hearing my mum talk about this feels alien and fantastical all over again. She spoke of worlds, more than just here and there.

'How did you know it would work?'

'I didn't, but it was better than the alternative. I couldn't stay after my eyes had been opened.' She stares up at the ceiling like there is something up there. Neither of us turned on a light as the evening turned dark and now we sit in near darkness with just a faint glow from the moon. 'I never heard of another Siren escaping. But you know, I really thought Tristan would do it for you. When he didn't, well, I was just glad he left you alone. I respected him at least for that.'

I close my eyes not wanting to think about Tristan, but deep inside that's a question I can't stop asking myself. If Tristan really loved me, why didn't he make the same sacrifice as Mum? He certainly knew it was an option. The hurt I continually feel when thinking about Tristan was changing everyday. Now, it felt dominated by anger rather than desperation.

'Where are these doorways?'

'I only ever found one, it wasn't easy to reach, but I found the closest one to the village so I decided to risk it.'

'Where?'

'At the bottom of the lake on the edge of the meadow. There's an underwater cave.'

'That must have been hard to risk drowning to find it.'

'It was.' She nods as she remembers. 'I used to practise holding my breath just so I could last long enough to find the cave.' She gives me a speculative look. 'You know a lot more about Sirens and the village than I realised.'

I change the subject. 'Weren't you afraid of giving it all up?'

'I was terrified,' she admits. 'But the thought of losing your father was worse.'

It's the middle of the night. Those hours where time seems thin and stretches the longest. I wake up with a start. Disorientation is chased away by anxious thoughts that grip me as strongly as when Tristan first broke my heart. I'm living on borrowed time. I can't shake the feeling that Tobias knows I'm here. He's playing with me. He's just waiting for the perfect moment. For what could be hours or only minutes I feel too afraid to move, afraid of what hides in the shadows of my room. I practise deep breathing. I practise golden thread breathing like Mum taught me. I think eventually it must help as I feel able to slowly creep out of my bed and cross the landing to Mum's room. I quietly enter. I see the form of her curled up in her bed. She doesn't speak, but she shifts to the side and lifts the covers. I slip in beside her.

CHAPTER 21

It's April and spring finally feels like a possibility. It's always been one of my favourite times of the year, when the days feel longer and winter is finally shaken off. My exam results will arrive soon in the post and assuming I don't completely fail, I'll be invited to the summer graduation ceremony. We'd planned one big final party that weekend at the house. And then the dreaded clean up of the three storey terrace. Parent's would arrive, often with younger siblings in tow, and we'd pack up our stuff, clean and pray we'd get our deposits back. There was a huge sigh of relief across the city as another year's worth of students left and a quiet summer lay ahead. And then the next load of students would move into the student halls and houses and make a corner of the city their home. I wondered if I'd be there to see it all. I could already see Beth complaining if I didn't do my share of the cleaning.

It has been two weeks with no sign of Tobias, but time passes differently for Sirens. Each day didn't feel like a victory, it only heightened my fear. I didn't let my guard down. I practised every day. I felt stronger, but also I felt untested.

'You're daydreaming.' Mum says as she joins me outside, wiping her hands on a dishcloth.

It happened so easily. I would start my breathing exercises, try to clear my mind and then different variations of the future would play through my mind.

'You need to think less and let yourself just be.'

'I'm trying!'

'You're better than when you started. More focused. You're an anchor, focus on your connection with the ground. You will scare Tobias.'

I doubt that will ever happen, but I just smile gratefully. 'How long did Abbie take to get the hang of all this?

Mum pauses. 'Oh, well I worked with her for months, even now I check to make sure she isn't slipping. But we never practised as much as you and you're-'

'Months?' I wish I hadn't asked. I tried not to think about how I was investing a lot in Mum's method and yet I wasn't like Abbie. I've lived in the village. I'd built a house. I'd been accepted by these creatures. I was in so deep. The uneasiness was like an itch across my skin.

'You don't need months. Only belief.' Mum is firm.

Another thing she said sticks in my mind, *even now I check to make sure she isn't slipping.* I think about Abbie alone in her house down that dark tiny lane. I wonder if she's truly beaten her demons or if she's just got really good at hiding.

I see it watching me.

At first I think it's just flower heads bobbing in the breeze. I refuse to look. I refuse to mistake flowers for yellow eyes. But I can feel them too. Their presence on the periphery feels like it did before. A gentle lure, a tantalising promise. The truth behind a secret.

It's colder again today, but I had wrapped myself in one of Mum's thick cardigan creations as I preferred to meditate outside. At the bottom of her garden screening a compost bin and a dilapidated shed are a row of tall Leylandii trees. The Leylandii were once Mum's height, but now they are huge and encroach in every direction they can. Amongst their shade, I see movement. A shadow shifts impatiently, it unfolds itself and hulks forward like it might break cover.

I really don't want to look. Just leave me alone. But I can't help it,

I sneak a look and see the yellow eyes trained on me.

Liv.

I screw my eyes up tight. This will pass. Clear thoughts. Free from fear.

Tobias is angry.

I am free from fear. I am anchored to the earth.

You should come home.

Free from fear. This will pass. I am anchored to the earth.

Tristan misses you.

My thoughts stutter and I forget the words. I open my eyes and see them. Eyes upon eyes. Eager and leaning towards me.

We will always be watching you.

Come with us.

Give us a chance.

Come and play.

Tobias and Tristan want to play.

I shiver, feeling sick anticipation curl in my stomach. Tobias and Tristan. I should resist. If I can't stand against Shades, what hope do I have against Tobias? But, would Tobias hurt Tristan? What if Tobias is punishing Tristan because of me? I am standing directly in front of the trees, though I'm not aware of moving.

That's right, Liv. Come and play.

I nod faintly. Only to check on Tristan I think. Just to make sure he's ok. Through the Leylandii, I know the meadow is waiting for me.

'Liv!' Mum's voice snaps me awake. 'What are you doing?' She grabs me by the shoulder and spins me around. I lower the outstretched arm that I don't even remember raising.

'I …' But no words follow. I have nothing. The Shades have vanished and I feel strangely disappointed.

Mum bustles around the kitchen. I can tell she's upset. There is a direct correlation between her mood and her cooking. The worse her mood, the more distractions she needs and the worse the food ends up. Several pans simmer and no inch of work space has been spared. She's even dragged out her ancient blender that weighs a ton. I watch from the kitchen table, not even daring to offer my help. With the return of the Shades an idea is crystalizing in my mind and getting harder and harder to shake. I need to go back.

'You were going back,' Mum accuses me suddenly as if she can read my thoughts. She keeps her back turned to me, fighting with the blender. Despite years of use, it is impossible to remember how the blender pieces fit together and every time is a struggle. Her attention appears focussed on forcing a piece to click into place. 'If I hadn't stopped you, you'd be there now.'

'I saw the meadow,' I say lamely, watching the piece in her hand. I don't think it fits. It's probably the wrong one, but she is determined.

'All your practice and you're still so willing to go back to Tobias.'

'No! It's not like that.' I react to his name. 'I just wanted to—' I pause to think. 'I want to make sure Tristan is ok, but now—'

'Liv.' Her voice holds a warning. She finally looks up, slamming the plastic down in defeat with a shaky sigh. She looks at me briefly and I feel the sadness in her eyes before she lowers her gaze and moves to the stove. 'You need to let go. Tristan made his choice. He chose to stay. Your life is here.'

'I know.' I say through gritted teeth. 'But I'm afraid Tobias will hurt him.' I can't bring my voice to speak the words too loudly, as if saying his name will summon him.

'Siren's can take care of themselves,' Mum replies, stirring one of her pots viciously. 'If you go back there again, it will be your last. You won't come back this time.' She abandons her cooking and whirls over to me. 'Don't let him win.' Her palms hit the surface of the table as she confronts me. 'You're as good as dead if you go back. Can I be any blunter? I don't know how to get through to you!' Her eyes are pleading. She thinks she's already lost me I realise.

'I know that Siren's can die. Do you really think Tristan is safe?

You know Tobias better than me. Do you really think he won't hurt Tristan if I stay here? Do you really think *you're* safe if I stay here?' I think we both know what I'm really saying. *Be my mother. Reassure me. Tell me everything will be alright. Tell me Tristan is safe. Tell me you will be safe. I'll stay if you tell me everything will be ok.*

Her eyes widen and she sits down with a sigh. Behind her something hisses and a timer starts beeping. We ignore it all.

'I can't,' she finally admits. 'I can't promise Tristan, or any of us, will be safe. Tobias has killed his own kind before.'

'I'm done being afraid of him.' I say calmly into the silence that follows her omission. I already knew Tobias was a killer, what difference whether it was humans or Sirens. My father or Tristan. I know what I have to do. 'I *was* thinking of only going to check on Tristan when you stopped me, but now I know that's not enough.'

'What are you saying?'

'I am going back. I'm going to kill Tobias.'

If you knew it was your last day, would you do anything differently? I end up spending mine planning how to kill a monster.

I think part of me knows today is the day. Mum too.

We're extra nice to each other over breakfast. Extra careful. Something silly in the newspaper Mum still gets delivered triggers an old memory. We smile over stupid jokes and things we once misheard in song lyrics. Each memory reminds us of another. The passage of lonely time can make it easy to forget all the good times we had. All those times we did seek each other out. They aren't grand times or amazing stories, but they're warm and they're ours.

Mum decided not to argue with me anymore about going back. And so interspersed with silly memories from our past we talk about how to kill a monster. She wants him dead as much as I do, but I know she feels guilty that she's letting me risk my life to do it. 'You can't stop me, you know?' I promise her. 'You can only help me.'

The only way to kill a Siren is by drowning. We discuss various methods, but the lake is the obvious location and knocking him out first and then weighing him down so he sinks seems like the most effective way. Just as I called forth drinks in the Night Cafe or imagined what clothes I wore, Mum said I should be able to create rocks and ropes. What a sinister edge this skill had taken. 'But how do I stop him from unimagining the weights or just disappearing to escape? The laws of physics aren't on my side.'

'Get him drunk.'

'You're kidding?'

She shakes her head. 'Did you ever notice in the Night Cafe that as the night wore on the shifting changes slow and stop?' I nod, suddenly remembering Cillian explaining in the Night Cafe.

'Alcohol dampens everything. It'll make him slower. You'll have to give him the drink to make sure it's really alcoholic. Some Siren's like the idea of drinking and think it makes them look sophisticated, but their glass will often be water.'

The more we plan the more scarily real it all feels, but there's no turning back for me. If this is Tobias' only weakness, I'll take it.

'Do you think Tristan would help?' Mum asks.

'Maybe. But I can't rely on him.' It feels sad to say out loud. Mum just nods and moves on to talking about my practice. I go through the motions of the exercises. We breathe through the exercises, we discuss mental barriers and the power of positive thinking.

'Repeat after me,' she says. 'I am the master of my fate. I am the captain of my soul.'

Mum loves this poem. I repeat the words. And today they finally sound true.

Mum nods approvingly like she can feel my strength. I don't let on that I see figures writhing in the edge of my eyes. Yellow eyes blinking in dark places. There are glimpses beyond her garden of beautifully tall shimmering grass waving in the wind like fur being stroked by an invisible giant hand.

I dig out my phone from where it fell down the side of the bed days ago. The battery is dead, so I decide to go old school and write emails using Mum's laptop. There are so many things I want to say to so many people. But most importantly, I want to apologise to Nina and my other friends. The words come surprisingly easily. I ignore the phantoms and Shades that occasionally drift by me. I ignore their reflections on the computer screen as I type. I even manage to write an email to Miss Salter. I wonder if she ever thinks of me? Mum finds me at the computer and looks absurdly relieved to find me doing something so normal.

'Come and help me make dinner?' she asks.

We're still being careful with each other. She gives me easy jobs like washing vegetables and talks about her day. The hum of the Shades outside is quiet but incessant. Mum talks about a village play that she's helping to make the costumes for and jokes lamely about the lead who keeps complaining that she's making the costumes too small despite putting on a stone since Christmas. She talks about a village council meeting where the main order of business was dog fouling and whether the council budget could extend to pink spray paint for residents to spray rogue poos in their area. It's all rather mundane, but I can see all of it makes her content. The innocuous topics of conversation continue through dinner and all the while the impatient eyes of the Shades press in and their noise increases. There are too many of them all talking over one another to be able to pick out any of their words. I think they know I'll be theirs soon. Still, I make a good show of eating dinner and I do enjoy Mum's stories of village life. As we finish dinner, there is a silent pause between us, where I listen to the racket the Shades are making outside.

'Mum, I think it's time.' I suddenly say, surprising both of us.

'Liv, no.' She jumps up, her chair scraping back against the floor tiles. 'Why don't you give it another day?'

'We both know there is only so much planning I can do. I can't go on like this. It's time.'

Mum's breath is shaky, but her eyes are resigned. She doesn't try to change my mind. She knows that she can't. 'I don't want to run away,' I continue. 'Even now there are so many eyes watching me. So many Shades begging me to return. I have to face him.' I point out the window, but when we look there is nothing outside but darkness and a slender moon in the sky.

'I just wish I could help you more,' Mum finally says. There is a catch in her voice that it breaks my heart to hear it. 'I wish I could go back and confront Tobias. I wish I'd ended him back when I had the chance.'

'This isn't your fault.' I reach out and grab her hand. She brings her other hand over mine. It's far from a hug, but it's a lot for us. My eyes sting with tears as I look at her. I know she'll be fine without me, living life in the heart of this village. But how will she cope with the absolute loss of me? Another person she loves, stolen by Tobias. I hate to think of her all alone in this *Otherside*. 'You know, I'll do everything in my power to return.' She nods, but doesn't speak. She just stares at me for such a long time like she's memorising my face. She thinks this is the end. I try not to let her certainty that I won't return affect me. I am the master of my fate.

I am brand new.

I try to pull my hand away from beneath hers, but she holds on a moment longer. 'I'm so proud of you, Liv. Of the person you've become. Your father would have been too.' She releases me then and steps back once, then twice, until she's resting against the door frame. 'I can't watch you go,' she whispers. She spins and runs out of the room. I hear her climb the stairs. A door slams. Part of me - most of me - wants to go after her and crawl in bed beside her. To close my eyes and pretend everything is alright.

I open the back door and the Shades greet me louder than ever before. Excited eyes move closer and their shadowy forms swarm. I step into the night and the air feels frosty and damp for a moment, until I close my eyes and feel it shift and warm around me. I open my eyes and the meadow greets me, golden in the sunrise.

CHAPTER 22

At the edge of the meadow, furthest from the lake, trees line the border. Shafts of warm morning light steal through the branches and light up floating seeds. From a cold April evening, this is what I open my eyes to. It's easy to see why I loved this place. The grass brushes against my bare legs as I wade through toward the lake.

When I'm knee deep in the water and feeling the smooth pebbles beneath my feet, I think now is the time to test myself. To take Mum's lessons and use them to see how I can manipulate my surroundings.

I am the master of my fate.

Any hope I have of beating Tobias rests on this. I'll need rocks. One to hit him across the temple and a large one to help him sink once he's unconscious. I could almost smile at how calmly I consider killing a man.

Not a man. A monster. Not a Shepherd. A Siren.

I feel something smooth in my hand and look down to find a rock grasped between my fingers. This is no different to creating my house up in the mountains. This is easy. I can do this.

I will the rock away and it's gone. I focus on the far side of the lake. I'll need to think bigger for the rock I place on his chest. Large, almost like stepping stones. Trying to call forth rocks feels ridiculous for a moment and reminds me of Ludo from the film *Labyrinth*, but I don't have time to second guess myself as a rock emerges from the lake. It stops an inch above the water into the perfect stepping stone. I step onto it and without looking take the next step out across the lake. Another stepping stone meets my foot and I smile. This is what I've been waiting for all the times when I couldn't figure out how to get back to the meadow, all the times that I couldn't control how I looked or what I wore. It's all so easy now. I run across the lake and rock meets me every step of the way. I feel calm. I don't know what it is, this strange numb blanket that has settled over me. Either being in the meadow again or having finally made a decision to confront Tobias has cured my anxiety. I think of the fallen Sirens beneath me as I run over the water and wonder how many litter the lake bed. Tobias said Sirens who broke the rules ended up at the bottom of the lake. But I wonder if there really are 'rules' or just those that annoyed him.

The sticky jungle heat greets me after the lake. I want to find Tobias before he finds me, but there is one other place I need to go first.

*

Tristan is sitting on the edge of the pier when I get to *The Refuge*. His feet dangle in the water and I'm reminded of when he told me lakes reminded him of his mortality. I understand why now.

'You're so predictable, Tris.' I say as I approach. 'I knew I'd find you right here.'

'Maybe you're the predictable one,' he replies. 'I knew you'd come back.' I stand beside him, I can't bring myself to sit. Something feels different between us, like the power has shifted. It feels a little less his and a little more mine.

'Was it all a lie right from the start?' Not the question I was planning to ask. I lift my hand to shield the sun from my eyes as it slants in from over the mountain.

Tristan sighs. 'Would that make you feel better?'

'Why can't you ever just give a straight answer?' I breathe slowly. Not just rocks, manipulating the space feels easier than ever. Reflective sunglasses cover my eyes and I drop my hand. 'Look, I didn't come here to fight with you, Tris.' He looks up at me, squinting against the sun.

'You don't want to be a Shepherd anymore, so why are you here?' He turns away again, kicking his foot in the water.

'You don't know what I want.' I feel my temper rising again. This could be the last time we ever speak. Again, I swallow my annoyance. I don't want to have regrets. I lower myself to sit beside him and stare out across the water. 'I came to ask you one last time if you're willing to leave with me.' I see his fingers clench, gripping the edge of the pier tightly. I want to tell him the truth, that I'm here to kill Tobias, but I can't trust him anymore. I ball my fists and feel a smooth pebble in my hand. Just thinking of how I'll kill Tobias makes me will stones into existence now.

'You know, I love you more than anyone,' he says after a moment, almost against his will. 'As much as I know how. Leaving you was the bravest thing I ever did,' he continues.

'Brave?' I hurl the pebble into the lake as hard as I can.

He watches it hit the water before he replies. 'I'm a joke here for losing you. For failing. I knew what it meant for me when I let you go. If I fail again, my fate will be set in stone. Tobias is already looking for a reason. Why couldn't you just let me be brave?'

Set in stone. That phrase has a new meaning.

For the first time, I consider things from his point of view. He loved me. He gave up his reputation among his own kind to spare me. Me living my life and the bravery of that act were his only consolations. Until I showed up to risk his existence and demanded bigger sacrifices.

'All the more reason to leave.' I reach my hand over to cover his. 'You could be more than a Siren.' He starts at that name and looks at me sharply. 'I can help you escape. You could live a human life, free from Tobais. Like my mother chose.' There is no surprise, he already knew what my mother was. Another lie between us.

Finally, he meets my eyes. He is full of sadness. 'I want to, Liv. Believe me, I want to. But I can't. I'm afraid. I'm not like your mother.'

I think it all makes sense now. He loves me *as much as he knows how.* And it's not enough. I raise my hand up to cup his cheek and lean over. When our lips meet, it's soft at first. I think we both know this is probably goodbye. My mouth opens and I taste the salt of tears, but I don't know if they're mine or Tristan's. His arms come around me tightly and there is an urgency in both of us as we continue kissing.

I'd always thought I could kiss Tristan for hours. It would be so easy to slide onto his lap right now. To let him pick me up and carry me inside. We could be like this forever.

Living in stolen moments between ensnaring and falling for humans.

Living between moments of brutality and killing.

The reality turns everything sour in my stomach. I break away from him and push out of his arms. I jump up and start walking away before I can change my mind.

'Liv!' Tristan calls from behind me. I turn around to face him, but keep walking backwards. I have to keep moving now. I have to remember why I came back. I'd hoped Tristan could help me. Mum had asked if he could be relied upon to help me with my plan to kill Tobias. Leaving with Tristan had been my plan A and now it was time to accept plan B.

I don't feel one little bit of it, but I manage a smile. 'Yeah?' I can remember him like this, sitting in the sun at the edge of the pier. Tears tracking down his beautiful face.

'Don't become a Siren. For me or anyone else. Promise?'

I can't speak. I wipe at my wet eyes and nod shakily. I give him a thumbs up and immediately feel ridiculous and like my old awkward human self. I turn and walk away.

I can feel all eyes on me as I enter the Night Cafe. Hostile or curious, I can't tell. I try not to pay attention. I just need to find Tobias. I don't care what they think of me anymore. When I see Cillian and Orla standing, heads together, I hope to pass unnoticed.

'Liv!' Fail. Cillian's voice calls me back. I pause, debating whether I can ignore him. The last time I saw Cillian, his hands were red with blood. 'Liv?' he calls again, his tone sharper this time.

I plaster my most confident smile before I turn and approach them. I'm grateful for the sunglasses that still hid my eyes.

'Cillian. Orla. Sorry, I didn't see you there. I'm a bit preoccupied.' I tap my head lighty and pull a face. They don't smile back and I feel a spike of panic that they're against me. They know why I'm really here. They can stop me.

Cillian smiles suddenly with a slight shake of his head. 'I haven't seen you around lately. I thought Tobias was hiding his newest prize away somewhere. But-' he frowns, 'you're still human.'

'I thought you'd gone home.' Orla chips in with hard eyes. 'To the *Otherside*.' She looks me up and down and then looks away into her drink. It's like I disgust her, like I'm a Shade.

I choose to face Cillain. He's easier to deal with than Orla's mood swings. 'Tobias hasn't been hiding me,' I say lightly. 'He's been wonderful. So patient. I needed some space to think things over and he granted me a few days.'

Cillian nods sagely. 'Yes. To get your affairs in order. Humans have so many affairs.'

'Speaking of *human affairs*. How's your Galway adventure?' I know from the moment his eyes light up that I asked the right question. They're such vain creatures happy to talk about themselves for hours. Cillian launches into stories of rocky beaches, romantic rainy evenings and a shy Irish girl who's beginning to trust him. It's hard to listen now that I know the truth. Cillian is like a cat lazily playing catch and release. The mind games are so similar to how Tristan played with me at the start. Orla is watching though, her green eyes intense and fixed on me, so I force myself to look interested and ask the right questions. Cillian pauses to pick up his Guinness, it's all he drinks now, and takes a gulp. Orla pounces on the gap in our conversation.

'And you, Livvy, you've made your decision, yes?' Her stance is relaxed as she leans back against the bar behind her, but there is an edge to her voice. She's wearing a lime green crop top and black shorts, revealing her perfectly tanned stomach. Looking at her resting casually against the bar, it would be so easy to believe she was just a normal girl. An attractive girl that knows it, but still just a girl. Instead, I see the alertness in her eyes and the tension held in her muscles. She's waiting to figure out if I'm the thing to be hunted or the hunter.

'Oh yes,' I smile right back at her. 'I'm ready now.' I sound so convincing, even I believe myself. 'I'm ready to make the final cut.' Both Cillian and Orla stand up a little straighter, their eyes gleaming with excitement like they've just caught the scent of blood.

'Excellent,' says a smooth familiar voice from behind me. I shiver involuntarily as his hand comes to rest on my bare back and I feel him lean in. 'No time like the present.' His breath tickles my neck. I turn to face him, knowing everything rests on these next few moments. He has to believe that I accept becoming a Siren is the only way. I place my palm flat on this chest and he grins as I push him gently away from Orla and Cillian.

'Excuse us,' I smile at them over my shoulder. My smile disappears once we find a quiet corner. 'You win, Tobias.' He inclines his head graciously. 'If-' I pause trying to sound confident. 'If you swear my mother is safe and left alone.'

'Liv!' He looks wounded bringing his hand to his chest. 'I already gave you my word. You doubt my word?' We stare at each other and the glint in his eyes tells me he enjoys baiting me. This is a game to him. 'I need to make sure.'

'A Shepherd's word is his honour.' His eyes crinkle at the corners and eventually he relaxes into a full on grin, flashing white teeth. I've seen this smile before, only coated in blood. 'You don't really have a choice here, Olivia,' he reminds me.

'I know. So, I'm trusting your honour.' Two shots materialise in my hands and I hold one out to him. I've finally mastered this place now that I know I can't stay. 'Let's celebrate.' Tobias is impressed I can tell and takes a glass from me downing it one. He grits his teeth against the taste and lets out a whoosh of breath. If it's anything like the alcohol I was aiming to materialise, it's strong. A shot I used to give to customers when they asked for the strongest thing we had.

'You're making the right choice.'

'What choice, right?' I say humorlessly before tossing my shot back. I'm so relieved when the inoffensive taste of water hits my tongue. The occasional customer had requested a fake shot of water to save face among their friends. For the first time since returning I actually think my plan might work. I grab Tobias' hand to pull him back to the bar. 'Come on, no one ever drank just one shot to celebrate, right?' And this time my smile is real.

Cillian and Orla gladly join our celebrations. Others drift over drawn by the noise and sound of our glasses banging down on the bar. Mum said a lot of Siren's only pretended to drink alcohol, but I can tell Orla is drunk as her sing-song voice grows louder and louder. She's a sloppy drunk and I'm surprised she's not given away her inner turmoil over John before. Cillian and Rowan lean on each other as they snigger over some nonsensical joke. Zara has curled up in a chair and fallen asleep already. But it's only Tobias who matters. He's the one I need to be stronger than. I see him across the room. He's talking with Tal. Last I saw her, she had blood on her nose and still managed to look cute and adorable. Tobias slouches, leaning slightly against the wall, his head dipped. He looks relaxed, but Tal looks unhappy at what he's telling her. He reaches out a hand to stroke her face, but she ducks away and replies with an angry scowl. Her eyes meet mine as I approach and narrow coldly. She walks away from Tobias and as she passes me she grabs my arm tightly and speaks while looking straight ahead. 'I hope you're happy. You've destroyed Tristan.' She storms away before I can reply. I stare after her for a moment. She's not important. Once I've got rid of Tobias, Tristan will be safe.

'Tobias,' I say, coming up behind him and bringing my hands to wrap around his waist. My insides recoil at the contact, but I am so close now to destroying him that it makes me brave. 'It's time. I can feel it. Let's go.'

◆ ◆ ◆

'I knew you'd change your mind.' Tobias says as we make our way to the meadow. He holds up a hand to stop me from interrupting even though I wasn't speaking. 'No, no, you can say it's all for your dear mother. To protect her. Fine. But I know you, Olivia.'

No, you don't. I seethe as I trudge behind him.

'This is in your blood. You try to fight against it. But deep down you want this. You were born to be a predator. And you know it. It's the reason you've always felt like you didn't quite fit in. The reason your mother withdrew from you. It's the reason you were drawn to Tristan.'

'You know nothing about my Mum.' I try to stay calm. But anticipation and anger war my stomach.

'I know enough,' Tobias replies, looking back at me. 'If she'd trusted you with the truth a long time ago things would be different now.' I look away, it's something I've thought myself too many times. Why hadn't Mum told me the truth years ago? 'You'd be a Siren already.'

'No.'

'Yes,' Tobias laughs. He pulls a branch from the path and steps aside to let me pass first. 'She knew if she told you, you'd seek us out. You would have needed to know, needed to learn about your kind to finally feel accepted.'

I pick up the pace, desperate to get this over with. Tobias will be vulnerable in the lake. His reactions are dulled by the alcohol and arrogance. He'll be slow to understand what's happening, slow to react when I strike the side of his head with a rock.

He thinks he knows me? The only comfort as we walk is knowing that he really doesn't.

The lake is a welcoming sight. It reminds me that this is nearly all over. That a house at the bottom of a hill on the edge of a northern village awaits. Mum is waiting for me. Tobias' words still sting though.

Did she really not tell me because she was afraid I'd choose this life? Does she think I'm more Siren than human? Maybe she already mourns me, thinking that I'm not coming back.

Tobias passes me as I'm lost in my doubts. He turns and swims a confident backstroke through the water and I realise I've just lost my first chance. We could have done the final cut here right by the water. On the other side, he strides away, without waiting for me, into the long grass.

'Wait!' I call as he walks away from the lake. 'Can we do it here?'

Tobias turns and for a moment we're both dripping wet, chests heaving from the effort of the swim and then the next moment we're dry. Tobias smiles and runs a hand through his dark hair, pushing it off his face. He takes a step back towards me, but still in the grass.

'Yes, if you prefer. Here works just as nicely.' He holds out his hand and I hesitate, debating if we're still close enough to the water. How can I get him deep enough to drown? 'Liv,' he coaxes, misinterpreting my hesitation. 'I'm sorry for making you feel threatened. It was for your own good, but you're here now. This is what's best for you and you'll soon come to realise that this final cut is not the end. It's just the beginning.' He wears his most hypnotic smile. The hair he pushed back moments ago, falls forward as he dips his head and watches, waiting for me to take his hand. He really is beautiful. I step closer offering my hand.

'So, how does this work?' I take a deep breath, closing my eyes a moment and trying to recall why I'm here. He brings his other hand over to trap my hand between his palms.

'You'll locate what's left of the threads holding you to that damaged body. They're invisible until you call them forward, but once we can see them, it's time to cut.'

Siren's appear across the lake and out from the trees

'What are they doing here?' I asked, startled, pulling my hand free. There are so many of them. I only ever saw this many gather for the completion.

'Olivia,' Tobias says patiently. 'They only want to watch. You're so special to us. Forgive them for being eager.' I feel the first stirrings of panic. I can't escape this. There's too many of them. I think my knees will give out at any moment. 'Olivia, don't be afraid,' Tobias continues gently. 'This is the easy part. Think about where your body lies and think about your essence here. Then, call forth the bond between the two. Once you have it, cut it. It's as simple as that and then you're free.' Grey spots swarm my eyes. I fall forward dizzy. I can't do this. Tobias catches my forearms and holds me up. 'Come on, Olivia,' he says gently. His hands tight on my arms are the only thing keeping me up. I see the Sirens drawing closer out of the corner of my eye. 'Concentrate, call forth the connection. Where is your body and what binds you to it?'

Almost against my will I see through the meadow. I see the truth like a dream. I'm lying on the sofa covered in blankets. Mum is sitting beside me, asleep in an awkward position. It's dark outside. I imagine her having to move my body from outside to the sofa and hate what I've put her through.

'Yes,' Tobias breathes and his voice pulls me back to the meadow. I stumble away from him. I need to get closer to the lake. He releases me and as we part, we both see the shining brilliant threads pulled from my chest. They flicker, fade and then resume stronger than before binding into a united golden cord. This thread finds my body and connects us in the way a body and soul are meant to be.

I never knew it would be like this. I feel so vulnerable, so raw and exposed. Tobias and I stare in awe. They're so much like the bright thread of light I saw pulled out of the girl at the completion. I know the other Siren's can see it too. The only thing I know, more certainly than ever, is that I do not want to sever myself from this life. I have to fight back.

'The lake,' I manage to whisper. I stagger back and eventually feel the water around my ankles. I reach out for him. 'Tobias, I need you.' Deeper, I need to go deeper. Tobias is by my side in an instant.

'Of course, I'm here. I'm here.' He's so gentle with me. 'Take a breath, you have time. Take a breath and then make the cut. You're so beautiful, Olivia.' I would trust him, if I didn't know any better. Tobias has always been kind so long as he's getting his own way. He flits between the Shepherd and the Siren so easily, but he's always the monster. When did he turn on my mother? My father? Tristan? They are the reasons I chose to confront him. Remembering them spurs me on and I breathe the way Mum taught me. I imagine the rock I will smash into the side of his head. I drop down into the water pulling him down with me, until we're crouched. I imagine the boulders that will roll atop his chest to hold him down once I've knocked him out. I look into his eyes, so like Tristan's. Behind him, I see water lapping against a boulder that wasn't there moments earlier. The boulder trembles and shakes keenly when I ask. Tobias smiles at me, he's still waiting for me to make the cut.

My hand reaches down into the water. I find the rock and curl my fingers around it. 'Tobias,' I whisper. He leans closer to catch my words and the golden threads burn between us. The Sirens will try to have me after this, but if I can take him down first I'll still have won. I might have time to get myself back home before they reach me, but now I have to focus solely on Tobias.

I raise my hand out of the water, the rock is heavy. I breathe trying to pull all my strength together in one place, into the strength of my arm. The threads spark and spit with the effort. I smile at Tobias as my arm swings down.

There is a split second moment, where Tobias' eyes widen a fraction in shock as he realises what's about to happen. My hand crashes and the air changes around us and I know he's controlling it. My palm strikes his temple, but the rock is gone and all my force is transformed into a gentle caress. 'Olivia, that could have been nasty,' he admonishes softly.

'Tobias.' I don't know what else to say. My only chance and I blew it.

'Shh,' he interrupts. 'Here, let me help you.' He reaches for me.

His fingers are like knives as they reach swiftly inside and make short work of my life. In one cut, Tobias shears the brilliant cord still burning between us. And I am a kite set free. I am scattered through the air.

I realise I've made a horrible mistake. Tobias lifts me up like I'm nothing. My horrified eyes meet his as he wades out of the lake and places me carefully in the grass. The Sirens swarm closer like the bloodthirsty monsters they are. They are excited. They are eager. Their fingers reach as they hope to touch the sheared brilliant threads. How could I ever have thought I could take on Tobias and win? Behind them all, he is there. Calm, satisfied and triumphant.

I shrivel. I'm dying. I can feel myself fading away. Fading and floating away like I'm nothing more than dust. I was never meant to be a Siren after all. I was always going to end up a Shade. I feel the world tilt as I fall back and face a sky, framed by their monstrous grins. I close my eyes. I am nothing.

And then I feel it.

The tiniest coiled thread of energy remains, unspooling and falling away from me. I grab hold of it without thinking, without even knowing how. It slips between my grasp and I'm frantically trying to grab hold and claw it back. It's my essence, it's what makes me *me* and I can't lose it. Without it I truly am nothing. I take hold. I gather it desperately to me, the ruined pulsing threads of myself. I can't make it go back the way it was. The threads of energy flail and come alive around me. They grow and weave in on themselves, turning brilliant and strong. I feel a new force flow through me. The panic recedes all at once. And I feel new. I am brand new. It's like I didn't know I was asleep and suddenly I'm awake. I am reborn. My eyes flash open and they all take a step back. I am lying in the long, long grass. I am spread like a star.

I am a Siren.

CHAPTER 23

Nothing will ever be the same again. I will never be the same again. What I've broken cannot be repaired. Yet, I've never felt so strong.

They all watch me. Curiosity, glee, and a tense anticipation that could go either way between hostility and festivity. I climb to my feet and am distantly aware of Tobias talking. The blood roaring in my ears drowns him out. There is a war within me and I fight the urge to revel in my new strength. Strength that is fearless and laced with ruthless anger to....to what? I'm not sure. To control, to dominate, to win. To get what I want. I back away from Tobias as if he's the source of these insidious thoughts. The crowd move aside to let me pass. I make no eye contact with any of them as I strive to control my breathing and my anger.

I run back to the lake. Chase me and I'll rip your throat out. You just try. No one follows, but I hear their cackles and howling voices. I crash into the water to drown them out and swim. I dive under the water kicking hard to propel myself. It's too dark to see the stone faces I know are down there. Certainly too dark to see any glimpse of the doorway to the Otherside that Mum spoke of. If I let myself sink Tobias would win. I consider drowning for only a moment. Tobias has already won. I rise out of the water on the far side of the lake and look back. They are dancing and celebrating. They've lost interest in me, except for Tobias. He lifts a hand in greeting. He just ripped the soul from me like it was nothing. He severed my life and now he waves at me like a neighbour across the road. He helped me do what I was unable to. I retreat into the jungle, unwilling to turn my back on him while he's watching me. He knows what I'd just tried to do to him. Would he seek revenge? Maybe, he'd hoped I'd shrivel up into a Shade. I'm sure I nearly did. My heart pounds and I need to be alone to figure out all the feelings raging through me. Underneath the shock, the confusion and the anger, there is the strangest thing - I feel victorious.

Did I really come back here to kill Tobias or was that just a lie I told Mum and even myself? Maybe for some part of me becoming a Siren was always the real goal.

I surge up the mountain. I make no sound and my surroundings are perfectly still. I've never been so graceful.

Liv. I hear the low voice and stop short. I can't see her yellow eyes, but I know she's out there.

Liv, how could you? I helped you. You were supposed to be better than this. You were the one who got away. You were the proof that I was more than nothing. But, look at you. She sounds so agonised, so broken.

'Rip! Wait, let me explain.' I was going to say more, but am struck by how different even my voice sounds. Smooth and lilting.

We're done. You will grow to despair of this choice.

'Rip!' But she's gone. Being surrounded by cheering Sirens and Tobias' smug expression hadn't managed to overcome the sense of triumph or stifle this tiny part of me that felt it was being called home. Yet somehow Rip's devastation did. She stripped me bare and left behind all the failure. Bile rises up my throat. I will despair of this choice. What I've broken cannot be repaired. I will never be the same again.

My house is exactly as I'd left it. Tucked away up the mountain, off the track and sheltered by the trees. I slam the front door behind me as I rush inside. Immediately, I hear the normal sounds of cooking from the kitchen and then Tristan's voice. 'Liv? In here,' he calls. I walk into the kitchen nervously. Tristan is bent over a bubbling pot on the stove. He's smiling, but when he looks up and sees me his face falls instantly. I feel my legs start to shake.

'Liv, no,' he whispers aghast. 'Why?'

'Tristan,' his name and all the words that follow are wrenched out of me as my chest heaves. 'I didn't...it's a mistake. I didn't want to. Tobias, he- I thought I could stop him. I thought I could beat him. And now, it's all ruined. It's over. I can't fix this, can I?' The tears run down my face and I feel my legs buckle. Tristan drops the wooden spoon in his hand and rushes to me, crouching down to join me on the floor.

'Oh baby,' he sighs and gathers me to him. I cry, while he holds me on the kitchen floor.

It's a long time later when I finally stop crying. My breathing slows until all I'm aware of is the rhythmic stroking of Tristan's hand on my back.

'Feeling better?'

'No.'

'Liv,' he says gently, pulling back to look at me. 'Isn't this what you wanted?'

'No!' I recoil. 'I don't want this. I don't care if it's in my blood. I didn't want to become a ...'

'You can say it.'

'... a monster.'

'I don't understand why you came back.' He takes my face between his palms, using his thumbs to wipe away the tears

'I thought I could trick Tobias.'

'How?' His voice carries a note of uncertainty.

'I came back to kill him. In the lake.' I close my eyes feeling my face grow hot between his hands.

'Oh, Liv. I wish you hadn't done this.'

'It was the only way to keep Mum safe. Why are you even here anyway?' My voice turns sour and accusing.

'When did you make the cut?' Tristan asks abruptly, ignoring my tone.

'I can't do this.. .be this - I won't hurt people.' I babble, feeling the panic rising again. 'What will he do to me if I refuse?'

'When did you make the cut?' Tristan repeats more forcefully, his hands dropping to grip my shoulders.

'Not long. Less than an hour ago? Oh, Tris,' I feel my face crumple again. 'I keep thinking of Mum back home having to deal with all this. My body. The funeral. She'll be all alone.'

Tristan rises pulling me up with him. 'An hour? That's good. You might still be able to get back to your body. You remember how to escape from here, the doorway? If you go through so close after the cut I think you'll be returned to the body you left behind.' I can't believe I'd forgotten about the door at the bottom of the lake.

'I can go back?' I'm hesitant as I think it through.

'Yes, just like your mother. You don't want to be here. So, go back. I'll help you.'

'And if it's too late, where will I end up?'

'I'm not sure. It could be anywhere in the world I guess.'

'Mum came through and ended up with my father.'

'I don't know, Liv.' He looks helpless. 'She hadn't just left a human life behind. She was starting from scratch. I don't really understand how it works.'

'What body would I end up in if not mine?

'Your mother is the only Siren I know who did this and we didn't exactly talk about the specifics. It's a risk. Time moves differently here compared to the Otherside. The sooner you return I think the better your chances.'

I sigh. 'Going back doesn't change anything though. Tobias will still be out there. What's to stop him going after Mum? Or dragging me back?' I pull free from Tristan, realising I'm back where I started. I stand up and notice for the first time the soup boiling over on the stove. I move around the kitchen island to turn off the heat. Tristan was making me soup, just like when I got sick that time.

'Liv?' Tristan frowns at my smile.

'About how, despite everything, you were making me soup.'

'We don't have time for soup anymore.'

'You burnt it anyway,' I say and he laughs. The sound reminds me of better times. It reminds me I have one more chance to protect my Mum and Tristan. It's a risk worth taking for them. I'm stronger now. This time Tobias has to die and only then can I go back.

◆ ◆ ◆

For the first time the Night Cafe seems flat. The same tedious conversations all around me. The same plots and schemes wrapped up in stories of Shepherds being the saviour to poor human souls. It's like someone's cleaned off the sheen and everything left behind is duller than before. How could I ever have thought I wanted this repetitive and cruel imitation of life? 'Don't know how you managed it, but guess you joined the club.' Seph sidles up beside me. I don't think I'll ever see his face without remembering how he looked with blood smeared around his mouth.

'Get away from me,' I move away to join the vapid discussion being held between Luna, Zara and Rowan. They're reminiscing about their favourite humans. Their favourite dead humans. One good thing about being a Siren is now I'm no longer afraid or in awe of anyone. Any spell they had over me is broken. I glare at Seph over my shoulder to make sure he doesn't follow me, but he just smirks and walks away.

This is the third night in a row I've come here looking for Tobias. Any hope of returning to the life I left behind is dwindling. Every now and then stray thoughts surface, whispers that I should run away home before it's too late and whispers that it's already too late. The worst thoughts are the traitorous ones suggesting I stay here, that being a Siren isn't so bad. I was born to do this, maybe I could pave the way for a different kind of Siren. One that didn't hurt humans. One that visits her mother on a regular basis. I dismiss it all and steel myself to refocus. This is all about Tobias now.

'Liv?' I realise Zara has been trying to get my attention.

'What?'

'Where were you?' Zara's laughing.

'Oh? Just thinking … about what kind of Siren I'll be.'

'You know, Shepherd is our preferred name.' Rowan comments.

'Really?' I say innocently. 'I prefer Siren, a bit more accurate I find.' I no longer care about pissing them off.

'Liv's right.' Orla interrupts dramatically, joining us in a ridiculously sheer black long-sleeved dress. 'You'll find out just how accurate once you get out there and start hunting.'

'Orla.' Rowan looks uncomfortable, even Zara's smile dims. 'We're not hunters, we're helpers.' Zara nods, 'a helping hand in the dark,' she echoes.

'Oh, drop the act. Livvy understands exactly what we are.' Orla laughs, but it has a high-pitched brittle edge that lets me know she's not far from breaking.

'There's no act.' Luna says quietly. 'We leave all the theatrics to you, dear.' The others laugh and Orla's eyes narrow. She turns to me with a fake smile.

'You see, Liv. They don't make any sense. He has them brainwashed. They actually think they're angelic Shepherds. It's pathetic—'

'Orla.' Tobias is suddenly by her side, his voice impatient. 'Walk with me.' He pulls her away from us without an acknowledgment. He's finally here.

'What was that all about?' Rowan frowns after them.

'You know what Orla's like.' Luna replies. 'She's getting worse though.'

Zara links her arm through mine before I can chase after Tobias .'Leave her to Tobias, Liv. He'll see she's alright.'

'Is she seeing someone right now?' Rowan asks.

'I think so?' Luna shrugs. 'But she's been so quiet about it. She's been weird since … oh, I don't know. Forever!'

Since John, I think. It's happening slowly, but Orla is unravelling. Tristan isn't the only one breaking the rules. I wonder how many more of them are unhappy. How many more of them don't realise they're the hunters?

Their chatter fades into the background as Tristan enters the Night Cafe. I haven't seen him since he left my house days ago. He's angry that I'm still here. He acknowledges me with a sad nod, but comes no closer. He takes a seat in a quiet corner and around him I see glimmers and snapshots of the Nectar Lounge. Faded green velvet cushions and gold trim. Tristan is the only one who still holds the same spell over me. He still makes my heart swell in my chest. His last words ring in my head, *you can't take on Tobias and win. You should run now while you have the chance.* I untangle myself from Zara and am about to excuse myself from the group when Orla and Tobias come back over to join us. Orla is smiling brightly and holding a drink, but her eyes are red-rimmed and strained.

'Hi guys,' she rests her free hand on Rowan's foreman. 'What are we talking about?' There is a brief silence where I wonder how any of them miss the signs that she is clearly not alright.

'Orla love, I was just clarifying first date text protocol with the girls.' Roman falls back into his placid smile and wraps an arm around her shoulders.

'Never text back after the first date.' Luna affirms.

Rowan shakes his head. 'But this girl was annoyed I didn't text to make sure she got home safe.' Seriously, this is all they have to talk about. I can't bring myself to have an opinion, but I remember the first date with Tristan where he walked me right to my front door and kissed me. Also, there are the memories of the days after where I waited and waited with not a single message. Orla slips back into comfortable territory and assumes the lead role of the group.

'Rowan, Rowan,' she tsks. 'When will you learn, what they think they want and what they really want are two different things.' And just like that her mask is back in place. I wonder what Tobias said to her or how he threatened her. I glance back over to Tristan who still sits alone staring into his drink. Without Tal around, he really does seem unpopular among the Sirens.

'We'll have to deal with him.' Tobias murmurs from behind me.

'What do you mean?'

'He broke the rules when he let you go.'

I swallow. 'Well, I'm here now. So all's well that ends well.'

Tobias shakes his head. 'Too many know the truth. *I* know the truth. When I look at him all I see is failure. Lacking even the courage to do as your mother did.'

'Don't talk about her.' I snap before I can stop myself, but Tobias only laughs quietly.

'Yes, yes. Her pathetic little life is of no interest to me. She has nothing left. Leaving her to live with that knowledge really is the best medicine. But Tristan, no. His time is done.'

Any lure Tobias ever held is dead. His voice makes my skin crawl and it's all I can do to not let the revulsion fill my eyes. Now that I've found him, I need to find a way to get him back to the lake. Or could I knock him out and transport him unconscious to the lake another way?

'Can we go somewhere private to talk about this? I ask turning to face him. 'There are things you don't know about Tristan. I want to tell you everything.'

'Of course, Olivia. I always have time for you.' He lifts my chin up lightly with his fingers and stares into my eyes. We're locked in each other's eyes for a moment. It confirms that any power he held over me is gone and I think my eyes stare defiantly back.

'Tobias,' Cillian cuts in. 'It's Orla.' I see her, on the other side of the room with a different group now, she's gesticulating wildly, her drink sloshing over those standing closest. 'She listens to you. We should take her home.'

Tobias growls under his breath and drops my chin. 'Yes, let's see to Orla.' He looks back at me. 'We should finish our conversation tonight. I want this business cleaned up. I'll find you,' he promises and walks away with Cillian.

I have to warn Tristan, but when I look around he's already gone.

◆ ◆ ◆

Tristan answers his front door grimly. I've been banging my fists against the door ever since I raced around the rest of the pier and garden looking for him. He steps aside to invite me in.

'He's coming for you.' I say immediately, without moving.

'I know.' Tristan walks back inside leaving the door open behind him. 'I've been living on borrowed time for a while.'

'You need to leave. You don't have a choice now, you can't stay here. Go through the door under the lake. Let me help you. I can handle Tobias. We should go now. He'll be looking for me soon. I can delay him. But then he wants you.' I'm rambling as I follow Tristan through his house. In contrast, he moves calmly, drifting through the corridors like he's barely there. 'Tris, are you listening to me?' I look ahead and throw up a wall to block off the corridor forcing him to stop. It's as easy as moving pebbles now. He laughs lightly, 'You've gotten good at that.'

'I've been practising.' I say sourly. A moment later, a door appears in my wall blockade. Tristan opens it and steps through. 'Why don't you care about what I'm saying?' I cry after him.

'Follow me, Liv.' he simply says and we pass through the kitchen out into the evening air.

'Could you hide from him instead?' I ask as I follow him through the garden. 'As soon as I've killed him you can stay here if that's what you really want.'

'Liv, shut up. I want to show you something.' He takes my hand without looking back and leads me along the wooden pathway down towards his lake.

The lake is peaceful in shades of blue and black. The brown mountains look soft in the faint light. It reminds me suddenly of being in the woods surrounded by wild garlic and bluebells. The feeling of peaceful simplicity is the same. This is Tristan's calm. Tristan stops at the end of the pier and stares out. I've run out of words and feel a lump form in my throat. He doesn't say anything.

'Tris, there isn't time for this.' I say quietly.

'A touching scene.' Tobias steps out through the trees and the wood beneath his feet creaks as he approaches. 'I had a feeling I'd find you two together.' My mind races, I have no reason to explain why I'm here. How can I get Tobias back to the meadow lake?

'Tobias, can we have our talk now? Not here.' I say. Tristan's hand squeezes mine suddenly, but when I look at him I don't understand the meaning in his eyes.

'Get lost, Tristan.' Tobias' voice is low. 'I need to speak with Olivia alone.' I think Tristan will stand his ground and refuse to leave my side, but he nods and drops my hand. He walks away skirting around Tobias as he goes back along the deck. I watch him leave, biting my tongue to stop from calling him back. Tristan's good at leaving. I turn back to the water. It's inky darkness now seems inviting with Tobias behind me.

'Tristan,' I hear Tobias call. 'Don't go too far. I'm coming to see you next.' Then, I hear his voice softer and right behind me. 'Olivia, shall we take a seat?' I turn to see him pointing at the chairs under the veranda where Tristan and I used to curl up under blankets. I nod and slowly make my way back along the pier. I try to think of reasons to make Tobias agree to come with me to the meadow lake, reasons to spare Tristan, reasons to not be angry. But each step away from the lake feels wrong. It feels like a step in the wrong direction. Tristan brought me out here for a reason. I glance back out over the water, reminded again of how invitingly refreshing it looks. As inviting as the lake at the meadow...I stop.

'Olivia?' There is a note of impatience in Tobias' voice. I ignore him and lower myself off the pier and into the cool water. It laps around my calves. Maybe, I need to stop waiting for the right moment. There will be no easy way. There will be no right moment to kill Tobias and I'm running out of chances. One lake is as good as another.

'Olivia, what are you doing?' I take a few steps deeper.

'The water feels really good.' I smile over my shoulder at his dark silhouette against the sun. 'Come and play.' I wade deeper into the water. Until my knees. Until my thighs. Until I'm beyond the pier and I feel an underwater shelf with my toes where the ground drops away and the cold water is a shock around my stomach.

'None of your games this time, I trust?' Tobias asks. The impatience has left his voice, replaced by curiosity. Siren's do love to play. I hold up both my hands innocently in response. I turn away from him and am satisfied to hear the splash as he enters the lake.

If I held him and refused to let go we could both sink like a stone. It would be the end of both of us. Just another two stone statues to litter a lake bed. But Mum and Tristan would finally be safe from Tobias.

Maybe, this is what I deserve.

Deserve. Deserve. Deserve.

I think it would be worth it to die protecting the people I love. To protect countless others from a monster. Deciding to die is a calmer thought than I expected. All my fear is gone. I turn to face Tobias as he reaches me, stopping him from going any further.

'You know, being a Siren feels different than I expected.' I say, pulling my hands through the water.

'How does it feel?' He comes closer. He's topless now. His skin shines where the sun hits beads of water.

'It feels like ...power.'

You have no power over me.

'It feels like...strength.'

I am the master of my fate.

257

His fingers skim across the water, making circles in front of me. 'Yes,' he agrees. 'It's both those things. You're stronger now than you ever could have been as a human.' My smile almost flickers when I realise he actually expects me to thank him.

'I wasn't finished,' I reprimand, shifting back out of his reach. Only my toes remain balanced on the ledge. 'I feel brand new.' His hands find my waist under the water and he draws closer. 'It feels...nothing can stop me.' I slide my arms around him until the length of our bodies are pressed together. I look him in the eyes when I add 'including you.' I step back off the ledge with the slow, almost lazy, resistance of water. I think of the rocks tied about my ankles. I lean back, pulling him with me. I take a deep breath.

And then we're under. Pulled deeper and deeper. Sinking faster than I expected. Tobias' eyes widen, bulging out of his face. He tries to push free of me, but I wrap myself tighter around him. An embrace so tight, as if I love him. I press my face into his chest as I cling on. Every rock he removes, I add more. I feel him struggle, but I'm the one thing in this environment he can't control. I feel him fight me, but I'm the one thing he can't change.

Suddenly pain explodes in my head as I realise he's hit me with something, but I don't let go. I screw my eyes shut and dig in my nails. Don't let go. Don't let go.

We're still sinking. Sinking and shaking and struggling. I start to feel the pressure in my lungs, but I don't let go. The pain in my head strikes again, and this time across my back and legs too, but I don't let go. Everything burns and swells and hammers. Just when I think it's unbearable and my lungs and head are about to burst, it stops. Shimmers of pain pulse in the wake and Tobias changes in my arms. He goes heavy and loose. I'm still too afraid to let go. We're pulled faster down into the depths. I still can't let go. Even as everything grows hazy, the mantra repeats. Don't let go. So I don't let go.

Until the body in my arms turns hard like stone. I pull back immediately, unwinding my arms from him. Tobias' opaque eyes, permanently furious and panicked, stare back at me. His beautiful face rendered ugly. I push back clumsily in the water, desperately wanting space between me and him. The rocks pulling me down fade out of existence. Without them, I stop sinking and Tobias sinks deeper. It's only moments before he's lost through the water, swallowed up by the darkness where the light never reaches.

I look up and see the surface is far away. I have no energy left to reach it. I think I'm about to black out, but Tobias is gone and that's all that matters. For Tristan, for Mum, for my father. I feel tired, but oddly calm.

In my last moments.

It's peaceful down here.

It's not so bad.

And I *do* feel brand new.

So I'll die next, but at least it'll be with a smile on my face.

CHAPTER 24

'You never told me what you wanted to be when you grow up.'

'Didn't I?' Tristan frowned thoughtfully. 'Well, I want you to be safe. I want to be healthy. And I would like my family to be proud of me.'

'Tristan!' I dismissed his answers. 'Everyone wants to be happy, healthy, and safe. World peace would be nice too. I meant what dreams do you have for your future?'

Tristan closed his eyes like he was trying to conjure it up. 'I've never thought much about the future. When the future is endless, the present is much more enjoyable.'

'I know what you mean,' I sighed into his shoulder. 'Sometimes the future does feel endless.'

The burn of water scorches my throat. It rushes up flooding my mouth and nose. An agonising gaping breath rattles through me.

Tristan, why me?

Give back what you stole from me.

◆ ◆ ◆

Cold air shivers over my wet skin. Lips press against mine. Fingers thread gentle through my hair. I don't know where I am or even what I am anymore. But the hands are kind and the lips soft.

'Liv?'

'Am I dead?' I groan.

'No, you're not.' A soft chuckle I know so well.

'Where am I?' I open my eyes to see Tristan. It's dark and only a flickering light illuminates his face.

'You're safe. This is my refuge.' I pull myself up, twisting to brace against my arms. We're in a cave. The roof is low, barely enough for me to stand straight. The only light is a lantern on a rock shelf beside Tristan and beyond him I can't tell how deep the cave goes. The darkness swallows the light whole. The blackness beyond our little circle of light feels tangible.

The last thing I properly remember is Tobias' stone eyes staring at me.

'Tobias-'

'Dead.' Tristan confirms. My breath washes out in a rush. I reach my hand up to touch the back of my head. My hair is wet and tangled, but no sign of his attack remains. Tristan shifts to take hold of the lantern, bringing it closer and for the first time I notice he's wet. The light reveals the inky black lake water, waiting patiently, in a large hole beside us.

'Tristan, did you pull me out?'

He frowns back. 'I was watching. I watched right up until you both disappeared under the water. I jumped in after you, but I wasn't quick enough and you were sinking so fast I couldn't reach you. I thought I was too late.' He falls quiet and it's just the sound of our breathing and the smell of stale air.

'Thank you, Tris.' I try to smile, but I don't know what comes next. I'm still so confused. I'd made peace with everything. I never expected more time.

'Thank you, Liv.' Tristan smiles back and my heart thumps a little. It feels more like nostalgia now. 'You did it,' he continues. 'He's gone. You are so brave. So much braver than I am.' I shake my head, but words fail me. It didn't feel brave, it just felt right. 'You know, your mum told me about the door in the bottom of the meadow lake? That time I found you in the snow and carried you home. I think she thought I'd make the choice so easily to be with you. I really wanted to be the man she thought I was. I wanted to be the man you thought I was. So badly.'

'Where are we? Is this the cave Mum found?'

Tristan shakes his head. 'I built *The Refuge* here on purpose. I put my lake here on purpose. Your mum didn't know that I'd already found another doorway. That I'd already made the choice to stay here. I put the lake over it so no one would find it by mistake. I kept it my secret.'

'There's a way out?' I crawl to my feet, stunned. 'Can I still go back? Can I be human again?' My eyes well up and bands of emotion grip my chest like a vice until my breath shudders. I'd given up hope of ever returning. Killing Tobias had felt like the best ending I deserved.

Tristan nods, climbing to his feet. He stoops to keep from banging his head. He points a hand to the water. 'A cold swim back to *The Refuge*,' he points in the other direction, deeper into the cave. 'The Otherside. Home.'

I laugh. It's not what I expected to do or even within my control, but I can't stop. I'm going home. Tristan's eyes warm and I remember a time when he told me he loved the sound of my laughter. A time when he told me I deserved to laugh everyday. He looks back towards the darkness and our escape. 'I may have come down here quite a few times and considered going through that door.' His voice is solemn. 'I came down here when I wanted to hide from all the Sirens. It's stupid, but I came down here to feel close to you. You were just there, around the corner, waiting for me. Looking at me the way you used to,' he laughs, but it's got a bitter edge now.

'Come on,' I hold my hand out. 'Tobias is gone. We can walk through together?'

Tristan shakes his head. 'No, Liv. I belong here. I don't make sense in your world.'

'No one makes sense, you'll fit right in,' I joke, but I can feel what's coming.

'I don't even know where I'd end up. It might not be in the same place as you.' Tristan argues weakly.

'You don't need me. Anywhere is better than here. Just knowing you escaped is good enough for me. We could try to find each other?'

'I'm sorry, Liv.' He looks down, his cheeks burning red.

And I finally run out of reasons. We both look at my outstretched hand, empty and still waiting for his.

Why am I always waiting? Waiting for summer. Waiting to graduate college. Waiting for university. Waiting for Tristan. Waiting to be wanted. Waiting to figure out my life. Waiting for Tristan to love me the way I loved him. Waiting for someone else to tell me who I am and where I belong. Always waiting for things to start. I will be happy once I have this. I will be happy once I get there. I will be happy once my life begins. I'm eighteen. So, why do I feel like my life hasn't started?

What am I really waiting for?

I have everything I need right here. Inside.

Staring at my empty hand, everything feels different. I feel like my head has just broken above the water and only now do I realise I'd been drowning for so long. Tristan looks different. Still gorgeous. Still a regret I'll hold, a memory I'll treasure, but suddenly everything is clear. 'You don't deserve me.'

He frowns unhappily, but I think I see a dawning realisation cross his features. I study every part of his face. Committing it to memory. I see such fear in his face.

Give back what you stole from me.

'You know what?' I finally say. 'You can keep it. You need it more than I do.'

'What?' He's confused. I turn and walk away. 'Liv?'

I don't look back. I can't. Even as I feel the tears blur my vision. Even as they break free and fall and every step feels heavier and harder than the one before. 'Liv!'

What I'd give to see your face again, Tristan.

But I don't look back. If I look back I'll stay a moment longer. Moments longer, days, years. A lifetime wasted. I don't look back. I walk into the blackness. I have to do this. I am done waiting. I walk through the darkness, until I'm through the door. I walk and I don't stop.

I walk until it starts to feel easier.

THE END

One month later

The sun is strong, as bright as it's been for ages. It slants in through every window it can get hold of. It brings the house to life. Spring feels like a possibility.

There is an envelope waiting for me on the doormat. My college's logo is stamped in the corner. For a moment I just stare at it. The next chapter of my life will be decided by what's inside this envelope. I go through the routine of boiling the kettle and making proper coffee with the cafetiere.

The envelope sits quietly on the doormat waiting.

I open the French doors. I push the coffee plunger and inhale as I pour. It smells like mornings. It smells like time, like lazy relaxed drawn-out time.

And finally I pick up the envelope.

I take my coffee and go sit outside on our old painted wooden bench. The white painting has been peeling off for the last few years. It creaks and threatens to collapse as I sit down. When it eventually does collapse I know Mum will just fix it again. I set my coffee mug down by my feet. The sun beams all around me, pouring into me like I'm a glass to be filled.

I think briefly of Tristan. Of where he might be now. I feel sorry for what he's missing. I feel sorry for him. I wait for more. But that is all I have left. I wish him well wherever he may be. For the first time since I met Tristan, I finally *see* him. I see him without the blinkers. I see him without the clouds and storms of devotion. He was just a boy who was afraid. He was a boy who was lost. He was a boy who wasn't strong enough to fight for what he wanted. He was a boy who didn't deserve me.

I smile. It feels good. My hands tighten and I hear the envelope crackle between my fingers.

And I finally understand.

The Beginning

ACKNOWLEDGEMENTS

My first and biggest thanks go to anyone who reads this story and makes it all the way to the acknowledgements section. Thank you, thank you, thank you, you legend! Tellings stories for other people has been something I've loved for as long as I can remember. So dear reader, I hope this book was enjoyed by you.   This story took me a long time to finish and so many thanks go to all the family and friends who were willing to read, advise, reread, critique, support and reread again! I'm especially thankful (and sorry) to my Mum who I think has read this novel more than any human should ever have to read anything. Thank you also to Jean and Martin Gill, Jo Musgrove, Marta Kurzawa, and Sean Woodall. Thanks also go to all the people who let me borrow little bits and pieces of their personality or mannerisms to help build my characters (you know who you are).

Finally, special thanks to Daniel, Ruby, Yoshi and Gata for giving me the time and space (and occasional distractions) to get this done.

ABOUT THE AUTHOR

Alexa Cleasby

Alexa has a PhD in chemical biology, but has since left academia to write about medical research and rare diseases. She currently lives in north west England with her partner, daughter, dog and cat.

Printed in Poland
by Amazon Fulfillment
Poland Sp. z o.o., Wrocław
27 August 2023

2099d29c-0155-454a-b27f-370ed2b12951R01